Two boys fall in love in a deadly world, but it's the secrets they keep that might kill them.

Seventeen-year-old Zach was visiting his uncle in a small Montana town when a mysterious illness ripped through the world. Most died, but those who survived the Infection became mindless killers, spreading the disease with a single scratch. Now, a year later, civilization lies in ruins, and Zach is the town's sole survivor. Desperately lonely, he longs to return to his family in Seattle, but his fears hold him captive.

Eighteen-year-old Aiden is on a critical mission for the covert Scientific Collective, delivering vials whose contents could cure the Infection. Tortured by his boyfriend's death, he welcomes the risks of the perilous journey. When a militia attacks Aiden, he flees to Zach's town.

The boys escape together and soon form a bond as they comfort each other in this desolate and broken world. The farther they travel, the more their affection grows, as do the forces pulling them apart. But their greatest threats are the secrets they keep. Zach hides details of his uncle's death, and Aiden conceals the vials' sinister origins. In order to survive, they'll have to confront the truths that could tear their love apart.

TOGETHER IN A BROKEN WORLD

PAUL MICHAEL WINTERS

A NineStar Press Publication
www.ninestarpress.com

Together in a Broken World

CONTENT WARNING:

This book contains sexual language and content that is fade-to-black, which may only be suitable for mature readers. Depictions of graphic violence, guns, abduction, death of family, mourning; discussion of attempted rape/non-con (past, off page), social anxiety, and past and present trauma.

Chapter One

A Broken World

AIDEN

It's hard to get over how desolate the world is now. I haven't seen another soul for over a week. And if I want to stay alive, I hope to keep it that way.

The road cuts a winding path through a dense forest, the cone of my headlights revealing just enough to see ahead. Everything else is stark blackness. Daft Punk and GRiZ blast through the car's speakers—an EDM mix I made last year as a DJ for my high school. Back when DJs and high schools existed, that is. The bass rumbling through the seat makes me feel connected to the car.

With one eye on the road, I paw at the backpack resting on the passenger seat. It's the third time this hour I've checked on the vials. The familiar shape of the protective aluminum case through the nylon fabric helps ease my anxiety. For the moment, anyway. It may be a little obsessive, but the vials are my critical cargo. They're what I'm risking my life for. *And I'm doing this for Marcus.*

The slightest thought of him sends waves of grief flooding over me. I fight those feelings and bury them away. Letting emotions control me is the surest way of getting killed.

When I pull up to a rest area, the car cuts a path through an inch of pine needles spread over the parking lot. Weeds spring up through every possible crack, and vines are well on their way to swallowing the restrooms whole. The sheer relentlessness of Mother Nature is startling.

Since man-made light is a thing of the past, it's impossible to see your hand six inches in front of your face, especially on a cloudy, moonless night in rural Montana. The headlights are my only guide through the darkness, so I leave them turned on.

As I open the door, I'm hit with a cold blast of air and the smell of sap. It must be low forties out. My breaths puff out in misty clouds.

Looters often overlook vending machines at rest stops, so I always check them out. I'm pleasantly surprised to find the machines undamaged and nearly full. With a few pries of a crowbar, the lock springs open. I load what I can into my backpack and stuff the rest in a black plastic bag.

After doing my business in the restroom, I return to my faded red '97 Integra, crunching through the thick layer of decaying pine needles. I stop suddenly, staring at another pair of footprints that cross over mine, head up to my car door, and then into the woods. They were *not* here before.

I'm sure of it.

Did I remember to lock the door?

In a flash, I run to the car and reach for the handle. *Locked. Thank god.* The second I'm in, I fire up the engine. Debris kicks up from the tires as I hit the gas and speed away.

For the next several minutes, I'm hypervigilant, keeping my eye on the mirrors and looking ahead for a potential ambush. Those footprints could have been from a member of a local militia. Their scouts are notorious for spotting lone cars and radioing for backup.

Or the footprints could have been from one of the people sick with that damn disease. The Infected. It's unlikely since they went right up to the car door. Once the fever has done its damage, the Infected don't really have that level of cognitive ability. The path would have been more random.

Either way, I'm glad to put the rest area behind me. As time passes, my nerves start to settle. Guess I got lucky. Maybe it was nothing, like a local survivor passing through.

As the minutes drift by, my eyes get heavy. It's no use fighting sleep, so I scan the highway for a side road with enough cover to pull over and rest for the night.

That's when headlights shine in my rearview mirror.

Goddamn it.

Carjackers.

Their standard MO is to drive up beside you and point guns at the car until you pull over. But I'm not planning on letting them get that close. The trick is to go slowly at first and make them overconfident. Let them think they've got easy prey. Then floor it. Take curves so fast, they'll piss their pants. With any luck, their car will spin out, trying to follow. It's half skill, half psychology.

And here comes a curve now. I find just the right speed to keep traction. The tires squeal but hold. Right at the apex of the turn, I punch the accelerator. It pushes me back into the seat as the tires grab the tarmac, and the car blasts down the road.

Those guys *should* be long gone, but somehow, the headlights shine in the rearview mirror again.

Shit.

These guys are good.

I floor the accelerator, but the engine groans in protest. A distinct smell of burning oil drifts into the cabin. That can't be good.

Whizzing sounds fly past the car. Are those bullets? Are they shooting at me?

A bullet hits the rear window, shattering it into a million pieces, making my heart rate spike. These aren't carjackers. They're trying to kill me.

I turn off the music. Drawing in a deep breath, my training kicks in. One wrong move, and I'm dead. I sharpen my focus and clear my mind, each action deliberate and calculated.

I weave the car back and forth to evade the next round of bullets and take the next turn faster than the last. The subtle sliding out of the back end translates through the wheel. With the slightest shift of steering and a barely perceptible change of speed, the car holds to the curve.

Another round of bullets sprays the car, and the left rear tire explodes. The steering wheel lurches violently. Trying to steady it takes every ounce of strength, fingers clenched, my life on the line. The car veers off the road, and I slam on the brakes. Dirt kicks up everywhere but decelerates the vehicle gradually enough that the crash doesn't kill me. The front bumper comes to rest against a tree.

Ninety to zero in five seconds. And somehow, I'm still alive.

I grab the backpack and my mixtape as headlights approach. With no time for anything else, I jump out and run for the cover of the forest. The sounds of screeching brakes and slamming car doors are right behind me.

I'm in total darkness.

Brambles rip against my face and arms as I stumble through the woods. The knobby end of a tree branch hits me hard in the ribs. The pain is blinding, but I grit my teeth and push forward. Bullets stream past, some hitting nearby trees, covering me in an explosion of splinters.

A voice yells out from behind. "Aiden! I know you're there. Hand over the vials, and you can walk away."

Who the hell knows my name? Worse, how do they know what I'm carrying? The only other person aware of my mission is the woman who sent me. She handpicked me because I was the only courier who could get the job done. Willing to do what most would call a suicide mission. And maybe that's what this is.

Behind me, the gunshots and shouts are relentless. My lungs burn, and my ribs scream. Every part of my body is telling me to stop. To my left, the ground slopes slightly. I fumble in that direction, following it downward. As it gets steeper, the slope forces my pace to quicken. I'm barely able to keep my feet from sliding under me. A wet patch of leaves sends my legs flailing forward, and for the last thirty feet, I'm on my backside until my boots splash into a running stream.

My burning lungs force me to pause for a moment. Beyond the babbling of the stream are the sounds of gunshots and shouting, but they're far off to my right. So, I head in the opposite direction with slow and deliberate footsteps, favoring silence over speed.

After several minutes of painfully slow going, the sound of the stream is gone, and the gunshots have fallen silent. But I don't dare stop yet.

Time has lost all meaning in the darkness. It could be twenty minutes. Could be an hour. My aching feet and burning muscles are my only gauge, and they just hit empty. I sit down hard on the forest floor.

How did that get so bad so fast? My mind races, playing out all the scenarios that could have happened. If the car lurches the other way, or a bullet flies six inches to the right, then I'm dead.

Focus, Aiden.

I close my eyes and force out unwanted thoughts, clearing my mind. Okay. Survival.

When I open my eyes, they've adjusted to the darkness. The moon has risen, providing the slightest bit of light. Vague details emerge. Scrapes run up and down my arms, but nothing is too deep. I'll live. My ribs are tender at the spot where I hit the tree. The slightest touch makes me wince in pain. Yeah, that's going to suck for a while.

Inside my backpack, the small aluminum box has a minor dent in one corner, but beyond that, it's undamaged. This is what my pursuers were after.

But who in the hell were they? I know the territories of every militia group between Boston and Seattle. Standard training for couriers like me. This is the turf of the Freedom Liberation Army—the FLA. Grabbing every bit of territory after the Great Collapse, their influence runs from Montana to Central Washington. But how could they know anything about my mission?

There'll be time to figure that out. Right now, my focus needs to be on staying alive. Besides the box, there's not much in the backpack—a bottle of water and the granola bars and pretzels I looted. Of course, my flashlight, compass, and gun are all back in the car. I wasn't expecting to have to ditch it like that. Sure glad I took the time to get my mixtape. *Shit.*

It's not a lot, but it'll last me until tomorrow. No sense in stumbling around in the dark, so finding shelter is the first order of business—something with cover and warmth. A small, protected hollow under a tree fits me perfectly. A layer of moss and leaves act as my blanket, and I soon fall into a restless sleep.

The same dream haunts me every night. Like some sick cosmic joke, my worst memory replays in my mind, a horror movie in excruciating detail.

I'm returning from an ill-fated mission. My fellow courier Connor has died, sacrificing his life to save mine. But things get even worse at home as I discover my boyfriend, Marcus, has fallen ill. He's lying in bed, sick and dying, the Infection in its vicious final stage.

I stand by his bedside, a protective barrier separating us. The undulations in the plastic distort his face. A face that is pale and worn out, with deep creases marring what was once beautiful. He looks more eighty than eighteen.

"Aiden," he utters weakly, putting a hand up to the barrier.

I press my hand against his, with tears streaming down my face. "I'm here, Marcus."

His voice is only a whisper. "Connor. I know—" His words are cut off by a fit of coughing.

I pull back in shock. Marcus couldn't know what happened on the mission. I only just returned, and Connor didn't make it back alive.

"What about Connor?" I ask.

He's too weak to speak. But the look in his eyes is sadness and hurt. I want to explain and tell him what happened—tell him I love him. But he's used his last breath. He coughs up blood, and his body thrashes as the Infection claims its latest victim. The only small mercy is him not turning into one of those—*things*.

Consciousness tears a hole through my nightmare, and I wake up with a start, my eyes damp. No use in trying to bury this memory. My subconscious won't allow it. It's been six months since his death, but the dream keeps returning as vivid as if it were yesterday.

The box. In a panic, I reach for the backpack, but of course, it's still there. That same familiar shape.

I'm under no illusion that the vials in the box will erase my torment or somehow bring Marcus back. But if they help find a cure and save a single person from the Infection, or spare a single loved one from feeling the misery I feel, maybe I'll have done my penance. Maybe *that* will dampen the pain.

And if this really is a suicide mission? Well, that'll dampen the pain too.

Chapter Two

Longing For Home

ZACH

Day 378. With the end of a flathead screwdriver, I scratch another notch into the ever-growing rows of hash marks on the wall of the abandoned bank lobby.

Taped next to them is a picture of Mom and Dad standing outside my childhood home on Vashon Island, west of Seattle. They are smiling and blissfully ignorant of what the next year will bring. I put two fingers up to my lips and kiss, then touch each of them.

"Miss you guys. I'll find some way to get home," I whisper to the empty room. A deep pit of loneliness wells up in my chest. I hate being alone.

The last bit of twilight shines through the door of the bank, casting a long ghostly rectangle across the lobby's marble floors. Time to check the perimeter defenses before it gets too dark. It's the first thing I do when I get up each morning and the last thing I do before bed. Every. Single. Day.

Big Sky Bank is the most defensible building in the little town of Elk Springs, Montana, so I've made it my home. The inside is all stone and marble, with drab furnishings suited for—well—a bank lobby, to be quite honest.

I run my fingers against the seams of the sheet metal I've welded to windows and the front door, looking for imperfections. All looks good— no sign of cracks. I'm pretty secure in my little cocoon.

With a flashlight in hand, I head out into the cool evening twilight, walking past the white granite blocks and Roman columns out front. Elk Springs is nestled between mountain peaks on either side and surrounded by a dense forest of evergreens. I rub my hands against my arms as goose-bumps form on them. Even in June, with days in the seventies, it can get chilly at night at high altitude.

Boarded-up businesses pass on either side as I head to the edge of Main Street. That damn town sign always glares at me each time I pass it.

Welcome to Elk Springs, Montana

Sportsman's Paradise

Population: 597

It's taunting me. Should read *Population: Zach.*

I'm not even from this miserable town. School was out, and I was on summer break, learning to fly-fish with Uncle Max. Bonding time, he called it. Then the power and Internet went out and didn't come back. Lots of people left town. The ones who stayed started getting sick from some mysterious disease. Most died within days. Watching my uncle die was the hardest part. I don't like to think about it.

But not everyone *died* of the disease. The few who fought through the fever and lived—those are the ones who scare me. They've lost all reason and wander around looking for anything to eat to survive. A single scratch from their nails is a death sentence. But it's been a while since I've seen one.

Past the town sign, a row of aluminum cans spread out across the entrance to Main Street. People can't help but clatter through them as they enter town. My first line of defense. Cars block the street behind them, strategically placed to appear random, but they keep people from driving through.

Next, I head to Elk Springs General Store. Inside, barren shelves and empty refrigerators greet me. The rifle pointing out the window is rock solid on the stand I built. I duct-taped a volleyball on top, emblazoned with the name Wilson on it, complete with a handprint drawn with a red Sharpie.

"Hey Wilson." I chuckle and wave to the volleyball. It's the little things that keep me going. Wilson says nothing back. As long as it stays that way, I know I'm still good.

With three shells loaded, the rifle angles slightly upward so people will hear and feel the bullets flying by them without being hit. The idea is to scare people, not kill them. Wilson isn't a monster.

The wire attached to the trigger is secure. It runs to a pulley, up through a hole in the ceiling, and across the street to Big Sky Bank, to a remote trigger. The tension feels right. No kinks or snags in the line.

After the general store checks out, there are two more Wilsons to inspect. One's in Leo's Garage next door. The other is in The Prospector, the dive bar across the street.

The Wilsons have saved my skin a few times. Bands of thugs come through town now and then. A single gunman holed up in a building is an easy target. But if they're surrounded by Wilsons, well, that's a different story. And the noise from the guns seems to scare off the sick ones too.

I'm headed across the street on my way back to the bank when a branch snaps someplace nearby. I stop in my tracks and stay totally quiet, shining my flashlight into the darkness and straining to hear. It's dead quiet. The only noise is the beating pulse in my ears.

A moment later, the clattering of aluminum cans cuts through the silence. The sound I most dread.

Out of the shadows, a man comes barreling toward me at full sprint. He's severely emaciated—almost skeletal. Purple veins bulge from his neck and forehead. Telltale signs of a man who fought off the disease but lost his mind in his battle to stay alive. A surge of adrenaline runs hot through my veins.

He's closing too fast.

I'll never get back to the bank in time. Squaring my shoulders, I face him, knowing standing my ground is my only chance for survival. I fight back every instinct telling me to run. His dead eyes stare at me, getting closer by the second.

Don't fricking run.

As he lurches clumsily toward me, the reek of decay overwhelms me, and I nearly retch. But I hold my ground. Remembering the self-defense techniques my mom taught me, I grab his outstretched hand, narrowly avoiding his jagged nails. I pull him forward with everything I have, using his momentum against him. He's so startled he loses balance and sprawls to the ground.

With him down, I race to the bank in a full sprint, but he gets up quickly and closes in fast. Just feet from the door, his footsteps are right behind me, the heat of his breath on the back of my neck.

The moment I'm through the bank entrance, I strike him hard with the door, knocking him in the head and pushing him backward. But this guy is relentless; he rushes forward again as I slam the door shut. His fingers get trapped in the doorjamb, and he lets out a howl that sounds more like a beast than a man.

He bangs his body against the outside of the door. I hold back the onslaught with all the strength I can muster, trying to get traction as my feet slip against the marble floor. He drives into the door again, pushing it inward the slightest bit. With that momentary slack, he wriggles his hand out farther, but I shove the door back hard. Now, only his fingertips poke through.

I reach up to the hinged beam to barricade the door, but it won't quite slot into place. The fingers wedged in the door make the gap a hair too big.

Drawing from some inner strength, I slam my shoulder against the door hard enough to see spots. I do it again. The third time does the trick. The door slams shut, and the beam falls into place with a large thud. A terrible shriek comes from the other side. Blood trickles from the doorjamb where his fingers were stuck. The smell is horrendous, like something rotting.

I collapse to the floor, safe for the moment. I'm sweat-drenched and gasping for air.

That was too close.

I've never been caught that off guard. Never been out in the open like that. It's been so long since I've encountered anyone sick that I've gotten complacent.

I quickly scan every inch of my exposed skin to check for any scrapes. As far as I can tell, I'm okay.

Risking a peek out of a porthole cut into the window, I slide the metal shutter aside and strain to see in front of the door. But the moment I look out, I get his attention, and he runs right over. I jump back just in time as he jams his fingers through. Luckily, the portholes are only a couple of inches wide.

I put my rifle up to his hand. But I can't do it. A gunshot wound is a death sentence. These are people, after all—the few who were strong enough to survive that damn disease. Their humanity is gone, operating on pure instinct in a never-ending search for food and water. They'll attack anything—human, animal, and even other sick ones. The weak die fast. That leaves the strongest, like the one outside at this very moment. *Lucky fricking me.*

Maybe putting the poor soul out of his misery would be more merciful. But what if a person still exists behind all that rage? It shouldn't be my call to decide if he lives or dies.

The shrieking continues as the man slams his body against the door repeatedly. With each blow, the beam shudders. But the wood is thick. It should hold.

I *think* it will hold.

It had better hold.

Chapter Three

Paths Cross

AIDEN

I'm woken by the sound of chirping birds and the sun streaming through the trees. I push away the moss and leaves that served as my blanket. My nightmares of Marcus are a fading memory. Almost gone.

The slightest movement sends a flash of pain radiating from my ribs. My arms look thrashed, covered with angry red scratches and streaks of dried blood. Stretching my legs is a mixture of pleasure and pain, the muscles sore from last night's escape. A quick massage loosens them up.

I drink a few gulps of water to wet my parched throat, but it does little for my thirst. With no idea when I'll find more, I use it sparingly. The granola bar is stale as hell, as are most prepackaged foods these days. All are well past the expiration date. But it's calories, so that's all that matters.

Okay. Lost in the forest, with no map and no compass. No use trying to get back to the car. It's trashed, and I'm sure my pursuers already picked it clean. The best way to get unlost is to go in a straight line. So, I keep the morning sun to my right, which keeps me headed north.

After a while of trudging through the forest, I bump into a river that blocks my path. It's swift and full of spring runoff. Churning and bubbling rapids cascade over large rocks and fallen trees. I know better than to drink from it. Puking up precious calories because of a stomach bug is a bad idea.

There's no hope of crossing the river. The strong current would knock me over in a second, so I follow it downstream instead. As I navigate boulders and branches, it's slow going along the jagged bank.

Frustration builds as I plod along. My legs ache, and my ankles keep rolling on the uneven rocks. I'm about to give up and return to the forest when my persistence pays off. A bridge appears ahead, around a bend in the river.

Whew.

You never know how long it'll be when you're lost in the woods. It could be hours or even days. *Or never.* Finding the bridge is a lifeline to civilization. But just because I'm no longer lost doesn't mean I want to be found. With civilization comes danger. Ever since the Infected ravaged the world, everyone left wants to take something from you. Take your possessions. Take your freedom. Or take your life.

The road is quiet. No humans or vehicles. Only the chirping of birds and the roar of the river break the silence. The road heads through a dense forest of Ponderosa pines and maples. All roads have been getting worse since the Great Collapse a year ago when most of the world's power grids and communication networks toppled like dominoes.

But this road is in good shape. Covered with branches and pine needles, it appears rarely traveled on. That's good news in my book. Less chance of running into people.

I turn right onto the bridge and cross the river going north. At some point, this should get me to Interstate 90, which cuts across Montana. And I-90 leads to Seattle, my ultimate destination.

In a few minutes, I pass a sign.

Elk Springs—5

Never heard of Elk Springs.

Perfect.

Hopefully small enough that militia groups have overlooked it. And hopefully abandoned. It's best to avoid running into anyone. Maybe I'll find another car to scavenge. Then hit the road again and try to get this godforsaken box delivered.

*

ZACH

I wake with a start, lying on my bed behind the teller's desk. Dust motes float through the beams of sunlight streaming through the portholes as the sun rises over the hills around Elk Springs.

Last night, the constant banging went on for over an hour. It was hard to believe, but the four-by-six beam barring the door showed some strain. Slight cracks formed right at the doorjamb. But the force and frequency of the banging slowed until it turned to nothing. When I worked up the courage to peek out of the porthole, the town was empty again.

Somehow, I managed a few hours of sleep last night, but it wasn't particularly restful, broken up by nightmares of having my door beaten down by that sickened man.

That's it. I've had it. I grab the backpack I keep fully packed with enough food and supplies to last a week in the wilderness, then shut the bank door and head north on the highway. After last night, I've got to get out of this town.

A forest of evergreens lines both sides of the road, dense enough that I can't see more than twenty feet in either direction. Out here in the open, if I run into anyone, I'd be vulnerable, so I clutch my rifle like it's a lifeline.

This isn't the only time I've tried to leave. But each time I do, it dredges up memories of being lost in the woods when I was seven years old. I wandered in the forest for hours until I collapsed from exhaustion, spending the night shivering next to a tree. I woke the following day, my mouth parched and stomach aching from hunger, sure I was going to die. It was two days before a search and rescue ranger found me. I cried into his chest, never wanting to let go.

From that point forward, I would freak out if I ever got lost in a mall or lost sight of my mom in the grocery store. A therapist taught me to manage my anxiety, but being alone in the woods sends these memories flooding back.

The first time I tried to leave Elk Springs, I didn't even make it out of town before my anxiety kicked in. A week later, I hiked out far enough to spend the night. The last time, I made it three days out. That's when I ran into Ezra. He's an old, grizzled guy holed up in his junkyard. My first contact with another person in months. When I met him, he was in awful shape, on the edge of starvation. I gave him some food, and in return, he gave me the sheet metal and showed me how to use a welding torch to fortify the bank. He brought the supplies in the car that he keeps in running shape.

He'd come by about once a month, and I'd trade him food for sheet metal and other building supplies. He told me if I ever wanted to make a run for it, he'd trade his car for all my supplies. He said he was too old to travel, and the junkyard was all he knew. That was back in November before winter made driving impossible. The last traces of snow melted over a month ago, and I keep expecting him to show up. But so far, no sign of him. So that's where I'm headed. To take him up on his offer.

I only get a mile before my frazzled nerves from last night get the best of me. I jump at every sound in the forest. There's no way I can make it any farther. Not today, anyway.

So I turn around and run the whole way back, only stopping when I'm within the town perimeter. I'm such a damn coward, slinking back to the bank with my head hanging low. I let out a deep sigh and stow my back-pack, resigned to my fate as Elk Springs' lone inhabitant.

After another failed attempt at fleeing the town, I'm wrapped in a deep malaise. With nothing else to do in this miserable town, I start my daily routine.

I smooth the cans disturbed last night, check the Wilsons, and head to the vegetable garden. It's my favorite place in town, and it helps to calm me.

The moment I enter, my tension eases. My mom kept a garden at home, and it reminds me of her. Green shoots poke up from the tilled rows of soil. The damp earth between my fingers feels just right as I take in the moldering smell of compost. Soon, I'll have fresh tomatoes, carrots, celery, and a handful of other produce. Before the Great Collapse, my parents had to force me to eat vegetables, but after months of canned food, my body demanded something fresh. Now, vegetables from the garden are a special treat.

Snare traps line the garden. Two of them hit their mark, with rabbit carcasses lying motionless, necks trapped. My heart aches for the little critters. Never saw myself as a hunter, but your perspective on things can change once you're hungry. Speaking of which, rabbit stew sounds good tonight. With the traps reset, I grab the carcasses and head back to Big Sky Bank with my haul.

I set the rabbits on the cold marble of the teller's desk, then head back to the vault where I keep all my food and supplies. The vault entrance dominates the back wall of the bank lobby. It has a circular door about eight feet in diameter with an old-school manual combination lock in the middle. Luckily, one teller was nice enough to write the combo on a Post-it. Or stupid enough, depending on how you look at it.

As I walk down the vault, I do a quick inventory. There's a pile of cash left over from when people cared about things like paper money. I use it for kindling. Plus, it's fun throwing a stack of twenties on the fire sometimes. Like I said, it's the little things that keep me going.

Looking at my food supplies is always a little depressing. I looted everything from all the nearby homes, so there was a lot at first. But after a year, the supplies are dwindling. I've supplemented the food by canning the extra vegetables from last year's crop and learning to hunt. But the inventory is still trending downward. For now, I have enough that I'm happy to live in denial. But it won't last forever. Making it through another winter will be pushing it.

My camping supplies, survival gear, and a pile of weapons are at the end of the vault. I keep the weapons sorted by type—rifles, shotguns, pistols, crossbows, compound bows, knives, swords, and machetes. If you can kill with it, I've got it. I don't even like guns, but better to have them locked up than looted by some stranger and used against me.

I grab a buck knife and head back to the lobby to work on the rabbits. I've got one rabbit skinned, and I'm starting on the second when a noise from outside makes me jump.

It's those damn aluminum cans.

*

AIDEN

After a few hours of walking, I come to a faded wooden sign by the side of the road with lettering scrawled across it in peeling paint.

Welcome to Elk Springs, Montana

Sportsman's Paradise

Population: 597

There's a homespun drawing of a fly fisherman casting a rod in a stream.

A handful of sad-looking businesses line the road ahead, with a few blocks of modest homes behind them. A smattering of cars lines the streets. Most are burned out or smashed, but a few look mostly intact. There may be hope for me yet.

I'm so focused on the cars that I don't notice the wide patch of aluminum cans until my feet clatter through them. The noise echoes throughout the quiet little town.

Well, shit. Now somebody knows I'm coming.

Chapter Four

Elk Springs

ZACH

I bar the door and grab my rifle, adrenaline coursing hot through my veins. Probably that sick man from last night. I should have known he'd be back. These encounters are always terrifying and unpredictable. It's like being in an earthquake. You never know how long it will last and how bad it will get—a singular point in time where your life is at risk.

Peeking through the porthole, I spot a lone guy wandering into town. *Hmm.* Not the guy from last night, and he doesn't look sick. That calms my nerves a bit. But a few things are odd about him.

First, he's not holding any weapons. That's extremely unusual.

Second, he's alone. Every encounter with looters and thugs has always been three or more. Safety in numbers and all that. And they're usually doing some poorly executed tactical drills, jumping behind cover, and yelling "clear" a lot. Third—and this is by far the most interesting—he looks… normal. Like the Great Collapse has had no impact on him.

Most people I encounter are somewhere on the spectrum, from dirty and ragged to full-on mountain man. But this guy looks clean-cut, like he's had a recent shave and a real haircut. His dark hair is clipper short on the sides, the top longer and kind of messy. He's about five foot ten and young. I'd guess around my age, maybe a bit older, eighteen or nineteen. He's muscular but not too bulky, his skin medium olive. And he's dressed all in black, wearing boots, cargo pants, and a V-neck T-shirt.

He doesn't have that desperate look everybody has now. The look you get after living on your own for a year, not knowing where your next meal is coming from. Or if you do, you're worried somebody will take it.

Usually, I'd be firing off warning shots and yelling at him to clear out of town by now. But instead, I watch him and wait. Curiosity replaces my apprehension. His confident and fluid movements captivate me. He's trying to be stealthy. It's kind of funny to watch, actually. Especially after the way he clattered through the cans on the way into town.

There's a strange feeling in the pit of my stomach. A little fluttering.

Oh crap.

I forgot this feeling existed. This doesn't happen anymore. Nowadays, it's survival or nothing—zero guy distractions. But this guy is fricking cute.

He continues down the road, peeking into each shop, then approaches a 4Runner parked on the street. He tests the doors, and they open.

But he's wasting his time. It has no keys, a dead battery, and an empty gas tank. That's true of every car for miles.

Well, there's that *one* car at the junkyard. It's ever-present in my mind. My escape hatch to Seattle, where I used to live with my family, where I left my ex-boyfriend and first love, Felix. I don't even know if they are dead or alive. They must all be dead. Everyone I've ever known or loved is dead.

Cute Guy must have figured out the car was useless because he exits it and continues on. As he approaches the general store, I panic. He'll find Wilson.

Damn it, Zach.

The defense system doesn't work if I don't use it. If I set it off now, there's a good chance I'll hit him.

Without taking time to think things through, I open the bank door and run out with my rifle.

I shout across the street, "Hey! Don't move or I'll shoot!"

*

AIDEN

A voice calls out behind me, and I swing around fast. A guy is pointing a rifle right at me. That's a sight you never want to see. My hands shoot skyward. This isn't my day.

He has a haggard look about him. Long and frazzled light-brown hair goes almost down to his shoulders. It's matted into clumps, like he's not combed it in months, and he's got a wispy, unkempt beard. A few patches of pale, freckled skin show through what's probably weeks of dirt covering his body.

It's hard to tell through his grizzled exterior, but he looks young.

He's shorter than me, around five foot eight. I've got thirty pounds of muscle on him, easy. If it came to it, I could take him. But I hope it doesn't. Violence is always my last resort and *always* nonlethal. There's enough death around already.

This calculation is required for each new person I come across. And I hate that. I used to enjoy meeting new people and could strike up a conversation with a total stranger. Now, I assume all strangers are trying to kill me. Everyone's a murderer until proven otherwise. So, let's see what this guy is.

"Don't mean any harm. Just passing through." I stretch my hands up farther.

His eyes narrow, but he says nothing. He stares at me like he's not sure what to do next. His hands quiver, making the barrel of the rifle shake slightly. Maybe he's new to this whole "holding a person at gunpoint" thing.

I clear my throat. *It's your move, dude.*

"Well—uh—keep passing through, then." He points his rifle down the street as if to show me where to go. Based on his voice, he's definitely young. And definitely scared.

"Look, some guys ambushed me." I wave toward the road I came in on. "I lost my car and all my supplies. Can't make it much farther with what I've got."

"Well, you won't find anything for miles. Everything's picked over. *Including* the cars." He nods toward the 4Runner I just checked.

I keep my face calm, but my insides churn. This is bad. It's hard to say how long I'll last if I leave this town with nothing.

But this guy doesn't strike me as a killer. I could try taking his gun, but a nervous trigger finger mixed with a loaded weapon is a recipe for getting shot. He came out here for a reason and hasn't killed me yet, so he must want *something*.

"Any chance I can trade for some of your supplies? Got nothing of value, but I can work off anything I take. I'm handy with tools, and I'm pretty strong." I flex my bicep and point to it.

He makes a snorting laugh and rolls his eyes. But quickly refocuses and steadies the gun. "Keep those hands up."

But that's good. For a second there, he showed a sense of humor. I can work with that. I need to make him feel at ease and trust me.

"You're the boss here," I say.

"Um—turn around. Do you have any weapons?"

"Nope, no weapons." I do a slow three-sixty, keeping my eyes on his gun the whole time.

"Why?"

"Why what?" I ask.

"Why no weapons? Seems kinda stupid walking around without any."

I laugh. "Sorry to disappoint you. But it's not by choice. I had to ditch my car in a hurry. Like I said, I lost everything."

He grips the rifle tighter. "Turn out your pockets. Slowly."

Man, this guy is really on edge. Gotta figure out how to calm him down. I reach into all my pockets and turn them out. "See? Nothing."

"Let me see in that backpack."

Shit. The last thing I want is him snooping around in my backpack. I take it off, unzip it, and show him the inside. *Please don't notice the box.*

He leans in to look. "What's in the box?"

Fuck.

"Just medicine." I keep my voice steady, fighting back rising panic.

"What kind of medicine?"

"Antibiotics," I lie.

"Show me."

Deep breath, Aiden. It'll be okay. I remove the box with the utmost care and crack open the lid. Sunlight glints against the three vials of pale-green liquid packed tightly in padding. I figure he's only looking for weapons. But if he tries something stupid, like trying to take them, that would get ugly, fast. My entire body tenses, expecting the worst.

But all he does is nod and take a step back. I let out a deep breath and put the box away.

Shit, that was close.

"No *hidden* weapons?" he asks.

"Nope."

"Then drop your pants."

I bark out a laugh. "Excuse me?"

"I said drop 'em." He gestures with his gun. "Better not see any guns or knives strapped to your legs."

Wow. He's not kidding. "Like I said, you're the boss." I unbutton my pants and lower them to my ankles. Sure glad I wear underwear. A breeze tickles the hairs of my exposed legs, giving me goosebumps.

"See? No weapons," I say. "Only one place you haven't checked." I slather that last bit in sarcasm, trying to crack through his nerves with some humor.

He jerks his head back, eyebrows raised as if he can't believe what I said. We both stand frozen for a moment. Did I miscalculate?

"Not on the first date," he says in absolute deadpan.

He lets out a short laugh, and then I do, too, which cuts the tension.

"Alright, pull 'em back up."

As I do so, he lowers his gun, and his stance relaxes.

Whew.

"So, where did you say you were headed?" he asks.

His tone is noticeably calmer. Almost friendly. The sudden change is a little startling.

"Seattle. I'm looking for family. I was on the East Coast when all this shit went down."

Family is *not* why I'm going there, of course. But keeping my answers vague and close to the truth makes it easier not to get caught in a lie.

But when I mention Seattle, his eyes go wide. "*I'm* from Seattle," he blurts out. "I'm admitted to University of Washington—uh—I mean, I was admitted."

Cool. Another way to win him over. He'll think we're best friends in no time.

"Yeah. U-Dub is great," I lie. Never been there. Yet. But that's exactly where I'm headed. UW Medical Center. "So, how'd you end up here?" I gesture around the small main street.

"You mean ass-end-of-nowhere, Montana?"

We both laugh.

"Yeah, that."

"I was visiting my uncle. But he's dead now." He says it so matter-of-factly. But there's sadness in his eyes.

"Where's everybody else in town?"

His eyes shift downward, but he says nothing. That's all the answer I need. It's only him.

I nod. "I can relate. It's tough."

"Yeah, it sucks."

"How have you survived out here on your own? With the Infected and all," I ask.

"The Infected? Oh, you mean the sick ones?"

"Yeah." I nod. "That's what I call them."

"Being in the middle of nowhere has helped. Off the radar. The rest is being resourceful. And lucky."

Surviving alone is no simple feat, and it's impressive he's made it this long. But he's right about being lucky. And it's hard to say how long that luck will last.

He's getting more comfortable with me. With his gun lowered and guard down, this would be the time to act. And I almost do it. But something holds me back. There's something about this guy. Out on the road, I've learned to judge character quickly. Not everybody is ruthless. There are good people out there. If I can, I'd rather work with him instead of against him. And to be honest, some company doesn't sound like the worst thing. It's been weeks since I've talked to a soul. I'd guess it's been longer for him.

"My name's Aiden."

"I'm Zach."

Aiden. Zach. A to Z. Mnemonics help me remember names.

"We've got the whole alphabet covered." Zach chuckles.

I snort out a laugh, more from surprise than anything. Great minds think alike, I guess.

"So, was that true about the cars?" I ask. "Nothing for miles?"

"Yep. Checked them all out myself. No gas. Looters took care of that long ago. But none of them run, anyway. No keys and dead batteries."

I let out a sigh. "So whatcha think? Trade supplies for labor?"

"Look, you seem like a good guy." His eyes soften. There's kindness there, and it's a bit disarming. "I'll share some supplies. I'll figure out how you can pay me back. Maybe some things around town you can help with."

The tension in my body releases. If he turned me away, I don't like to think about what I'd have to do. He must understand that too. He seems smart.

He starts to turn around but then faces me again quickly, gun slightly raised. "But don't try anything. I've got my eye on you." He's trying to sound tough, but it comes across more as scared. I nod solemnly, but inside I laugh a little.

With that, he heads to a building with the words Big Sky Bank carved into the granite facade and gestures for me to follow. "Come on."

"Thanks," I say. "You're a lifesaver."

Zach glances back. "Don't make me regret it."

Chapter Five

Rabbit Stew

ZACH

I walk into the bank and gesture for Aiden to follow me. It takes my eyes a moment to adjust from the brightness of the outside to the relative darkness in the lobby. I turn around to see the silhouette of Aiden coming through the door.

Am I stupid, bringing a total stranger into my little cocoon? The last year has been nothing but building it up and defending it. Letting someone else in makes me feel exposed. Maybe his good looks are clouding my judgment. Being cute isn't a proper reason to trust someone. But maybe it's an *improper* reason? As in, I'd like to do improper things to him.

Man, I'm lonely.

That whole lowering-the-pants thing—I saw that in a spy movie once. It may have been a little over the top. But it *was* fun.

Still, there's something about Aiden. I'm pretty sure I can trust him. It was an experiment, when we were outside, and I lowered my gun. Made it look as if my guard was down. If he made a move, I was ready. But he didn't. He passed the test. I saw that in a spy movie too.

It's not absolute trust. I'm not totally naïve. My guard is still up, and I'm keeping the vault locked. Plus, there are things he isn't telling me. Like where did he really come from, and why does he appear so unaffected by the Great Collapse? And what's really in those vials? It was obvious how nervous he was when he showed them to me. Antibiotics, my ass. Something's not adding up.

Then again, he's not the only one with secrets. He doesn't know what happened to my uncle. And I haven't told him about the one working car I know about. There are some secrets best kept to myself.

The real reason I let him in? We each have something the other needs. And I'm not talking about trading supplies for some work around the town. I couldn't care less about that. I've tried to leave this place so many times, and I don't think I can do it alone. If he's heading all the way to Seattle, that could be my ticket home. If I trust him enough, I'll lead him to the car at the junkyard, and we can travel to Seattle together. I just need to find the best time to mention it.

Standing inside the bank lobby, Aiden looks around, eyes wide. He admires the steel sheets I welded onto the windows. "You did all this yourself?"

"Yep."

"Impressive."

"I'm handy with a welding torch." I smile.

"I'm getting a picture of how you've survived this long. What do these do?" Aiden reaches for the cables that fire the guns.

"Don't touch those!" I launch between him and the cables, and my arm strikes his chest. My first human contact in over a year, and it sends an unexpected little wave of electricity through me. My cheeks heat. "Maybe—just—don't touch anything."

"Sorry." He backs away, hands raised.

"It's okay. It's just—I'm not used to having anybody in here, and this is all a little strange for me." I rub the back of my neck. "Plus, I've got a few—um—defensive measures set up around town."

"Got it." He points at a chair left over from when this was a bank lobby. "Is this safe?"

"Yes. The chair is safe." A weird laugh escapes my lips. "Please. Sit down. Hang on for a second. I'll be right back." I gesture for him to stay as I scurry to the vault. There was a time when I could handle myself around a cute guy. But now I'm awkward and indecisive. It turns out flirting is a skill like everything else. Use it or lose it.

I grab a few items from the vault I suspect Aiden will want. I need to make a good impression on him, so he'll trust me. While I'm here, I also grab ingredients for the rabbit stew. With everything loaded onto a gray plastic cart, I shut and lock the massive vault door. It makes a satisfying booming sound as it closes, echoing through the bank. My stash is safely locked inside.

Back in the lobby, Aiden still sits in the chair, hands on his legs, looking around the room.

I haven't had a moment to truly look at him. He's not just cute. He's gorgeous. Stunning, in fact. He has piercing, pale-blue eyes. Almost silver. They're a striking contrast to his olive skin. His square jawline frames full lips and perfect teeth. His nose is just the right proportion with a cute little tip, enough to make him adorable.

God, I must look so terrible right now. Personal aesthetics haven't been exactly on top of my mind recently. Let's be honest. I've entirely let myself go. But what am I stressing about? I've got more important things to worry about, like convincing him to take me home. But the feeling in the pit of my stomach is hard to ignore. I'm going to have to find some time to get cleaned up.

"Brought you a few things." I hand Aiden a stack of cotton wipes, some antiseptic, a bottle of water, and a granola bar. "I notice you have a bunch of scrapes. You should get those cleaned up so they don't get infected. And you must be hungry and thirsty."

"Man, thanks." He beams at me, then chugs the entire bottle of water.

The way he looks at me makes me melt inside. How am I going to operate around this guy?

Aiden inspects the cart. "Wow, you're pretty well stocked."

"Yeah, I found most of this stuff around town."

"Quite the looter, aren't you?"

"Yeah." I let out a forced laugh.

The whole looting experience was horrific, to be honest. After my uncle died, I stayed locked in his home for as long as I could. But after a few weeks, my dwindling food supply forced me to venture out and start scavenging. I could tell the instant I went into a home if the owners had skipped town or stayed and hunkered down. It was the smell. I don't like to think about it.

Looters had already done a number on the town. They took every car with keys and siphoned the fuel from the rest. Picked every shop clean. Luckily, most of the houses were still untouched. Probably because of all the corpses. And the sick ones.

Going into each house was terrifying. Some were empty or only had dead people. In a few, one sick person remained, but never more than one. Survival of the fittest, I guess. They don't seem to have qualms about killing each other. When I found a house like that, I'd open the door and run to the bank. They would eventually find their way out and wander into the forest. That sick man last night may very well have been one of the ones I set free, surviving in the forest somehow.

Once the houses were empty of people, I stripped them of everything useful and carted it all back to the vault. It turned out to be a good idea. Over the next month, looters took care of anything I left behind. Every time I saw somebody stroll into town, I'd go hide in the vault. That was all before I had the Wilsons and my armor-plated bank lobby. Now, I don't put up with that crap.

With Aiden occupied, I'm free to start cooking. "Hey—um—I'm going to be making some rabbit stew. Let me know if you need anything else." A weird laugh escapes my lips. *Geez, I'm like a giggling schoolgirl.*

"Will do," Aiden says flatly, not noticing my awkwardness or just ignoring it.

He cleans up the scrapes on his arms and face while I finish skinning the second rabbit. The whole while, I keep stealing glances at him, half to keep my eye on him and half because I can't help myself.

With the rabbit cleaned and deboned, I cut it into chunks. The teller's desk is my kitchen. The long marble slab makes an excellent surface for prepping food. A stock of dishes, pots and pans, spices, and cooking supplies are all lined up along it.

Aiden's finished tending to his wounds, and now he's hovering, hands in pockets, watching what I'm doing. Those pale-blue eyes pierce into me. I'm so distracted I nearly cut my finger off.

"Hey, if you want something to do, you could get a fire started." I point over to the pile of firewood and wood stove set up behind the teller's desk, next to my bed.

"Sure. I can do that."

The cast-iron stove has a flat surface on the top. It provides heat and a space to cook. A pipe extends up to the ceiling to vent smoke. What fun that was getting the stove all the way to the bank, taking me hours to drag it from a nearby house.

I grab a stack of bound twenties off the cart and throw it to Aiden. "Here. For kindling."

It gets a laugh out of him, so it was worth every penny. *Every penny.* See what I did there? Yep, my mind tells jokes to itself. I've been alone for too long.

Once the fire has heated the cooktop, I sear the rabbit meat in a large Dutch oven. For the rest of the stew, I add a few jars of vegetables and potatoes. Some fresh thyme and rosemary from the garden help to enhance the flavors. I mix it all up and let it simmer. It's a beef stew recipe I used to make with my mom but substituted with rabbit. It reminds me of her.

The scent permeates the room, and Aiden breathes it in. "Wow, I haven't smelled something that delicious in a long time."

"Thanks." I'm trying hard not to blush at *every* nice thing he says.

He comes up right next to me to get another sniff. My mind fills with conflicting emotions. Attraction and repulsion are all mixed into one. He's too close, and it's freaking me out. I lurch back, unconsciously grabbing for the rifle slung over my back.

Aiden backs off, hands up and eyes wide. "Sorry."

"I'm—Look, I'm gonna need some space."

"I'll keep my distance."

"Have a seat." I point to the lobby chair. "The food will be ready soon."

I've spent the last year surviving on my own, not trusting anyone. Caution has kept me alive. I can't turn that off like a switch just because some cute guy rolls into town, even if he's traveling to the exact place I want to get to. It'll take some time to get used to this. I have to let things run their course.

I clean up the kitchen in silence as the stew cooks. Once the flavors have melted together, and the meat is tender, I ladle out a decent portion into two bowls and hand him one.

"Thanks," Aiden says as he takes the bowl. Now that he's cleaned up his scrapes, it's easy to make out four long scratch marks running down his right arm. They look like defensive wounds.

Oh god. What if he's sick and doesn't show it yet?

I move quickly to the other side of the lobby, hoping he doesn't notice my reaction.

"You don't need to worry about those." Aiden points to the scratches. "I'm immune. That happened a week ago, and I'm fine. You're probably immune, too, if you've made it this long."

Immune? Is that even a thing? I suppose it explains why some people have survived. I assumed they were all isolated and lucky, like me. Being immune would be nice and all, but I've never been scratched. So I'm not so sure.

"How do you know you're immune?" I ask.

"There's a blood test. I was one of the first subjects. One in ten thousand are."

I do some quick math. Eight billion people in the world. That's only eight-hundred-thousand immune people. Around thirty thousand in the entire US. Not even enough to fill half of Seattle's Husky Stadium. Isolated in Elk Springs, I could only guess how bad things were for the rest of the world. Those are slim odds for my parents and ex-boyfriend being alive. My throat is thick as I fight back emotions welling up.

That's also slim odds for me being immune. What if my isolation has only made me lucky? Then again, what makes me think I can trust anything this guy says?

"What do you mean 'blood test'?" I ask. "Are there, like, hospitals around still or something?"

"Something like that."

Another annoyingly vague answer. "How do I know you're not lying?"

"What reason would I have to lie?"

"To kill me and take my supplies."

He raises an eyebrow. "If I had the Infection, and I wanted you sick, we'd *both* be dead soon. And me before you."

"But maybe you can still spread it. Even if you're immune."

Aiden shakes his head. "That's not how it works. It only spreads when you have symptoms, or if you're one of those *things*. And symptoms start within twenty-four hours of being infected. These scratches are over a week old, so we're good."

"You sure know a lot about it." It comes out a little sharper than I intended.

"I do." His tone has an edge, as if he's done talking about it.

This isn't going how I wanted. I take a deep breath. "Look, I'm sorry. I'm worried about my family back in Seattle. I haven't seen them in over a year."

"I understand." His eyes soften a little. "It's been tough on everybody."

The fear of the Infected is too ingrained in me. Still, I guess he has nothing to gain by lying, but I'm still not ready to throw away all my precautions or admit I'm wrong. "Eat your stew before it gets cold."

Aiden shrugs and starts eating. The way he wolfs the food down, it's like he hasn't eaten in weeks.

"This is so good." He barely stops chewing while he's talking. "Where did you learn to cook like this?"

"My mom. She's an amazing cook…" Any time my parents enter my mind, it makes me a little melancholy.

"Neither of my parents could boil water without burning it. We ate out a lot." Aiden snorts out a little laugh, not reading my mood. "Your mom taught you well."

"Thanks." An awkward silence follows. Aiden must have figured out it's a touchy topic for me. He doesn't probe further.

I change subjects to something that's been on my mind since I saw him wander into town. "So, what's your deal, exactly?"

"Um—can you be more specific?"

"The way you look. Most people look like mountain men. Worn out and frazzled. You don't. And to be honest, it's kinda freaking me out."

Aiden lets out a little laugh, then pauses for a moment. When he speaks, it almost sounds rehearsed. "Where I'm from, there's a slice of civilization left. A group of people who were in the right place at the right time. Scientists. Good people."

"So that's where you got the blood test?"

"Yes."

I hadn't dared hope a place like that existed. The very idea gets me excited. From my limited perspective, the entire world is anarchy. A hundred questions enter my mind, but he continues before I can ask any.

"I can't tell you a lot about it. Part of what's kept us safe is secrecy."

I'm dying to know more, but pressing him doesn't seem like a good idea. Not yet, anyway. I'll respect his boundaries for now. "Well, it's good to know it's not all anarchy out there."

"It's not much. But, yeah, the world's not *all* anarchy."

"Do you guys at least have ice cream?"

Aiden laughs. "No. No ice cream."

"That's too bad. I really miss ice cream."

"Yeah, me too." Aiden looks up at the ceiling wistfully. "I miss sushi."

"Roller coasters. Oh, and sailing! My family owns a sailboat."

"Nice. I always wanted to learn to sail."

"Maybe I can teach you some time." Realizing it's a little quick to make future plans with him, my face gets warm. "Uh—I mean, if there were any water around here."

"Heh, yeah. Too bad." Aiden smiles. "I miss movies. And popcorn."

When Aiden says movies, I'm so excited I literally can't contain it. An involuntary squeak comes out of me, and I cup my hand over my mouth. *Giggling schoolgirl.* Aiden shoots me an incredulous look.

I reach for a remote control next to me and make an exaggerated, "*Ah-hem.*" A sixty-five-inch flat-screen TV flickers on. Dramatic *Star Wars* orchestral music pipes through the speakers. It echoes around the lobby. Various cut scenes of Han, Luke, and Leia running around the Death Star play on a loop.

Aiden's jaw drops open, and he laughs. "You have *electricity?* And *movies?*"

"You'd be surprised what you find when you loot houses. A lot of guys around here had portable batteries and camping solar panels. Wanted to keep their beer cold in the woods, I guess?" I point to a bunch of heavy-duty extension cords. They're jammed through a hole in the corner of the ceiling, extending down into the room. "I've got about ten of them on the roof. They can't power too much, but at least I can watch TV."

Aiden shakes his head. "You're a clever one, aren't you, Zach?"

I wave him off and shrug. I'm getting comfortable enough with Aiden's compliments, so the blushing isn't an instant reaction this time. But it still tingles a bit.

"But *Star Wars?*" He feigns disapproval. "Nothing from this millennium? Not even *Mandalorian?* I'd love to see some Baby Yoda."

I scowl. "First, it's Grogu, not Baby Yoda. Second, *Star Wars* is a classic. Shame on you. Third, I got electricity working. Not the freaking Internet. If it ain't on DVD, it ain't on this TV." I fold my arms and glare at him for as long as I can hold it until a smile cracks through.

Aiden lets out a short laugh. "You had me for a sec."

And then we both start cracking up, the sound of it echoing around the lobby. Oh man, it feels great to laugh. And speaking of which, Aiden's laugh is amazing. Heartfelt and genuine. Not too noisy or hissy. I missed having company so much.

"For the record, I knew it was Grogu," Aiden says between laughs. "I just like the name Baby Yoda better."

"Sacrilege!" I point to him. "It's like I don't even know you."

At the ridiculousness of that statement, a fresh round of laughing erupts. My side hurts from it. A wonderful hurt.

As Aiden erupts with giggles, I contemplate my options. How can I get him to trust me? Agreeing to trade might be a step in the right direction. Plus, he could help with a bunch of things around town. An extra set of hands would make it a lot easier. I'll hold off on mentioning the car and me going with him. That will come later. All in good time.

"So I'll make you deal, Aiden. If you help me with some things around town for a few days, I'll stock you up with supplies to last you a week. And I'll even throw in a movie night. Sound good?"

Aiden pauses for a moment, then looks me in the eye. "Sounds like a deal."

We head out of the bank to tour the town. My comfort level is rising around him, but precautions are still important. I keep my distance, and the rifle is by my side. I don't think he's going to pull anything, but I'm ready in case he does.

We walk over to the rain barrels I've set up at the bottom of every downspout along Main Street collecting rainwater. May was a wet month, so they're all near capacity.

"These are fifty-five-gallon drums. But some tanks in town are over five-hundred gallons. Even empty, they're too heavy for one person. I'd like us to drag one over here."

Aiden nods. "Sounds good."

"And here are the drip irrigation lines that run to the garden. If I turn this spigot here, the water flows through them."

I follow the lines out to the garden and wave Aiden along.

"As long as there's enough water in the tanks, I get good pressure through the entire system. Until I get right here." Kneeling at the far end of the garden, I fuss with the irrigation tube. "Maybe it's too long of a lead—"

"Zach, don't move."

Aiden is towering over me, a rifle in his hands.

My rifle.

Chapter Six

Odd Jobs

ZACH

When did I even set my rifle down? It must have only been a few seconds. And that's all it took for him to grab it. He was playing me this whole time, waiting for the right moment. He'll force me to tell him the combo to the vault. Steal my supplies. Or worse. How could I be so stupid?

I raise my hands, my whole body trembling. "Aiden, please—"

"Quiet," he hisses.

And then he fires the rifle. It's impossibly loud. The shockwave from the muzzle blast hits me, and I freeze, waiting for the searing impact of the bullet. But there's no pain. Either I've gone into shock, or the bullet missed.

"Get behind me," Aiden yells as he widens his stance and aims again.

"Wha—"

"Slowly!"

Movement flashes in the corner of my eye. A giant cougar stands no farther than thirty feet to my left. Two hundred pounds at least. It's in full attack mode, staring intently with ears pinned back, ready to pounce.

Our eyes meet. The icy stare of this massive predator makes the hair on the back of my neck stand on end.

Time seems to expand; seconds feel like minutes. With my eyes locked on the cougar, I slowly get up from my crouch. But as I do, my feet tangle together, and I trip, falling back into the dirt.

The cougar acts immediately. Its entire body compresses, preparing to spring. Its jaws gape open, flashing massive fangs that could rip my throat out in a heartbeat.

As its front claws leave the ground, another rifle blast rings out. A fine mist of blood sprays out as the bullet grazes the cougar's left shoulder. The impact throws its jump off, and it lands short of me, making a loud screeching sound. The cougar is so close I could reach out and touch it.

Another rifle blast misses the mark, but the cougar recoils at the sound this time. There's fear in its eyes, the hunter becoming the hunted. Aiden makes himself big, raising his hands and yelling.

The cougar's had enough, so it turns to run. Even wounded, the speed of the beast is chilling. It retreats to the woods, tail lowered, favoring one side. Within seconds, it disappears out of view.

I turn to Aiden, stunned. In five seconds, my mind went from thinking he was killing me to realizing he was saving my life. I open my mouth to thank him, but no words come out. Yet my expression speaks volumes.

Aiden nods and smiles. "You're welcome."

*

AIDEN

For a while, Zach sits in the dirt, stunned. It's not surprising. I'd be blabbering like a baby after such a near miss. But now we're on level footing. We've both held a loaded rifle while the other stood defenseless, with each of our lives in the other's hands. The postapocalyptic version of a trust fall.

"I've seen cougars around before," Zach finally says, eyes still wide, hands shaking. "But never like that. Never caught so off guard."

"I was distracting you. Don't be so hard on yourself."

"You saved me." Zach has this earnest look in his eyes. "I think I might owe you my life after that."

"You don't owe me anything beyond what we agreed to. Supplies for labor."

I hope he doesn't lean too hard into this "owing his life" thing. The last thing I need is somebody following me around, thinking I'm a hero.

I keep alert, making sure the cougar is gone for good. Scanning around, a half-eaten rabbit in a snare trap at the edge of the garden catches my attention. "That could be part of the problem." I point to the mangled rabbit. "The cougar may think of this area as a food source."

"I put those there to keep the rabbits out of the garden. Never thought it would bring cougars." Zach laughs nervously. I'm glad he's getting over the shock and can laugh a little.

Zach wiggles a finger in his ear. "I still hear ringing."

"I'm sorry I had to shoot right at you. The plan was to shoot straight up to scare it, but then it started charging."

"I won't lie. The gun blast scared the crap out of me." Zach gets up and jumps around, shaking the tension out of his arms and shoulders. "But I think I'm okay now. Let's keep going."

"You sure?"

"Yeah. It'll help me take my mind off it."

He finishes the tour of the outside grounds, showing me the rest of the little world he's built here. His resourcefulness is impressive. He's what I'd call a hard-core tinkerer. A MacGyver. I've known a few people like that in my life. They're good to have around in a pinch.

"Where did you learn how to do all this stuff?" I ask.

"My dad owned a repair shop, and I helped him out a lot. I guess it rubbed off on me. He was also an amateur inventor."

"That explains some of it, but you clearly have a gift for mechanics."

Zach shrugs. "I guess I've always liked taking things apart and putting them back together. My mom would get so annoyed, until she realized things ended up better when I was done." He lets out a sad laugh and has a distant look in his eyes.

He really does have a gift. With luck, he could stay here indefinitely. But that's just it. He'll need a lot of luck. The world is a nasty place now. If you have something worth taking, people will try to take it. You *need* to protect it. His defenses are enough to hold off a few disorganized looters and an Infected or two. But he couldn't withstand a real assault.

For about five seconds, I contemplate taking him with me. Like I said, he might be good in a pinch. But then I'm hit by a wave of terrible memories.

I was traveling with Connor, a fellow courier. When we were attacked on the road, he fought back, but I froze up. All I could do was watch him die as he fell off a bridge a hundred feet to his death. He sacrificed his life to save me, and I've never forgiven myself for that. I can't ask anyone to die for me ever again.

Nope. I travel alone. No exceptions.

"Hey, Aiden, you there?"

I come back from that dark place. "Huh?"

"You spaced out for a second. You okay?"

"Yeah." Memory buried. Focused again. "Let's get to work."

*

Zach has no end of projects. First, we work on moving the huge rain barrel he told me about. It's awkwardly large and heavy. Lugging it over from the nearby house takes our entire combined strength. And it doesn't exactly make my ribs feel great.

Once it's next to an overflowing rain barrel, Zach sets up a siphon hose between them. The water in the small barrel flows into the big one until their levels equalize. He has this natural intuition for how things work.

Zach puts his fists on his hips and admires the work. "That'll hold ten times the water now. Thanks."

"You're the brains. I'm just the brawn." I smile.

The good news is, he's no longer grabbing for his rifle every time I get near. Closer up and in the sunlight, I get a better sense of what he looks like. He's not bad-looking per se. He's just—how did he put it—a mountain man? His wispy beard covers most of his face in weird patches. Layers of dirt cover every inch of his skin, and his hair is a disaster, constantly getting in his eyes. His clothes are all dirty and frumpy, really adding to his hobo aesthetic. But sometimes, in the right light, at the right angle, maybe he's kind of halfway attractive. Not that it's remotely relevant to my current situation. I simply need to finish his tasks, get the supplies, and then go. I'll never see him again.

Speaking of Zach's tasks, the next one is fixing the chicken coop. One entire side fell over and was too heavy for Zach to lift himself. It's easier than lifting the rain barrel, but it still doesn't feel fantastic on my ribs. Maybe agreeing to manual labor wasn't the best idea.

Rounding up the chickens is interesting. Many are still in the coop, apparently happy with the shelter and soft straw. Lots of others are milling about nearby. Some appear to be victims of certain predators we've recently become familiar with. Random feathers and miscellaneous chicken parts are all that remain.

We chase around after the loose chickens. We're both running around, hunched over, hands stretched out, looking like idiots. To be perfectly honest, we laugh a lot more than catch chickens. Teamwork works best. I distract them as Zach sneaks up from behind and nabs them. We keep at it until all the chickens are safely inside.

We save the most backbreaking task for last, of course—carrying large logs from the nearby forest. We use one of those two-man saws seen in old cartoons to break them down. By the time the shadows are getting long, we've got two entire trees cut into sixteen-inch rounds, ready for splitting. My muscles ache after the day's work. Zach is really trying to get his value out of this deal.

Back at the bank, he flips on some LED string lights illuminating the entire room in a soft white glow. He does it so casually that it makes me laugh.

"What?" Zach says with a sheepish grin.

"It's just—it's funny seeing you switching on lights like it's no big deal. Just another day in postapocalyptic Elk Springs."

"I can't help if I'm clever."

"Don't let it go to your head." I laugh. "Plus, if you're so clever, why don't you have electric heat? It's freezing in here."

With the sun nearly down, the temperature is dropping rapidly. And the stone floors and austere bank interior makes it feel that much colder.

"I've tried running electric heaters, but they drain the battery in no time," Zach says. "Some things are best done the old-fashioned way. Speaking of which, thanks for volunteering to start the fire?"

"*Fine.* I know what I'm good for." I roll my eyes but let out a big smile, walking back to the stove.

Once the fire's going, Zach reheats the leftover stew from lunch. We make small talk about our lives before the Great Collapse. He talks about his family and plans to go to U-Dub, but I avoid saying anything too revealing or personal. Anytime he probes too deeply, I find a way to change the subject.

When we've finished dinner, Zach springs up with a smile. "Okay, movie time."

We drag two chairs over in front of the TV mounted on the wall. With a press of the remote, the TV and the DVD player light up. The *Star Wars* intro loops, filling the bank lobby with the familiar themes of John Williams. Something about the music is so evocative to me, bringing back childhood memories.

"The TV was already here in the bank. But I found the DVD player and a bunch of DVDs in people's houses." Zach runs his hand along a collection of DVDs set up on a table below the TV. "We can watch whatever you want."

"*Star Wars* is fine. I haven't seen that since I was a kid, anyway."

Zach beams and rubs his hands together. I guess that's what he was hoping for.

"Oh, I almost forgot." Zach runs off into the vault with a big smile.

This weird little guy sure has a lot of energy and enthusiasm. It's silly but quite endearing.

A moment later, the whirling of a fan fills the room. What in the heck is he doing? Then loud noises start, almost sounding like muffled gunshots. I jump up from my seat, startled. But then, the popping noises get louder and more frequent, and I laugh.

Microwave popcorn.

Zach comes out carrying two bowls filled with fluffy golden kernels. "I've got just a few bags of these. Only for special occasions."

"I can't remember the last time I had popcorn." I grab one bowl. "What's the occasion, then?"

"My first visitor."

First? Dang. This guy really must be lonely.

"My lucky day, I guess," I say.

I toss a kernel into my mouth. And, *wow*. It's been a long time since I've had a treat like this. It's buttery, salty, and crunchy in all the perfect proportions. We have very few luxuries in the emergency medical bunker I've been calling my home for the last year. All our meal rations come out of prepackaged bags. Almost no entertainment. Everything is utilitarian and focused on two things only. Survival and medical research.

Zach dims the lights and starts the movie. I saw *Star Wars* as a child, but it's been so long that I forgot what a good movie it is. Zach and I feed off each other's reactions, from C3PO's first line until Luke destroys the Death Star. It's the most fun I've had in a long time. I've been transported away for a moment, almost forgetting the hellscape I live in.

When the world has shifted so much, life becomes all about survival. It's easy to only focus on the big things. But sitting here, watching movies, sharing a laugh makes me realize how important the little things are too. Even when Marcus was around, life was so altered that we almost never laughed or had any moments like this.

When the credits finish rolling, we sit in silence. I smile at Zach. "Thanks for that."

"Yep. I need a movie like that to lift my spirits sometimes. But I think you needed it more than I did."

What an odd thing to hear a stranger say about me. Not only because he barely knows me, but also because he's right. I *did* need this. It lightened me a little. This little hobo of a guy has known me for less than twelve hours, and he's already figuring me out.

"You're an interesting guy, Zach."

He grins. "You ain't seen nothing yet."

Chapter Seven

Campfire

ZACH

The sun has set, and the temperature is dipping fast. This time of night creeps me out the most. It's when I shut myself in. Seeing the massive beam of wood barring the door should make me feel better. Instead, it puts up a wall between the known and the unknown. Everything in the bank lobby is familiar and safe. But outside, in the darkness, who knows what's lurking? It could be building, growing, and getting ready to attack.

But tonight is different. Aiden's here, and it doesn't seem so bad. It's funny how the brain works. You can get disoriented when you close your eyes and try to balance on your own. But putting a single pinky finger on another person gives you a point of reference, and you feel steady as a rock.

Before he saved my life—and yes, he *did* save it—I planned to have him sleep in one of the other buildings. Or lock myself up in the vault and sleep in there. Before I installed all the steel plating, I'd done that plenty of times.

When he held my gun, I was at his mercy. It was my worst-case scenario. He could have forced the combination out of me, stolen what he wanted, and already been on his way. But he didn't. Aiden is a good person at his core. This is a person I think I can trust my life with on the road.

The cold is creeping in fast, so we stoke the fire a bit to get more heat going. Even with daytime temperatures in the seventies, it can dip into the forties at night.

"Aiden, you get the bed." I point my finger downward at it, a no-nonsense look on my face.

"I'm not stealing your—"

"I insist. You save my life. You get the bed. It's a policy of mine."

"A recent policy?" Aiden makes a wry smile.

"Yes, just enacted." I laugh.

After a little more grumbling, Aiden relents and settles into the bed. He keeps his backpack close by with one arm hooked around the straps. Guess he's worried about whatever's in that box of his.

After marking the day on my wall, I drag one of the lobby chairs near the stove, wrap myself up in a sleeping bag, and sit in it. This will let me keep my eye on things. I don't expect much sleep tonight, anyway. Too much to think about. Sitting up in a chair will help with that.

Before long, Aiden's chest moves in a rhythmic motion, and the soft sound of his snoring fills the room. Hearing another person after being alone for so long is so comforting.

On the outside, Aiden looks clean-cut and totally with it, unimpacted by the Great Collapse. But a distinct sadness weighs him down. I saw in full contrast as he watched the movie how his troubles slid away momentarily. He had joy in his eyes, and his smile was broad and genuine. He looked like a different person.

I stare for a long time, thinking of the best way to ask him to take me with him. At some point, I must have dozed off because the sound of yelling wakes me. It's Aiden. He's tossing around in bed and making unintelligible noises. The only recognizable word is the name "Marcus."

His dream continues for a while longer, and then he bolts up. I narrow my eyes to little slits to feign sleep. He tries to catch his breath and maybe even cries a bit. It's sad to see. The urge to reach out and comfort him overwhelms me. But I resist.

After a few moments, he settles back into bed and drifts to sleep.

*

The next morning, I let Aiden sleep in as I go about my regular routine.

Everything is in working order, like yesterday. The only difference is the extra bit of caution I take walking through town. I used to love the garden. Now, the tranquility of that place is lost. I'll always have a touch of apprehension.

No rabbits in the snares today, so I return to the bank empty-handed. When I get there, I find Aiden awake.

"You started without me." He scratches his head and yawns.

"Seemed like you needed sleep. But don't worry. I've got a great idea for a project today."

"Somehow, I wasn't worried." Aiden smirks.

Part of me thinks investing in Elk Springs is silly when all I want to do is get away. But the other part of me worries I'll be here for the rest of my life, and no matter how many cute guys wander into town, I'll never escape. So, for now, I'll hedge my bets and keep improving the place. Plus, that gives me a chance to show off my smarts to Aiden and demonstrate my worth.

Last night, I was thinking about all the extra water capacity, which gave me an idea. The whole town is on a composting septic system, so the drains work. But the town's well runs off electric pumps, so there's no water. Placing one of the large drums high enough—say a hundred feet—could create enough pressure to supply water to the bank.

Elk Springs nestles right up to foothills. A steep slope rises behind Main Street, where a mountain stream runs year-round. If we could carry the drum up there, keep it filled with stream water, and connect it to the bank's water main, it might just work. So Aiden and I spend the better part of the day lugging a large water drum on a trail that switchbacks up the hill.

It's a hot day, so halfway up, Aiden removes his shirt. I don't complain one bit. His sculpted form is intoxicating. He has strong, broad shoulders, and his arms make those fun little bumps at the triceps. He's got a few tufts of hair on his chest and stomach.

Aiden's looks remind me of my ex-boyfriend, Felix. Same general face shape and body type. Very similar eyes. That was part of what struck me about Aiden when he wandered into my town. I have the slightest twinge of guilt thinking about Aiden in this way while Felix may be alone back in Seattle. But I shove that guilt away. I broke up with Felix for a reason.

Personality-wise, Aiden and Felix couldn't be more different. Felix was soft-spoken and okay with doing whatever I wanted to do. I would always initiate things in our relationship. That worked for a while, but eventually, it got old. I wanted him to contribute more. Felix was also very loving and fiercely loyal. It broke his heart when I called it off between us.

On the other hand, Aiden strikes me as somebody more confident in how he carries himself and everything he does. Even though I've been giving the orders on the jobs around town, I get the sense that Aiden usually runs the show. And that's exactly the kind of guy I want to help me get home.

What is his deal, anyway? I've been getting flirty vibes from him, but something is holding him back. He hasn't said a peep about his personal life. The only hint I have is that name he called out in his dream. Marcus.

"I think this was the best spot, right?" Aiden's question brings me back from my thoughts.

We're at a flat section of the hill, below where the stream collects into a naturally forming pool.

"Yeah, this looks good. Let's set it down right over there."

With the tank situated, I run plastic PVC pipe from the pool of water to the top of the drum. An in-line filter in the middle removes the bacteria. It's amazing what you find when looting people's houses. The drum starts filling with water, as I imagined it.

In one of his trips down from the junkyard, Ezra brought me hundreds of feet of PVC pipe for irrigation. It was great, but way more than I needed for the garden. An enormous pile has been sitting next to the bank for months, with grass growing through it. Working from opposite ends, we glue the pipes together until they're long enough to go all the way from the drum, down the hill, to outside the bank. Several hundred feet in all. Navigating it up the slope through all the trees is an interesting challenge. But with a bit of coaxing, we line up the pipe. Next, I cut the bank's water main with a hacksaw and attach it to the PVC pipe.

Aiden does a drum roll on the counter in the bank's bathroom while I turn on the sink. Air sputters out for a bit, but then the faucet comes to life, pouring out water. We both let out a cheer. Caught up in the moment, we do a quick hug. Any observer would think it's purely platonic, and that may be what Aiden thinks too. But it's magical for me. Aiden's muscular body presses against mine. The heat of his skin warms me, and I take in his scent. There's a stirring down below, so I turn away from him, acting as if a dust ball in the corner is the most exciting thing in the room.

Then, the magnificent sound of the flushing toilet fills the room, followed by it filling back up. I turn to see Aiden next to the toilet, smiling. I cheer and pump my fists in the air. After a year of using outhouses, never has there been so much joy over a toilet flush. We attempt a high five but miss badly, then break up into a fit of laughter. *Man, do I like him.* I haven't laughed this much since I was a kid. And laughing seems so easy between us.

After our strenuous morning, we take a well-deserved break. While Aiden's snacking on cold corned beef hash from a can, I wander off to the bathroom. Staring back from the mirror is a person I don't recognize. I've avoided mirrors in the last year. Splashing water on my face from the newly working faucet does nothing. All it seems to do is smear around the dirt and get my beard wet.

God, that beard.

I need to get rid of it. That and this massive mop of hair on my head. What I need is some hot water and soap, a scrub brush and a razor. Tomorrow, I'll work on getting cleaned up.

After we've eaten, there's still a few more hours of sunlight. So Aiden and I break down the logs we sawed up yesterday. Watching Aiden swing the ax is another exercise in sexual restraint for me. With each swing, his shoulders and lats flex. And his butt pushes out each time he bends over to pick up the logs.

Only Aiden's wincing spoils the mood. Every few chops, he clutches his ribs and makes a grunting noise, which makes me feel a little guilty for forcing him to do all this strenuous work. But it reminds me of the sounds he made in his dream last night.

Between ax swings, I ask him, "Hey, Aiden. Who's Marcus?"

He buries the ax in a log and stares at me with a hardened expression. "How do you know that name?"

"You were calling it out last night. During a dream."

Aiden's face darkens. He pulls the ax out and starts chopping wood harder than before. Between swings, he says, "He's just a person I knew once."

Okay, that's a touchy subject. I take the hint and ask no more.

*

For dinner, I take the other rabbit from yesterday and put it on a spit. I make a campfire outside the bank and set up a stand so the rabbit can roast, rotating it occasionally.

We sit around the fire in two camp chairs I pulled out from my looted outdoor gear.

Aiden's been quiet since I asked him about Marcus. Which kind of sucks because I've been planning on bringing up my idea of tagging along. I hope to find the right time to slip it into our conversation. But that's hard to do when there is no conversation.

In a moment of inspiration, I run into the bank and bring out a guitar I found in a nearby home. What's a campfire without some campfire songs, after all? Practicing the guitar has helped to pass the time.

Mostly, I enjoy strumming chords and singing. I've learned a lot of Beatles songs from a songbook I found. Those songs are fun to play because the chords are easy.

I strum the intro chords to "In My Life", which is one of my favorites.

Singing is one of my joys in life. It's one thing I can say I'm truly talented at. When the first verse starts, my voice is clear and bright. This gets Aiden's attention, and he cracks a smile. Near the end of the first verse, he joins in and does the harmony. *He has a wonderful voice too.* We finish the rest of the song together, each with a big smile on our faces.

"I'm glad you don't think singing at a campfire is too cheesy," I say.

"Are you kidding? I was a camp counselor for years. Playing guitar and singing campfire songs were *requirements.*"

"You play?" I hand the guitar Aiden's way.

"It's been a while." He does a few strums to check the tune. Then, what comes out of the guitar is nothing short of magical. It's the complex and haunting introduction to "Blackbird," one of my favorite Beatles songs, and difficult to play. I know this from my own failed attempts. He sings the melody, and I join in with harmony. It's pure bliss being lost in the notes and hearing the luscious resonating chords. When we're done, I give Aiden a round of applause.

"You're amazing. I'm kinda ashamed of my playing now."

"You played wonderfully, Zach. Nothing to be ashamed of. But that voice. You've got me beat hands down there."

My cheeks are warming, so I change topics to get away from the embarrassing compliments. "Oh, looks like the rabbit is getting close to done."

I get some canned veggies from the vault and heat them with some olive oil and herbs from the garden. Oil gets used sparingly. Once it's used up, it's gone. But if everything goes according to plan, I'll leave all this behind and head to Seattle with Aiden. So I'm pulling out all the stops.

But as we eat, Aiden clams up again.

"How's your dinner?" I ask, trying to get the conversation going.

"Oh," he answers, but his mind is in another place. "It's good. Thanks."

This is going nowhere. The direct approach is my only option. "Back in a sec," I say.

He mumbles an acknowledgment, barely hearing me.

I come back with a backpack full of supplies. I packed it for him earlier in the day. In my last gesture of goodwill, I hand him the pack. "This should last you about a week."

Aiden sees the backpack, and his eyes come back into focus. He's present again, as if waking from a dream. "Wow. This is great." He looks truly sincere. "This means so much to me. You're one of a kind, Zach."

"So, when do you think you'll head out?"

"Well, that kinda depends on you. I could leave as early as tomorrow. But this is a lot, and I want to be sure we're settled up."

"Yeah, I've been thinking about that. I was wondering if maybe—

um—for final payment—" I'm trembling. I barely get the words out. Here goes. "You could take me with you. To Seattle."

Aiden looks down at the ground, takes a deep breath, then looks into my eyes. "No. I'm sorry. That's out of the question."

"Oh." The directness of his rejection hits me like a punch in the gut. I hoped he would say yes and might even like the idea. We were forming a bond. Or so I thought.

My disappointment must be transparent. Aiden tries to console me. "Why would you want to leave this? You seem to have a good setup here."

"This shithole?" I snap more forcefully than intended. "Are you kidding? I've hated every moment of being here. I have to get away."

Aiden keeps this infuriatingly calm tone. "Then why haven't you headed out on your own?"

"I've tried. But it's dangerous. I don't think I could make it out there on my own." Emotions are welling up inside me—emotions I've bottled up for months.

"Zach, you don't know how dangerous it would be to go *with* me. Look, I haven't told you everything, but those people that ambushed me? They wanted to kill me. They're probably still after me."

"And you don't know how dangerous it is *here*. I have to deal with looters and thugs all the time. Just the other night, I was almost killed by a man sick from the disease. It's only a matter of time before my luck runs out."

Aiden looks at me with tight lips and then down at the ground. He says nothing.

This might be my last, best chance to get back to Seattle. He *needs* to understand. Tears are welling up, but I fight them back. I can't look weak.

"Going to Seattle is extremely important to me. All I want to do is find my family and my boyfriend. I have to know if they're okay." I fight back panic. In my outburst of emotion, I outed myself to this near stranger. I've been out and proud since I was fourteen, but without the safety net of civilization, you don't know how people will react.

But he doesn't freak out. In fact, his face softens, and he looks me in the eye. "Look, I need some time to think it over, okay? Let's talk about this tomorrow?"

"Okay," I utter under my breath.

Fear keeps me from telling him about the car. As certain as he was about saying no, he might try to force it out of me, and I'd be stuck here forever.

With nothing left to say, we scatter the campfire ashes and get ready for bed. It's the same arrangement as last night—Aiden on my bed and me sitting in the chair. I'll make my last appeal to him tomorrow. He needs to agree to take me before I mention the car; that's my last bargaining chip if all else fails.

I'm not sure when I nod off, but the sun is streaming through the portholes when I wake up. The front door is closed, and the beam barring the door has been lifted. In a panic, I turn my gaze to the bed.

Aiden and all his belongings are gone.

Chapter Eight

The Real Peril

AIDEN

I wake up before the first light of dawn brightens the night sky. Moving as quietly as possible, I grab the backpack filled with the supplies Zach gave me and tiptoe toward the door. He's sitting awkwardly in the chair, sound asleep. With a delicate touch, I lift the beam of wood barring the door and sneak out of the bank.

He took me by surprise last night, not only in asking to go with me to Seattle, but also in coming out to me, a leap of faith on his part. There have been awful stories about how racism and homophobia have run rampant since the Great Collapse. I feel a little guilty not coming out to him, but what would be the point? I'd be out of his life before he knew it.

Him traveling with me is out of the question. I work better on my own, and I know the risks. Maybe in a different life, I might have let Zach tag along. He's a good guy. He's industrious, funny, and creative. All excellent skills for a travel partner. But it isn't going to happen. As certain as the sky is blue. People are literally trying to kill me, and I could never forgive myself if he ended up dead because of me, adding to the list of other unforgivable things I've done. I have a track record of people ending up dead around me.

I remember working at the local community center when I was fifteen. It was only a field trip to the local park with a group of fifth graders. Those kids were my responsibility. We were only going to be gone for, like, twenty minutes. Little Noah Lopez was only ten years old, with the cutest smile and big brown eyes. Bobby Wheeler, the troublemaker in the group, was whacking a tree with a stick. I went over to make him stop just as he struck a hornet's nest. There were hornets everywhere. Everybody got stung, but Noah was allergic. He was supposed to have his EpiPen, but he forgot it. I should have checked before we left. That was on me. His throat closed up, and he couldn't breathe. We called 911, but the ambulance took forever. I held on to him as his life drained away. By the time the medics arrived, little Noah was gone. I never forgave myself for that.

When Connor died on our mission, all those old memories bubbled to the surface again. Yeah, so people tend to die around me. It's why I work alone. Why I *am* alone.

Before leaving town, I make a quick sweep for anything useful to scavenge. The entirety of Elk Springs consists of five blocks. It takes almost no time to search every street. Half of the cars are burned out, have flat tires, or smashed windshields. And none of them have any keys. Like Zach said, people looted the cars long ago. One bag of spoiled potato chips in a glove box is all I find.

"Not a total waste, at least," I say to nobody. And nobody laughs at my joke.

So, time to leave Elk Springs behind. These supplies will have to last me. I'm bound to find something in a week. What kind of courier would I be if I couldn't do that? It's what I'm trained to do.

I hike along the side of the road, staying close to the forest in case I need to take cover. White mileage post markers, nearly lost in the weeds, mark my slow progress. It gives me time to think. A lot has happened in the last few days. That car crash and flight through the woods almost feels like a dream. And I still haven't figured out who was after me.

Sophia Hughes, the director of our bunker, is the only other person aware of my mission. Unless, somehow, somebody overheard our conversation or Sophia told somebody else I don't know about. But that doesn't seem likely.

Either way, it means there's a spy in our midst. It's hard to wrap my head around that. Everyone in our bunker is dedicated to our common goal. It's the single driving force keeping us all going. The thought that somebody is working to subvert that goal means we're in a whole new dangerous ballgame.

I think back to before my trip when Sophia called me into her office, asking about the brutal cross-country courier job I'd been assigned, checking that I was still up for leaving right away and that I understood the dangers.

What she revealed that day shook the foundations of my beliefs, and

I still haven't fully processed it. I'd be transporting vials that could lead to a cure for the Infection. The UW Medical Bunker in Seattle had discovered the ability to synthesize a powerful medication—effectively, a cure. But they needed something only we had—a sample of the *original* Infection called XT58, a bioweapon engineered in a military lab. The military had stockpiled XT58 around the world. One such place was in Boston.

"What are you saying?" I asked Sophia, almost mechanically, still absorbing the implications.

"I'm saying what you think I'm saying," Sophia said after telling me the news. "The Infection was man-made."

I felt ill. Connor had tried to tell me about this on our last mission together, but I didn't believe him. To me, it sounded like some wild conspiracy theory. When he died the very next day, I'd already put it out of my mind.

I flew into a rage, knowing everyone I loved, including Marcus, had died because the military decided to play god. When my anger faded enough to talk, I turned to Sophia. "Why didn't you tell me?"

"Because this knowledge is very dangerous," she'd answered in a calm, level tone. "XT58 was initially designed to control people, even though most died who were exposed. In the wrong hands, anything is possible. They could fix the flaws of the original XT58 and build an army of subservient people. It could be altered to get around people's immunity. Get around your immunity."

She'd assured me the Collective had nothing to do with the creation of XT58, and she'd only learned of it recently through a contact in the military. That was important to me. I needed to know I was working for the right people. Connor had believed otherwise, but Sophia convinced me.

And there was another complication: After informing the Collective about the breakthrough, the UW lab went offline five days later. That sounded like more than a coincidence. So, we didn't know what I'd be walking into.

No one else could do this mission. It had to be me. Connor was the only other courier with immunity from the Infection, and when he died, I was the last. For anyone else, it would be a death sentence. A simple crack in the vial, and they'd be dead. So, it was my job and my job alone. But I preferred it that way. I wanted to work alone, and work was the only thing keeping me going. Of course, I'd take the job.

I've been walking for over an hour with those memories heavy on my mind. Connor was right about the Infection being lab-made. When Sophia confirmed that, it was the first time I had any doubts about the Collective. Was I wrong to dismiss Connor's suspicions? He was so sure that the Collective was in on it—part of some big cabal. But I've seen firsthand the power of conspiracy theories on people's minds. And I trust Sophia and the Collective more than I trusted Connor. Especially considering what happened between me and Connor the night before he died. He broke my trust in a way that could never be repaired. I still believe the Collective is the only chance to find a cure. And I hope to hell I'm right about that.

The sun is well over the horizon now. I'd guess it's midmorning, and the chill is starting to ebb. I pause for a moment to snack on some trail mix Zach packed into my bag. Looking at all the nice things he stashed makes me smile.

Am I heartless to leave him? He's been so selfless and kind. And he's clever and resourceful. Leaving felt like the right thing to do. It *is* the right thing to do.

Even so, how many gay guys are left in the world? Don't I owe something to him from a sense of solidarity? Having more people like me to relate to in our shared common experience could only be a good thing. And I do enjoy his company. We have the same sense of humor, and I think back to some of the laughs we shared.

Okay, when I get to Seattle and finish this job, I'll head back this way and see how he's doing. I'll make it up to him. If he's not too pissed at me, that is.

Assuming he's still alive, that is.

Mind back on the job. Find a car. Get to UW in Seattle. Find the emergency medical bunker there. Hope that it still exists. It *better fucking* still exist. And drop off the vials. Simple. I laugh under my breath. *Yeah, simple.*

After a couple hours of walking and ruminating, a gas station appears. It has a garage and a store attached. It's an old building, probably built in the 1950s. Faded signs and a moss-covered roof add to the run-down ambiance. Cars litter the entire lot. Some are old junkers, but several others appear newer. Maybe I'll get lucky here.

The inside of the store is nothing but empty shelves and broken glass. Picked clean. Like pretty much everything, it has that musty smell. All man-made things in the world are in the process of either rotting or rusting.

Old broken car parts and discarded tools litter the garage. A half-disassembled car is up on a floor jack. There's a pegboard filled with hanging car keys on one wall. *Jackpot.* I grab them all and head out to the yard.

Matching the keys up to the make and model of each car is a pain. Most of them don't belong to any cars. Did this guy just collect keys? Going through them methodically is the only way to do it. I find the correct key one by one, and every single time, the car doesn't start. All the batteries are dead. I'm sitting in the driver's seat of the last car, crossing my fingers. I turn the key and—nothing. Zilch.

I have one foot out the door when the unmistakable sound of a car engine breaks the silence. An old Buick sedan tears into the station, brakes squealing as it stops. There's only enough time to pull my leg in and scrunch down behind the dash. The door is still open, and it's too late to shut it now. So I huddle in the front seat and wait.

Car doors slam, and two male voices argue back and forth.

"Well, crap, I didn't know we were almost out."

"You dumbshit, didn't you check the gauge?"

"I thought you checked before we left town."

"Well, now, we gotta siphon some gas. And guess who's gonna be doing the sucking?"

"Shit."

"And get at it. We gotta meet the others in less than an hour. Boss is sure he went that way."

"What about that little fucker in the bank, though?"

"We gotta root him out and find out if he's seen anything. He's been a pain in our ass for a while now, so it's about time."

Oh, god. How did it not occur to me that simply being there put Zach in danger? I have to warn him.

But it's too risky. The vials are too important. They could save so many lives. And they're far too dangerous to fall into the wrong hands. That would be a disaster.

And don't forget you're doing this for Marcus.

I'm hit with this wave of guilt. These people were trying to kill me, so they won't hesitate to kill Zach. But before that, they'll get him to talk. I was careful not to reveal too much. But that might even make it worse for Zach if he has nothing to tell them. They won't take no for an answer.

How do I weigh the lives of so many that *might* be saved with the life of somebody who's in danger *right now*? I was so worried about the risks of taking Zach with me. Turns out leaving him was the real peril. He tried to tell me that, but I didn't listen. I swore I would never take somebody with me. I couldn't stand another life on my conscience, but inaction now would be no different.

I know what I must do.

I open the car door opposite from where the men are, taking great care not to make a sound. A quick peek around helps me plan my attack. Two men, both forty-something. Neither looks as if they've worked out a day in their life. A guy with a bright orange baseball cap and a beer gut is heading toward some cars on the other side of the lot. He's got a hose and gas can in his hands. The other guy is scrawny and has a gray goatee. He's over by a tree taking a leak. Now's my chance.

My training has taught me to move in near silence, one of the re-quired skills for a courier. Without a sound, I'm right behind the scrawny guy. In a flash, my arm is around his neck, and a hand is over his mouth. I pull hard, cutting off his airflow. He tries to fight, but he's off-balance. His arms flail in the air. The critical moment when his body goes limp from lack of oxygen is an unmistakable feeling. Consciousness gone. He'll have one heck of a headache when he wakes up.

With him on the ground, I root through his pockets but find no keys. But I do find a .45 caliber pistol tucked into the back of his pants, which I grab.

The other guy is even easier. He's crouched and distracted by siphoning gas. It's a compromising position, and he goes down with almost no struggle.

Still no keys. Shit.

When I see the keys in the ignition of their car, I laugh. Guess I could have run up to the car and driven off. But better to have a head start. And better that they don't know what I look like or what they're up against.

I pour the siphoned gas into the tank. It's not much. I hope it'll last all the way to Elk Springs. The tires kick up gravel as I race out of the parking lot. My mind is playing out the different scenarios I may face. If I get there first, I'll warn Zach and convince him of the danger. Get him away and find a safe place to drop him off. Then continue on without him.

But what if I get there and people are already outside the building? Shooting from a distance is an option. Knock them off one by one. But I don't kill people. Never have. That's not a line I'm willing to cross lightly.

The last option I don't want to think about. They're already there, and they've taken Zach prisoner. Forced to choose between the importance of my mission and Zach's life, would I mount a rescue? I won't think about that one unless it comes to it.

After a few miles, the engine makes a sputtering sound. *Damn it.* The guys weren't lying about the state of the gas tank, and the extra didn't help much. The car rolls a few hundred more feet until the engine cuts out, the tank empty. I pull off to the side of the road and continue on foot.

It takes over half an hour to make up the distance. I run the entire way. Lightning bolts of pain shoot from my ribs with each foot strike on the road. I only stop once to empty the contents of my stomach onto the pavement.

When I enter Elk Springs, everything looks calm. But while running down Main Street toward the bank, my worst fear plays out before me. Two pickup trucks pull up a few blocks down the road. Thugs armed with rifles step out.

I dig deep and sprint the rest of the way to the bank. When I get there, I bang hard on the door.

"Zach, let me in! It's Aiden! We've got to go now!"

Chapter Nine

Heading Out

ZACH

I'm in the vault when shouts and loud banging come from the front door. I run to the lobby to check it out. As I recognize Aiden's voice, a mix of relief and anger courses through me.

When I found him gone this morning, I almost shut down as I thought back on being abandoned by my dad in the woods. Aiden leaving me has triggered these old feelings.

I was also filled with deep sadness. I was so ready to leave Elk Springs. And he left without discussing the possibility of my joining him. I didn't get a chance to tell him about the car. His leaving was the ultimate rejection.

He didn't even say goodbye. The pitiful thing is, I thought we had connected. I guess I can be gullible when a cute guy is involved.

But I won't let him fool me this time. He probably came back when he found out I was telling the truth about there being no cars. He wants to use me again. I'm sure as heck not letting him back in until I get a proper explanation, including lots of groveling.

"Didn't find a car, I guess," I snap at him through the porthole.

"Zach! Thank god! I'll explain everything, but right now, people with guns are headed this way. We have to go!" Aiden points down the street. Sure enough, five people armed with rifles are only two blocks away.

Crap.

With no time to talk about hurt feelings, I bury the pain, throw open the door, and drag Aiden inside by the scruff of his shirt. The moment he's in, bullets strike the steel plating, sending metal shrapnel in all directions. I slam the door shut and bar it.

"You just saved my life." Aiden's eyes widen as he feels around to be sure he wasn't hit.

"I guess now we're even."

"I'm so sorry, Zach. Those people are here because of me."

"You can beg for my forgiveness later. Right now, let's just survive."

Aiden nods. "Tell me what I can do."

"Grab that and be ready to draw their fire." I point to the rifle sitting against the wall.

Aiden checks the ammo and the safety and stands at the ready.

In situations like this, I'm normally a wreck. But this time, I'm filled with an iron resolve. Maybe it's because Aiden is here. I have more to fight for. Or maybe it's because I know how we'll escape. And this means my journey home can finally start.

We both peer through the portholes at the approaching people. They've gathered outside the bank, taking defensive positions behind cars and cement columns.

A tall man with short, platinum-blond hair shouts out. "Come out, Aiden. If you both head out with your hands up, we won't kill you or your friend in there." He has some accent I can't place.

"Screw that," I say to Aiden, but he doesn't hear me. He's staring out the porthole, and his face has gone pale. He looks as if he's seen a ghost.

He turns to me, deadly serious. "We have to go. *Now*. Is there another way out?"

"Yeah, but let's give them something to worry about first." I pull the Wilson wires descending from the ceiling. The sound of gunfire fills Main Street, and the people outside scatter. They're yelling and shooting at the decoy buildings. I tug on the wires again, and more gunfire erupts. Then a third time. Three shots are all the guns hold.

Aiden stares at me with widened eyes. "Wow. Just wow." A smile cracks through his otherwise drawn expression.

"Okay, let's head to the vault." I start back and gesture for him to follow.

Bullets strike the steel sheets on the windows. They make large welts in the metal, and one bullet finds its way through and hits the teller's desk.

"Holy crap. What kind of weapons do they have?" I glare at Aiden. He shakes his head and shrugs.

We make our way to the vault. As I reach to close the massive circular door, Aiden grabs me by the shoulder.

"With that kind of firepower, it won't take them long to get into the lobby."

I nod. "Hopefully, the vault door will hold them off longer. We only need a little time."

"What do you have planned?" The worry on his face is plain to see.

"I got this." My smile is all confidence, but Aiden doesn't seem too reassured.

Two fully loaded hiking backpacks sit in the corner of the vault. I spent the entire morning preparing them as I formulated a thorough checklist of items to pack. Going through the list was my therapy after Aiden left me. I kept telling myself it was useless and he wasn't coming back. But I'm glad I didn't listen to that voice in my head.

I take one and hand the other to Aiden. "Here you go. This is much better than what I gave you last night."

Aiden takes it and shakes his head. "You knew I was coming back, didn't you? I guess I underestimated you."

I flash him a smile. "Yep, you did. Don't do it again."

I hand an old Casio watch to Aiden. "Here, this shows the date, time, and has a compass. And the batteries last forever. I have one just like it." I point to the one on my wrist.

Aiden takes it and laughs. "Are our watches synchronized?"

I wrinkle my brow at his laughter. "Maybe."

From beyond the vault door comes the sound of shattering wood and the front door slamming open.

"Here, help me with this." I grab a crowbar and head to a large steel plate lying on the ground.

I wedge the crowbar under the plate, raising it about an inch. "Okay, now, let's both get our hands under it."

We lift the thick, heavy plate with all our might. Once it's lifted, I prop it up with a piece of rebar. A little divot on the floor and in the plate holds the rebar in place. Beneath the plate, a tunnel heads down into darkness.

Aiden smiles. "You're just full of surprises, aren't you?"

"Into the garbage chute flyboy," I say.

Aden shakes his head and laughs. "Okay, princess."

He got the *Star Wars* reference. He's awesome.

Loud impacts reverberate through the vault door. It *should* hold, but I'm not interested in waiting around to find out. I throw the crowbar down the hole and jump in after it.

It's about a ten-foot drop, and I hit the ground hard. Cold, stale air assaults my nose.

"Careful. It's a long way down," I say, cupping my hands to project my voice.

Aiden jumps in after me and winces when he hits the ground.

I take the flashlight from my backpack and flash it around. A narrow tunnel of rough rock and dirt stretches out in both directions. Thick beams of wood support the sides and gird the roof.

Aiden looks up at the hole leading back to the vault. "What's the story behind this?"

"A couple years ago, some guys figured out that this old mine shaft ran under the bank. They spent months digging the hole up to the vault floor. Got away with fifty thousand cash."

"Wow. Like a regular heist movie."

I laugh. "Lucky for us, they hadn't fully repaired it yet."

"Yeah, our lucky day." Aiden smirks.

I grab the crowbar and turn to Aiden. "Give me a lift?" I cup my hands.

Aiden hoists me up high enough to swing at the rebar, propping up the steel plate. As I strike it, the rebar clatters away. The plate lands hard on the floor above us, making a massive slamming noise reverberating through the mine.

"No going back that way," I say as Aiden lowers me to the floor.

"For more reasons than one."

I turn left and lead us down the mine shaft, knowing exactly where to go. Before long, we come to a fork in the tunnel. Without hesitating, I take the right fork and continue.

"You've had this all planned out for quite some time, haven't you?" Aiden asks.

"When you've had a year to yourself, you spend a lot of time making contingency plans."

We come to a spot where the entire right side opens up into a deep ravine, extending downward into inky blackness. With each footstep, the path gets narrower. Our shuffling feet send pebbles tumbling into the darkness.

"Watch your step here," I warn Aiden.

"No shit."

With delicate steps, we make our way past the treacherous edge. When we're on the other side, we exchange glances of relief. After a few more minutes, the mine shaft opens to a large natural cavern. Several shafts fan out in different directions. A metal ladder anchored to the cavern wall heads upward to a small outcropping. We climb the ladder and find a naturally occurring cave extending into darkness. The cave goes on for a couple of hundred feet before daylight shines ahead of us. When we get to the cave entrance, I poke my head out of it.

The sunlight is blinding, so I let my eyes adjust. We're in the woods north of town. The forest is quiet. I hop out of the cave with Aiden right behind me.

"That vault door should hold them for a while," I say. "But when they get through, they'll probably trace us back to here. We'll want to be long gone by then."

"Sounds good. Where are we headed?"

I smile at him. "For my last surprise, I know where we can get our hands on a car."

Chapter Ten

A Walk in the Woods

AIDEN

After we leave the mine, we hike directly through the woods for a while. It's turning into a beautiful day. Sun-dappled leaves create flickering shadows on the ground. Eventually, we meet up with a trail. Zach pauses for a moment, then turns left.

Boy, did I underestimate Zach. When I first met him, all I saw was this weird little guy, all disheveled with ridiculous hair, holed up in his bunker. Even though he's got this odd exterior, Zach is growing on me. He's a survivor, and he's clever. When he asked to come along with me, I thought of him as a liability. I came all the way back to save him, but it turns out he ended up saving me.

But that proves my point. I ended up going back, and it almost killed me. All because I allowed myself to make this connection in the first place. It's a weakness. He would have been fine without me.

He knows where a working car is, and that's great. We'll stick together until then. But once we're on the road, I'll search for another car and take the first opportunity to leave. He can make it back to Seattle on his own, and we'll both be safer away from each other.

"So, where exactly is this car?" I peer at the sun through the trees to get my bearings.

"It's in a junkyard. The owner is the only other survivor I know. Name's Ezra. The only guy I've talked to in the last year. I used to trade him food for supplies from his junkyard."

"You *used to* trade with him?"

Zach looks down at the ground. "Well, I haven't really heard from him in a few months."

That doesn't sound good. It usually means only one thing. An untimely death. Often from a militia or Infected.

Zach continues. "Anyway, he told me if I ever decided to leave town, he'd let me have his car."

Sounds too good to be true. But as long as we're still going in the right direction, I'll go along with it. "Okay, so how do we get there?"

"Just follow this trail north. It's a three-day hike. I know of a campground we can stop at tonight."

"Isn't a campground a little dangerous?"

"This was a popular backpacking area. There's a maze of trails around here and tons of different campsites. This one is hike-in only and miles off the road. Should be under the radar."

It's a little risky, but at least we're headed in the right direction. Zach's judgment has been good so far, so I won't make waves. When we get there, I can always reassess. "Lead on."

We continue in silence, but it's clear from Zach's face that he's thinking hard about something. I'm sure he's pissed at me for leaving. It gets worse the longer we go. It's better to hit it head-on rather than let it fester.

"Zach, about this morning. When I left, I was trying to do you a favor. Those guys back there? They're the ones after me. I was trying to protect you from them. If I had known for one second that they'd be coming for you, I would have done things differently."

"Look, you really don't owe me anything." Zach averts his gaze. "I mean, we've only known each other for a few days. It was foolish to think you'd trust me that soon."

"Zach, look at me." I grab his shoulders and wait until he makes eye contact. "Running off without talking to you first was shitty of me. I'm sorry about that."

Zach nods. "I was so ready to leave that town, and I saw my chance to get out. And I really need to get back to my family and my boyfriend."

The odds that Zach finds anybody alive at home are slim to none. But I'm not about to break that to him now.

"Well, looks like you're stuck with me for a while." I smile.

"Yep. But now that we're on the road together, we need to promise to have each other's back. Deal?"

"Deal."

Zach was right about what he said earlier though. I didn't owe him anything, and hearing him say it only solidifies my plan. I won't leave him in the lurch as I did last time. But I still have to break out alone as soon as possible. He'll be safe from all the dangers following me, and I won't have to be responsible for him.

As we continue down the path, he clearly has more on his mind. He starts and stops asking questions three times. I'm ready to ask him what's up when he finally speaks. "So, since we *are* on the road together, I want to know more about what we're up against."

"Okay." I'm a little worried about where this is going.

"Where are you from? Really. And who's chasing us?"

Zach has a knack for jumping right to the point. No small talk. I can't tell him anything that will risk my mission or expose too much about me. But I can keep things vague. Enough to satisfy him.

"I'm called a courier. There are only a few of us. We deliver things. Important things."

"Deliver for who?"

"The group I told you about. Who I ended up with after the Great Collapse. They're a group of scientists. There are a few other groups like us too. Scattered around the country and even the world. Sometimes things need to be delivered by hand. That's where couriers come in."

"That's what's really in those vials? Something important you need to deliver by hand?"

Zach's too smart for his own good. No use in denying it. But I can't tell him any more details, so I simply nod.

"And the tall blond guy we saw outside the bank. You know him, right?"

The mention of it sets me on edge. The guy who's been chasing me is Connor Bishop. Somehow still alive. I haven't had time to process that.

Seeing him outside the bank was like seeing a ghost. I saw him fall hundreds of feet to his death. At least, that's what I thought. Somehow, Connor survived the fall. And apparently, he's working against the Collective. He'd hinted about this the night before he fell off the bridge. I even got the impression he was trying to convince me. To recruit me, even. But after his fall, I put it out of my mind. And now he's back from the dead. After what transpired between us that night, I can't imagine a worse turn of events.

I'm lost in the past when Zach gives me a little tap on the shoulder.

"Hey, Aiden, you in there?"

I come back, shaking my thoughts off. "Sorry. Just recalling some unpleasant memories. His name is Connor Bishop. He used to be a courier like me. I thought he was dead. I haven't thought about it in forever. I haven't wanted to. But now I need to remember each detail. Figure out what I missed."

Zach nods and watches me, waiting. I have to tell him more. Maybe it will help.

"Connor and I were on a mission together about six months ago. I was excited to go because Connor was my friend and one of the best couriers I knew. I was eager to learn from him."

I don't tell Zach how upset Marcus was about me traveling alone with Connor. Marcus was the jealous type, and Connor had been more than a bit flirty on several occasions. Thinking of that dredges up memories I don't want to revisit.

"Connor was driving, and I was navigating. We were taking the back roads, trying to avoid people. In the middle of nowhere, we came up to a long, narrow bridge spanning a deep ravine. When we were halfway across, a large truck came out of nowhere, blocking the end of the bridge. Another one pulled up behind us. An ambush."

Zach's eyes widen. "What did you do?"

I stop walking and close my eyes, trying to recall every detail of the chaos that unfolded. "Connor jumped out of the car and told me to follow behind him. He started running to the truck behind us as a bald guy jumped out. I tried to follow. But by then bullets were flying everywhere, and I froze up."

As I reflect on the past events, I filter through the details I'm willing to tell Zach, wanting to avoid anything that would reveal too much about my mission. I'd reached into the glove compartment and grabbed the aluminum box we were transporting, but it popped open, and one of the vials fell out and smashed onto the pavement. Connor had kept the contents of the vial secret from me. But now it all made sense. It had to be XT58. Why else would they have paired up the two immune couriers to work together?

"What happened then?" Zach's quiet voice helps to ground me.

"Connor ran to the bald guy, shooting at him. When they got face to face, they started punching and kicking. It was so damn vicious. Both of them fighting for their lives.

"I finally forced myself to move and started running to help him. Before I got there, Connor kicked the bald guy hard, sending him over the edge of the bridge. But as he went over, his foot smashed into Connor's jaw.

"Connor was stumbling around like he was drunk. That kick really messed him up. I was about twenty feet away when he fell forward and tumbled over the guardrail. I was just in time to see him disappear into a bank of mist over a hundred feet down."

I shudder at the memory. Zach puts a gentle hand on my shoulder.

My first instinct is to pull away, but the look in his eyes is caring and earnest, so I take a deep breath and finish the story.

"The guys from the other end were running toward me, shooting. They had already passed our car in the middle, so I ran to the other truck. The guy had left the keys in with the engine running. So, basically, I got really fricking lucky and just got the hell outta there." I let out a long sigh. "I don't get it. No one could have survived that fall."

"But somehow Connor did," Zach says quietly.

"Yeah. Somehow, he did."

Chapter Eleven

Awakening

ZACH

The light is fading fast. The last time I hiked out this far, I had a much earlier start. On that day, the campground sign was plain to see. But thus far, we've found nothing. We come to a trail crossroads. No campground sign, but I'd swear this is the turnoff.

"I think this is it." I peer down the trail in the twilight.

"You *think* it is?"

"It looks *very* familiar."

Aiden sighs. "Well, let's go. But if we don't find it in the next fifteen minutes, we should find someplace to set up camp in the woods. I'm worried we'll be doing it in pitch black."

"Hey, I got this."

Aiden sends me a side-eye. "Um-hmm."

"Don't worry so much. You're as bad as my boyfriend." I keep leaving out the fact that Felix is my *ex-boyfriend*, and I'm not exactly sure why. Guess it sounds better. Has more impact. *Maybe to make Aiden jealous.*

We turn down the trail and continue for a while, with the forest getting darker by the minute.

"Look over there," Aiden says in a hushed tone.

"Where?"

"There. Up the hill." He points to our right. A small cabin peaks over the trees. It's a traditional log cabin style, with a round log exterior, a green metal roof, and a chimney on one side.

"Let's go check it out," Aiden says.

"You think that's a good idea?"

"I've never let a bad idea stop me before."

"What if somebody's in there?" I chew on the side of my lip.

"That's why we're checking it out, all quiet like. Now who's the worrier?"

"Touché."

As we approach the cabin, all looks quiet. No light comes from the windows, and a half-inch thick layer of dust and dirt covers the porch. Nobody's been here in a while. Despite that, it looks to be in excellent shape. The timbers are well-treated, and all the windows are intact. Not your typical run-down hunting shack. Whoever built this cabin knew what they were doing.

Before we get closer, we do a full orbit around it. In the back, a large propane tank is bolted to a cement slab. I lean over to check the gauge.

"It's half full!"

"That, more than anything, tells me this place is abandoned." Aiden cranes his neck around. "And remote enough that nobody has stolen the fuel. Should be safe to spend the night."

"*If* we can get in."

"Oh, we'll get in, alright." Aiden smirks.

We check the doors and windows, and of course, they're all locked. Aiden is about to smash a window with the butt of his rifle when I spot a conspicuous-looking rock resting against the foundation.

"Hang on a sec." I grab the rock. "It's fake. And there's a key in it."

"Good eye, Zach."

Opening the door, we're hit with a blast of stale air. But it's not the sickening scent of decay I've encountered during most of my looting.

It's a simple cabin. One big room serves as a living and dining area and kitchen. A small hallway leads to a single bedroom and bathroom.

The main room has a typical rustic cabin aesthetic with woven tapestries and shelves filled with knick-knacks covering the walls. Cast-iron pots hang above a stone fireplace, and an old, worn couch and loveseat sit in front of it. A basic kitchen with butcher block countertops holds a wooden dining table and chairs, a gas stove, and a sink. But there's no refrigerator, and I don't see any lamps around. So it isn't wired for electricity.

I turn on one of the stove burners. There's a sound of gas escaping, and the smell of propane floods my nose. I press a small red button on the stove, which creates a spark, lighting it up. "Stove works."

Aiden nods as he heads to the sink and turns on the faucet. A strong jet of water comes shooting out. "Huh, artesian well. Natural water pressure."

"Nice."

"But only cold."

"Challenge accepted." I smile, taking out a small bag of tools from my backpack. "There must be a hot water tank around here somewhere. I'll see if I can get it fired up. You get things situated out here."

"You had me at 'hot water,' Zach. If you can get me a warm shower, I'll give you a big fat kiss." He grins playfully.

My cheeks go hot, no doubt turning various shades of red. But I'm not going to just wilt under his teasing. "Careful what you promise," I shoot back.

I leave the room without looking at him, trying to act cool. But that little flirt was enough to send warmth radiating throughout my body.

It doesn't take long to find the tank in a small utility closet in the bathroom. Like the stove, it has a manual pilot light. I turn the starter knob, which makes a clicking sound. But still no flame. There's some corrosion on the electrode. With a long, flathead screwdriver from my box of tools, I give it a couple of scrapes. This time, the flame lights and the room fills with the roaring sound of the tank springing to life. I get goosebumps thinking about taking a hot shower. It means getting cleaned up is finally possible.

I strut back into the main room, looking triumphant.

"Ha! I got it working." I beam. "Once it's hot, I'm gonna hop in the shower. You can go next, so you'll owe me that kiss."

"I haven't forgotten." Aiden shoots me a smile. "And if I get a hot shower outta the deal, it'll be worth it."

Man. Aiden is so flirty. But these days, people are much more comfortable with their sexuality, right? Who knows if he's into guys. Either way, it's driving me nuts. I'm going to flat-out ask him tonight.

I head back to the bathroom with a small kit of toiletries and a fresh change of clothes. While waiting for the water to heat up, I go to town on my beard and matted hair with travel-size scissors. A year's worth of growth and grime falls into the sink in big ugly clumps. My eyes are visible for the first time in forever.

The water is lukewarm and could stand some more time. But I can't wait any longer, so I strip off my clothes and jump into the shower.

The warm water cascading over my body is like a dream. I scrub every square inch, watching the blackened water cascade down and swirl into the drain. The whole thing is emotional for me. Letting my personal appearance go like this reflected my mental state. I'd lost the will to care. And now I have something to care about again.

It takes several rounds of suds and scrubbing to remove all the dirt layers. And it's not always a pleasant experience. Some of my skin has dried out and cracked from neglect, and the soap stings. But I get through it. My skin has gone from a dusty brown to a rosy pink. I towel off and step out.

With the dirt washed out, I finish trimming my hair. Because of the mats, I have to cut it short. I finish up with a thorough shave. In the mirror, staring back at me, is someone I haven't seen in over a year and frankly forgot existed.

And suddenly, I'm wracked with fear at the thought of Aiden seeing me. The dirt and grime were armor for my self-esteem. It wasn't *me* who was being judged. It was my shoddy appearance. With it all washed away, there's nothing left to hide behind. Aiden will now see me for who I am. And it scares the crap out of me.

*

AIDEN

Then you'll owe me that kiss.

Of course, Zach won't let the kiss comment go. I know. It's mean of me to tease him like that. But it's cute when he squirms a bit.

It's clear he's got a thing for me. It's the little looks I get from him—the comments he makes. And I'm not exactly making things easy. I need to be honest with him. Tell him I like guys, but he's not my type. And I'm not looking for new commitments because of how complicated my life is. Be forthright. No game playing. I'll talk to him tonight.

In the meantime, he's run off to get cleaned up, and I'm looking forward to my turn. The very idea of taking a shower makes me excited. I have weeks of sweat and grime that need to be washed off, and some scrapes on my arms are looking a little too red for my liking. Cuts getting infected is no joke in a world without plentiful antibiotics.

While I wait, I explore the cabin more. A pile of firewood rests next to the fireplace, but I don't want to risk it. Smoke rising from a chimney is an invitation to be attacked. What with the warm day, the temperature in the cabin isn't too bad. We'll have to bundle up tonight if it gets cold.

It looks as if the cabin owners used candles for light. Ones of various sizes and shapes are spread throughout the entire room. I go around with a lighter and light them all up.

I'm surprised to find some actual food in the pantry. Most cans are long past their expiration date, but that's not something you worry much about post-Great Collapse. I find a box of dry spaghetti and some jars of pasta sauce. We'll have a nice little pasta dinner with some canned chicken. Might as well take advantage of having an actual kitchen. I find a large pot for the pasta and fill it with water.

I'm reading the instructions on the box of spaghetti when Zach comes out of the bathroom. At least it's somebody roughly the same size and shape as Zach because, beyond that, there is no resemblance.

Um, wow.

My brain forgets how to hold things as the box of spaghetti falls out of my hand and lands on the floor, sending dried pasta everywhere. It's like I'm seeing Zach for the first time.

His newly clean and short hair is a nice sandy brown. With it trimmed, his eyes are finally visible, and they're a gorgeous shade of emerald-green with long, dark lashes. How have I not noticed them before? His cheekbones are pronounced, and he's got a V-shaped jaw, full lips, and a cute little button nose. To put it simply, he's adorable. I was expecting him to look better cleaned up, but I wasn't expecting this. He cracked open a cocoon, and the real Zach popped out.

My surprise must be apparent because his face turns cherry red, and he looks downward.

"Your turn." He avoids my gawking.

"Sorry, you just—" I can't speak properly. "You—um—you clean up nicely."

"Thanks. The candles are nice."

"Oh, thanks." The change of subject is welcome. I rub my hand on the back of my neck. "I hope it's not too visible from outside. Oh, and I found some pasta we can make tonight."

But then I stare at the spaghetti noodles spread all over the floor and start picking them up.

"Never let a little dirt get in the way of some dinner, right?" I say with an awkward laugh.

"Right."

Everything I do feels awkward, so I get up to leave. "Okay, gonna go shower."

"Hey." Zach looks at me and taps his finger on his cheek. "You owe me. Remember?"

Now it's my turn to blush. I head over and kiss his cheek. Then I scurry off to the bathroom.

"Have a nice shower." Zach gives me a little wave as I walk away.

It's not like me to get that worked up over a guy. In fact, since Marcus died, I haven't allowed myself to get distracted by guys at all. When I'm attracted to someone, I immediately shut the feelings down. Have nothing to do with them. But Zach came in like a stealth missile. His frazzled appearance fooled me into a sense of complacency. I mean, I already like him as a friend. I care enough that I risked the mission to protect him. But I saw him *only* as a friend. Never anything more. *Right?*

I'm a little ashamed of my reaction, honestly. Am I so superficial that my feelings can change that fast? Maybe I *was* feeling something for him, but seeing him cleaned up nudged me over the edge. And boy, am I over that edge. I can't stop thinking about him.

Shit.

In the bathroom, I start the shower and undress. I run my dirty clothes under the showerhead, ringing out the dirt, and hang them up to dry. Plunging into the hot water, I relish the tingle of it cascading over my body. Weeks of dirt and grime wash down the drain. I scrub at the cuts and scrapes from the night in the forest, being sure to get all the dirt out.

As I wash, my mind drifts back to Zach, and I'm instantly hard. *Ugh.* I'm not ready for this kind of distraction. How could I ever be ready after losing Marcus? Given this world and my job, forming attachments is a bad idea. It's a weakness.

I take care of my urges, which helps a little. But not much. When I'm done in the shower, I change into a new pair of clothes Zach packed in my backpack. Blue jeans and a flannel shirt. Not quite my style, but they fit well enough, and they're clean, so that's a major improvement.

When I enter the kitchen, Zach has dinner well underway. I survey the room. Candlelight. Pasta dinner. Secluded cabin. Oh god, did I set us up for a romantic date night?

He pauses cooking long enough to look me over.

"You clean up nicely too." He's got a little smirk on his face.

I'm having a hard time looking at him without blushing a bit. But I have to hit this head-on. I have to be honest but also set up boundaries.

I look Zach in the eye. "Hey, last night when you told me about wanting to find your boyfriend…"

"You like guys," Zach says flatly. He's always a step ahead.

"That would have been the right time to tell you. But yes. I'm gay."

"Yeah, that got pretty obvious." Zach lets out a little laugh.

I can't help but laugh and smile too.

But a whiplash of emotions hits me as Marcus enters my mind, and I stop smiling. "Look, it's complicated. You asked about Marcus. He was my boyfriend. I lost him to the *fucking* Infection. And I'm not ready for any new attachments." A tear streaks down my face. I wipe it away quickly.

"I'm so sorry to hear about Marcus." Zach's eyes are full of understanding and sorrow. He's familiar with my kind of pain. The sadness in his eyes is the same I have in my heart.

*

ZACH

We finish dinner quietly, only talking a little about our plans for tomorrow. There's another campsite I want us to get to. Hopefully, with a full day of hiking, we can find it before nightfall. We avoid talking about the elephant in the room. The one where we both clearly have a thing for each other.

After dinner, we go directly to bed. Aiden insists I take the bedroom while he takes the couch since I slept in a chair the two nights before. Looking at the bed, there's plenty of room for two. *Sigh.*

I lie there, staring at the log cabin ceiling, counting the knots in the wood, unable to sleep. My head is still spinning from tonight. The way Aiden reacted when he saw me was exciting but also startling. I underestimated how dramatic my transformation must have been to him. Like I said, personal appearance has been near the bottom of my priorities lately.

Plus, he never made it clear that he was into guys until tonight. I had my suspicions, of course, with his friendly comments and occasional flirting.

So he's clearly attracted to me. But he also made it clear he hasn't gotten over Marcus's death yet.

And what exactly do I want, anyway? Even though I split up with him, Felix was my first love. We can't ever love each other as we did before. And that's probably my fault. But I still have to find out what happened to him. I have to see it through. Maybe it is better to keep personal connections to a minimum. I just have to keep Aiden around long enough to get me to Seattle.

Crap. What are the odds that two guys find each other after the Great Collapse, both attracted to each other but too hung up on their personal demons to make things work? It makes me want to punch the wall. Except punching the wall of a log cabin would probably hurt a lot. *Geez, I'm even overanalyzing my emotional outbursts.*

I fret over that until exhaustion finally forces me into a restless sleep.

Loud shouts wake me in the middle of the night, startling me until I realize it's Aiden again, haunted by his past. Maybe comfort is all he needs? Love and support to help him through this.

I slink out of bed. At night, every single sound is so much louder. The squeak of the mattress springs. The creaks of the floorboards as I make my way to the bedroom door.

Aiden is tossing around on the couch, shouting nonsense again, every tenth word making sense. Marcus's name is mixed in the yelling. Knowing who that name represents makes the whole thing more intense.

I'm nearing the couch to rouse Aiden from his nightmare when a new name floats out of the clamor. Perhaps it would have been indistinguishable if Aiden hadn't mentioned it earlier. Connor. Hearing it gives me a chill. The man who's hunting us.

Maybe shaking the hornet's nest isn't the best idea. There's no telling how Aiden will react. So I tiptoe back to my room. No sooner do I close the door than the yelling stops, replaced by the soft sound of crying.

Chapter Twelve

Uncle Max

ZACH

We wake up early the next day, pack up, and get going. Leaving the cabin makes me a little sad. A place like that is a rare find. I'd enjoy spending more time there, but we need to keep moving.

In the light of day, it's more obvious how I steered us wrong last night. We would have found my original campsite if we had hiked another ten minutes on the main trail. But I'm glad that it worked out how it did.

When we first start out, Aiden seems to be in a bit of a daze. But as the day goes on, he's more like his usual, confident self. I even catch him stealing glances over at me from time to time. I guess I'll need to get used to him doing that. Honestly, getting the attention makes me smile each time. Even when I found out he liked guys, there was no assurance he'd find me attractive. I guess that's one thing I don't have to worry about.

I want to learn more about his life now. Obviously, I'll stay away from topics like Marcus and Connor. But what about the group he comes from? Maybe I could join them. Help them out in my own way.

"Hey, Aiden."

Being deep in thought seems to be Aiden's typical mental state. His eyes focus, and he looks over at me. "Um—what's up?"

"Tell me more about the couriers. How did you become one?"

"Oh. I guess I was just in the right place at the wrong time?" He cracks a slight smile, which is encouraging. I'm glad he's willing to share some things.

He continues. "After the Great Collapse, Marcus and I were wandering around, trying to survive."

"So you and Marcus knew each other before, huh?"

"Yeah. We'd been going out for nearly a year. I was scratched a few times by the Infected but never got sick. Marcus was just lucky. After about a month, one of the Collective's couriers found us and took us in."

"Is that when you got the blood test for the immunity?"

"Yeah. Sometimes I wonder if it's the only reason they saved us, honestly. They needed people who could travel and not die from the Infection. So I was a valuable commodity. I think they only took in Marcus because of me."

"And the group you joined? Are they still doing research on the Infection?"

"Yeah."

I'm digging too deep when he starts with single-word answers. Okay. Direct approach.

"Since they let you join, do you think I could I join?"

Aiden's face scrunches. "It's a possibility, I guess. If you really are immune from the Infection, that'll improve the odds. You said your uncle died of the Infection, right?"

"Yeah." I hate this subject. I lower my head as sadness and guilt build in me.

"And you were with him?"

I nod but don't say anything, worried my voice will reflect my guilt. I was with him, but it's not the whole truth.

"If you were in close contact with him through the height of the Infection, that's when it's the most contagious. Even being near them can expose you. You *must* be immune."

He says it so matter-of-factly, as if the issue is settled. But thinking about what truly happened to my uncle makes me ill. I'm not ready to talk about it. Not yet. Maybe, never.

It all happened over a year ago, but I still remember it like yesterday. My uncle and I were fly-fishing. The mayflies were everywhere, and the fish were really biting.

I'd been trying for over a week and couldn't get the hang of it. But that day, something clicked, and I caught several fish. Satisfied with our catch, we packed up and hopped in his truck.

I remembered the conversation because Uncle Max brought up Felix. That was unusual. After some small talk, he broached the subject. "So I heard you broke up with Felix."

Uncle Max had always been great about accepting Felix into our family. Felix even made a few trips out there to visit. I knew Uncle Max liked him.

"Yeah. It was time. Long distance is hard and…I don't know." But I did know. Felix and I had grown apart. But I wasn't ready to go into details with my uncle.

"Gotta do what's right for you," he said. "Hopefully, you can still be friends."

"I think we will be."

That was all we said on the subject. Uncle Max was a man of few words. He lived all alone in Elk Springs. No wife. No *boyfriend*, as far as I knew. I often wondered about it. Some people simply didn't need other people in their lives. We never talked about it.

When we returned to the cabin, I could tell something was off as soon as I walked through the door. It took a moment until it hit me. There was no noise whatsoever. The furnace wasn't running, no hum of the fridge, no ultra-high pitch frequencies from electronic equipment. The power was out.

It wasn't the most unusual thing in Elk Springs. My uncle had a generator for such an occasion, so while I gutted the fish, he headed out to the shed to fetch it. But, soon, he came back.

"Hey, Zach, looks like I'm low on fuel," he said. "I think I'll run to Bozeman and stop at the Costco. I'll fill the gas tanks and buy us some supplies while I'm there."

"Oh—uh—sure." I wanted to go with him because I hated being alone. But my hands were all nasty, and I was halfway through gutting, so I tried to be chill and let it slide.

He could see I was nervous. "Don't worry, Zach. I'll be back in a couple hours."

I did my best to act normal. "I'll be fine. Can you pick up some Dr Pepper?"

"Will do." And with that, my uncle was gone.

Three hours had passed, and I'd finished the fish long ago. So I grabbed my phone to text my uncle. With no reception on the river, there'd been no need to bring my phone, so this was the first time I looked at it since we'd left for fishing at four a.m. When I unlocked the screen, my jaw dropped. Eight missed calls and forty-five text messages. Most were from my mom and dad and a couple from Felix. One incoming call was from 911, which was especially strange. But not a single one from my uncle. The texts were alarming.

Did you hear the news about the Great Collapse?

Are you OK?

Zach, call us!

I love you, Zach

What in the hell was going on? And what was "the Great Collapse"? I immediately called my mom, but the line wouldn't connect. I couldn't call anyone. Cell service must have been down as well. No voicemail, no Internet. Nothing.

I was totally cut off.

Uncle Max lived about a mile out of Elk Springs on five wooded acres, so heading to the town was an option to see if there was any news. I even put on my shoes and started heading out the door. But my legs froze. A full relapse of my crippling childhood anxiety literally shut down my ability to walk. I had to slide down the wall and sit on the ground to avoid falling over. I stayed there, unmoving, for hours until it started getting dark, and my stomach grumbled. The last thing I'd had to eat was cereal for breakfast. But my nerves wouldn't allow me to eat much. So I nibbled on a protein bar, then headed to bed.

The following day, there was still no power or sign of my uncle. Even with little fuel, some power might keep the food in the fridge from spoiling, so I checked on the generator.

The shed was about a hundred feet from the house, down the driveway, and set off into the woods. As I approached it, dread crept over my entire body. Somebody had forced open the shed and ripped off the entire locking mechanism. I swung open the door to see my worst fears realized. The shed was empty. Someone had stolen everything.

I ran back to the house, locked all the doors, and grabbed my uncle's rifle. I'd barely touched a gun in my life, but I figured out how to load it and turn on and off the safety. And then I waited.

Three days came and went with no power and no sign of my uncle. Each day, I would attempt the mile trek to Elk Springs to get news. Each day, I'd freak out from being alone in the forest and run back. On the fourth day, I was determined to make it, so I practiced the deep breathing and mindfulness I learned from my childhood therapy. I headed out with my rifle in hand, full of confidence, sure I could make it. I didn't get far.

Past the driveway, I spotted a figure about a hundred feet down the road. It was Mrs. Miller who owned the general store in town. But she looked different. Purple veins bulged from her neck, and she stared blankly into the distance.

"Hey, Mrs. Miller!" I waved to her. "Know what's up with the power?"

At the sound of my voice, she turned and sprinted my way. In total shock, I stood there, not knowing what was happening. Some instinct kicked in, and I turned to run. At that moment, a man came out of the woods and tackled her. Rolling on the ground, they fought like wild animals, scratching, biting, kicking, and ripping into each other. I nearly threw up.

I sprinted back to the house without looking back. *What the hell had happened to them? Were they sick?* After that, I locked myself in and didn't leave. My mind was wracked with worry about my uncle as I wondered what was happening out in the world.

On the morning of the sixth day, I was at the kitchen table when a noise came from outside. Footsteps on the gravel driveway. But it wasn't the typical rhythmic crunching you'd expect from somebody walking.

crunch cruuuuunch

crunch cruuuuunch

With my uncle's rifle in hand, I peeked out the living room window. A man halfway down the driveway was headed toward the house. Half of his body slumped badly to one side. On each step, he lurched one foot forward, then dragged the other behind him. His clothes and face were bloodstained, his body contorted almost beyond recognition. Purple arteries bulged out of his neck, and a trail of dried blood dribbled from his mouth. He looked like Mrs. Miller had. My pulse shot up, and I tightened my grip on the rifle.

As the man moved closer, a sick feeling formed in the bottom of my gut. *Those boots.* They were familiar. The shape of the body. The pattern of the plaid shirt barely visible under the blood and grime. *This man was my uncle.*

He shouted some noise I could barely make out. With his energy spent, he collapsed in a heap on the ground. The rhythmic movement of his chest was the only sign of life. But his breaths were clearly labored.

I stood frozen. Unable to move. The image of Mrs. Miller and the man ripping each other to shreds flashed in my mind. I wanted to help him, but my anxiety would have nothing of it. I collapsed to the floor, body shaking, weeping, unable to function as a human being.

Footsteps clomped on the porch. I cowered to the wall so he couldn't see me through the windows. Keys rattled outside. He was trying to unlock the door. If he got in here, I'd have to run, but I was frozen with fear. Small metallic clicks projected through the doorknob as he struggled to insert the key. Then the keys dropped and hit the porch. He let out a groan. There was a loud thud as my uncle fell over, followed by quiet sobs.

I didn't know how long I lay there. It must have been hours, but time had lost its meaning. Eventually, I worked up the will to crawl up and peer out the window. My uncle's body lay motionless, slumped across the front porch. No sign of breathing.

Waves of grief and guilt swept through me. How could I have done this to him? I let him die alone on the porch. But he clearly had some illness, and I had no idea what it was or if it was contagious.

It took me hours to work up the courage to go outside. Something had to be done to his remains before they attracted a wild animal. I put on latex gloves and my uncle's woodworking respirator mask, then headed out.

His face was deformed and barely recognizable. But the mole under his left ear and the gold chain around his neck meant it was undeniably him.

I grabbed him by his legs and pulled with all my might, but as I did, a slight gurgling sound came from his mouth. Uncle Max's chest heaved, and he started coughing violently. I dropped his feet and ran into the yard. *Uncle Max was still alive.*

Slowly, he got up. I stared in horror as he straightened his spine but still listed heavily to the left. He stared past me with a vacant expression. I called his name, but no recognition registered in his eyes.

In a flash, he ran right toward me, making an inhuman howl. He was faster than I could have ever expected but still limping badly on one side. I outran him to the back porch, but only barely, and slammed the door into him, shoving him away and setting the deadbolt just in time.

He bashed his body against the door, over and over, for nearly an hour, gradually slowing until it ended with the thud of him dropping to the ground. For the next two days, whatever shell of Uncle Max was left would get up every few hours and pound on the door. On the third day, he never got up. The monster Uncle Max had turned into had finally died.

With tears running down my cheeks, I dragged him to the shed and piled wood on top of his body. As I lit the match, memories flashed in my mind. He'd been a simple man living an isolated life in rural Montana. But he always loved and accepted me. I felt wretched for not helping him, and I'd never forgive myself.

Chapter Thirteen

Closing In

AIDEN

Zach and I hike for the better part of the day, only pausing a few times to hydrate and refuel. What am I going to do about Zach? His questions are getting more insistent and specific, and I'm finding it harder to resist answering them. Now he's asking about joining my group. I hold Zach off by sticking to short and vague answers to most of his questions. Eventually, he tires of not getting real answers, and we continue in silence for most of the afternoon.

It doesn't help that he suddenly transformed into this adorable guy. I keep catching myself looking at him. His captivating eyes. His cute little nose. He's smiling a lot more now, which brightens his entire face. Even the change of clothes after his shower is a big improvement. His old ones were dirty and frumpy, hanging on his body. Now, he's wearing well-fitting blue jeans that accentuate his butt. And his T-shirt clings tighter to his slender frame. When he lifts his arms to take on and off his backpack, his shirt lifts, showing off his stomach.

But mostly, what that's doing is dredging up feelings about Marcus, which I've been quite successful at burying. Until Zach, that is. In the last couple of days, Marcus has occupied more of my mind, forcing me to relive those terrible memories.

My original plan to strike off alone is still the best bet. The longer Zach stays with me, the more risk we are to each other. He's in danger as long as he's with me. And if I have to make hard choices, it'll be tougher with another person around. So it has to happen.

If this car thing works out, I'll stick around long enough to find another working car. Then we go our separate ways. He won't be happy. But that can't factor into my decision. He'll have to adapt.

The shadows are getting long when we finally make it to the campground. It's deep in the woods, off an unpaved Forest Service road. Zach was right. It feels remote, and we should be safe here for the night. It'll be nice to have well water and vaulted toilets. Much better than having to boil water and dig holes in the woods.

I'm still nervous about being right in the campground, so I convince Zach to set up a few hundred feet into the woods. We find a nice flat spot for our tents, butting up to a massive boulder with a slightly concave side. As I dig into my backpack, I'm impressed by all the things Zach packed for us. For tonight, I take out an ultralight tent and chair, a bedroll, a lightweight sleeping bag, a small pot for cooking, a dehydrated meal pack, and fire-making tools.

"Wow, you really know how to pack a backpack, Zach."

"Felix and I used to go backpacking for a week at a time. We had plans to do the Pacific Crest Trail at some point."

"You must miss him a lot, huh?"

"Yeah—I do."

Of course, he misses his boyfriend. Another reason to keep personal entanglements to a minimum. Getting in the way of his feelings for his true love is cruel. Even if we both know there's a good chance Felix is no longer alive. Until he knows, acting on any feelings for me would be like him cheating on his boyfriend.

After we set up the tents and chairs, we risk a small, smokeless fire and warm up some water to rehydrate our meals. We mostly sit in silence throughout dinner.

Zach's face is lit gently by the campfire light. He looks miles away. Probably thinking about Felix. I'm hit with this unexpected pang of jealousy. *Where the hell did that come from?* He turns and sees me staring at him. My instinct is to look away, but after looking down for a moment, I force my gaze back. We both watch each other for a bit with relaxed faces and warm smiles. No agenda. Just liking each other's company.

What in the hell am I doing? Am I falling for him? Every instinct tells me this is a bad idea. But the feeling in the pit of my stomach says otherwise.

"Hey." Zach breaks the silence. "You do know, when I'm sitting around a campfire, I can't resist singing."

"Zach, I would love to hear your amazing voice again."

Zach's face lights up with a big smile. It's so sweet I can't help but laugh.

"You're so good at harmony," Zach says. "Do you know 'The Sound of Silence'?"

"I love that song. But you have to do Garfunkel. I can't hit those notes."

"You got it. I'll sing the intro."

Zach's amazing voice rings out. His pitch is perfect, and his incredible timbre seems to hug every note. I almost hate to sing over that extraordinary voice. But when we hit the first verse, I come in with the harmony, and the notes combine beautifully.

At the end of the first verse, I close my eyes and let the music fill my entire consciousness. At this moment, I feel nothing but joy.

*

ZACH

The music we make together is so beautiful. Aiden said he wasn't ready for new attachments. But isn't it too late already? I saw the way he kept checking me out. And man, it was exciting. Every time I caught him looking my way, I had to fight back a smile. I haven't felt this way about somebody in a very long time.

The flickering firelight dances on his face. His eyes are closed, and he focuses on the notes. I want to get close to him so our voices can blend more thoroughly. So I scoot my chair over until I'm right next to him. His lips form into a smile as I do. We're almost touching.

When we get to the end of the song, Aiden opens his eyes, and I see nothing but joy. He looks straight into my eyes. I so desperately want to kiss him.

But then, his face transforms. The joy changes to something almost like fear. He turns his face to the fire and takes quick and shallow breaths. His fists clench, and he shuts his eyes tightly.

"Aiden?"

His face looks pained. When I reach out to touch his shoulder, he shrinks away from my hand as if it burns him.

"I'm sorry, Zach. I just—I can't."

He shuts his eyes again and takes slow breaths. When he opens them, they're downcast. Fear is replaced by deep sadness.

"I'm sorry." His voice cracks. "I need to sleep."

He gets up from his chair, with shoulders slumped down, and heads to his tent looking shell-shocked. I'm so stunned by the sudden change I can only watch him walk away.

I sit by the fire and contemplate what happened. In a matter of moments, Aiden went from joyous to almost panicked. There's something more there that he's not telling me. More than losing Marcus. That was terror in his eyes. The Great Collapse has spared no one from the beast called trauma. And some are in an active battle with it.

I'm lost in thought until the last embers die down to nothing. Then I head off to my tent and go to sleep.

*

I wake in the middle of the night. A noise woke me. I'm sure of it. But now, I only hear the sounds of the forest. Then it happens again, and I recognize it. The crunching of boots on gravel. But it's muted and far away. Through the window of my tent, flashlights shine around. My heart races, and I reach for my gun. But like the footsteps, the flashlights are several hundred feet away. *In the campground.*

There are two, or maybe three, people. They speak in hushed tones. The beam from a flashlight shoots off into the woods once or twice. Another heads in our direction. I flick off the safety on my rifle, ready for anything. More hushed voices. And then, the flashlight moves again, and the crunching of gravel fades away as the figures continue on.

The tension in my body releases, but I stay frozen in place until long after they are gone. Then I head to Aiden's tent. Dawn is not far off, with the blackness of the sky turning into a deep purple.

"Aiden, wake up," I whisper.

"I'm awake," he says through the tent flap.

"Did you see them?"

"Yes. We should go. Now."

We pack as fast as we can. Dawn is arriving quickly. If people are still in the area, we want to be mobile. Instead of returning to the campground, we take a wide berth around it. We meet back up with the northern Forest Service road but stay a hundred feet to the west of it.

The forest hampers our progress. After an hour of slow going, we risk heading back to the road. The junkyard is at least an eight-hour hike, and I want to be sure we have plenty of sunlight left to find the car, get it running, and hit the road. I'm also looking forward to seeing Ezra again.

We've barely spoken a word since we left camp. I'm almost afraid to say anything, unsure of what Aiden's reaction will be. If he wants to talk about what happened at the campfire, I'll let him make the first move. It needs to be on his terms.

After close to an hour of silence, he finally speaks.

"Zach. About last night. Sorry for how I reacted. I'm dealing with some stuff."

"You can talk to me about it if you want."

He gives a sad laugh. "Thanks. Maybe eventually."

"Okay," I say quietly.

He said he doesn't want attachments, but I'm getting mixed signals. And I'm as light as a feather each time he's nice to me. I try to convince myself that we shouldn't get close, and I should fight the attraction. But if I'm honest with myself, that's not what I want at all. I'm so confused.

We're both eager to reach our destination, so we only stop once for a quick break at lunch. As we head out of the mountains, the trees get sparser, replaced by rolling golden hills of grassland. That means we're nearing the junkyard, but it also means we're more exposed.

I survey the surroundings. "I figure we're less than an hour away."

"Okay. So tell me a little of what to expect when we get there."

"Well, it's just Ezra and his junkyard. In the middle of nowhere. He's on the outskirts of some town, but I'm not even sure what it's called."

"And you're sure he'll give us his car?"

"Yeah, that's what he said." In reality, he said he'd trade it for all my supplies. And I'd be glad to do that. But that assumes Connor and his gang haven't trashed the vault. I keep this little detail to myself. We can deal with it when the time comes.

"What kind—" Aiden cuts himself off, craning his neck to listen. "Car! Quick, hide!"

The trees have thinned out, but we find a drainage ditch with some scrub brush covering it. It's not perfect, but it'll have to do. I only hope we took cover quickly enough before anybody saw us. We're lucky Aiden has such good hearing and detected the cars quickly.

We both lie flat on our stomachs in the dirt. The sound of tires on gravel is now clear. The cold steel of the rifle in my hand is ready if the vehicles stop near us.

I push myself up enough to see several large trucks with enormous wheels speeding our way, kicking up a massive cloud of dust in their wake. Flags mounted on the rear of the trucks flap furiously in the wind. They're all black, with a golden image of a snake wrapping itself around a rifle.

As I hunker back down, my pulse quickens as the sound of the trucks gets louder. Aiden looks over at me, clearly alarmed by my reaction. His look of worry is making it worse. My throat constricts, and I'm finding it hard to breathe.

The trucks are driving right by us now, the engine sounds loud and throaty. Tires kick up the gravel, flying all over us, and we're blanketed with a cloud of dust.

I'm overwhelmed with the sudden urge to run, certain they will find us. I move to get up, wanting to get away as quickly as possible. Aiden puts a hand on my chest. I lurch from it, but he holds me down gently but firmly and whispers in my ear.

"It's going to be okay, Zach."

His touch and voice combined are enough to calm me and let me catch my breath. I inhale deeply, slowing my pulse.

And then they pass.

The sound of engines and gravel gets quieter. I exhale, relief flooding over me. My panic dissipates quickly.

Aiden looks me in the eye. "You okay?"

I nod. "Yeah. Thanks. Sorry I freaked out."

We lie there, unmoving and quiet, until the dust settles and the sound of the trucks has long faded.

"That was the flag of the Freedom Liberation Army." Aiden's eyebrows draw together. "They might have been the ones at the camp too. We can't assume these roads are safe anymore. Let's keep our guard up."

My fear from earlier is turning into low-grade anger. Anger for being chased and for not knowing why. And from being kept in the dark.

I turn to Aiden, my whole body tense. "I need to know more about what we're up against. My life is in danger, and I don't have a clue as to why. I barely know the first thing about you."

"I told you, Zach. It's for your own good."

"That's bullshit. You have to give me something."

Aiden stands there, his jaws clenched. He breathes in deeply a few times. "Okay. If we start walking again, I'll fill you in. But I'm going to start at the beginning."

Chapter Fourteen

The Great Collapse

AIDEN

After that close call, emotions are running high, and we're both on edge. But the promise of hearing more calms Zach enough to get us moving again. So we continue heading down the path.

I'm frustrated by Zach's insistence about digging into my past. I guess he has a right to know some of it. But I'm not willing to tell him about certain things. Things that are too important and *must* be kept secret. And things that are too emotionally raw for me to bring up. But there are some details I *can* share. Maybe it will be enough to satisfy him for now.

"Let me start at the beginning. I lived with my family in Brookline, a suburb of Boston. My mom and dad were visiting my abuelita in Chicago, and my brother was at college in California. I had the house to myself, so Marcus practically lived there. Then the Great Collapse happened."

Zach cuts in. "You know, I never really knew much about the Great Collapse. Power and Internet went out and stayed out. Stores went empty, and people started dying. That's all I know."

"Oh, shit. Really?"

"Really."

I feel a little stunned. "So you don't know about the earthquake?"

"What earthquake?"

"Wow. Okay. From the *very* beginning. Marcus and I were at home when it happened. We were watching TV, when an emergency message came up. Then our cell phones and the landline rang at the same time. The caller ID was 911."

Zach cuts in. "Yeah, I got a reverse 911 call too. But my uncle and I were out fishing all day, and I missed it. When we got back, power was out, and my voicemail had stopped working, so I never found out what caused it."

"Man, I didn't know how totally cut off you were. Didn't your friend Ezra tell you anything?"

"Ezra doesn't even have a TV."

"Huh. Well, the emergency was a massive earthquake—nine point one, I think—struck off the coast of Antarctica. It opened up this enormous trench in the ocean and created a hundred-foot tsunami heading north in every direction. Any place in the world within ten miles of a coastline was evacuated, and that included Boston."

"I can't believe I didn't know about this." Zach's face is a little pale.

"Yeah, I assumed you did."

Zach shakes his head. "So what did you do?"

"We packed all the food we could into backpacks and hit the road. The streets were a disaster, backed up for miles. But luckily, we were on a dirt bike, so I drove over lawns and took bike paths and things to get out of town. My family owned a cabin about fifty miles away. When we finally got to the cabin, we locked ourselves in, drew all the shades, and huddled by the TV.

"We couldn't believe what we were seeing. This massive glacier in Antarctica, the Thwaites Glacier, just liquefied. It's larger than the state of Florida and collapsed into the ocean in a couple of hours. Way faster than anybody thought it would happen.

"The tsunamis hit South America, New Zealand, and Australia first. Buenos Aires, Auckland, and Melbourne were all hit with a massive hundred-foot wave. The cities were gone. Wiped off the face of the earth."

I pause and glance over at Zach. He's been listening quietly this whole time, but now he's as white as a sheet.

"The coastal cities all got hit hard?" he asks in almost a whisper.

"Yeah, they did. New York, Hong Kong, Boston. All ruins."

"Seattle?"

Shit. I didn't think about how Zach might react to this news. Guess I could have eased him into it a bit more smoothly.

"Seattle fared better than most. It's not right on the ocean. But there was still a storm surge. And global sea level went up by ten feet because of the glaciers."

Zach's face is a tempest of worry.

"I can stop," I say, concerned about triggering him.

"No. Please. Keep going."

I scan Zach's face. "Okay. Let me know if it's too much."

"I will."

"Well, Marcus and I watched TV for as long as we could. Anderson Cooper coined it the Great Collapse. When he said it, he was talking about the collapsed glacier. But it ended up having a double meaning—the collapse of civilization. Before the TV went dead, most of southern Florida was underwater. Miami, Houston, and Los Angeles, gone. Then CNN stopped broadcasting. One by one, the other networks all went dark. Nine hours after we saw the first warning on TV, the power went out."

Zach shakes his head. "So when we got back from fishing, all this had already happened. God. We were out catching fish when the whole world was melting down around us."

I stop walking and look at Zach. I don't want to unload too much on him at once. I had no idea he was in the dark about this, and it's a lot for anybody. But he seems determined to hear more.

"So what happened to you guys?" Zach asks. "How'd you end up with the Collective?"

"We stayed at the cabin until we ran out of food. Then we headed out. We ran into a group of survivors and traveled with them for a few days. They told us how people were getting sick, and some people who survived were losing their minds. The rumor was that the water in the tsunami spread some disease. People on the coastlines were getting sick, but it was spreading inland fast."

"The Infection came from the oceans?"

"Yeah." I have a pang of guilt for not telling the whole truth. But there are things I can never reveal to Zach, like how the military created the damn disease. When the tsunami struck the stockpile of XT58 with a direct hit, it released into the world. It thrived in the ocean water and spread inland quickly. Other stockpiles on the West Coast, Europe, Asia, and the Middle East suffered similar fates.

"The world might have survived the tsunami and sea level rise by itself. But not with the Infection spreading and the world's power grid and communication networks gone—all governments effectively beheaded. Civilization collapsed quickly."

Zach's face has gone even paler. "It all makes a lot of sense now. I wondered how things got so bad so quickly. The disease spread so fast."

"Yeah, a mass migration of people leaving the coasts carried the disease inland in no time. The first time I saw an Infected man, I could barely believe it. He flat out killed three people in our group before we stopped him. And ten of us got injured enough to draw blood. I was one of them. By some stroke of luck, Marcus was back in our tent and didn't get hurt. Within a day, nine of the people injured started getting sick. Everyone except me. That was my first hint I was immune. Our whole group fell apart in a couple of days when one of the sick people started attacking the rest of the group. From that point forward, Marcus and I knew we were better off alone. So we kept traveling from house to house, looking for food. But it kept getting more difficult. That's when we ran into Connor."

Zach stares at me, eyes wide. "You mean the guy who's hunting us?"

I frown and nod. "Yep. We knew something was different about him because he didn't seem as destitute as everybody else we ran into."

"Just like when I first saw you," Zach says.

"Yeah, I guess so. He figured I was immune like him, since I'd been exposed a few times but survived. So he brought us back to this bunker deep underground. Over a hundred people, all doing medical research. They needed people like me who were immune, who could scout and deliver things. That's how I joined the Scientific Collective and became a courier."

"What happened next?"

"Hey, look." I point up ahead. "Our destination, I presume."

On the horizon, the junkyard comes into view.

Chapter Fifteen

The Junkyard

ZACH

It's midafternoon as we approach the junkyard. But my mind is miles away, processing Aiden's story. I immediately thought about my family when he mentioned the tsunamis and the storm surge. Our house is right on the water on Vashon Island. But it's fifty feet up on a bluff and in a protected inlet. That gives me some hope, but I'm still sick with worry. I shake off the thought and focus on the task at hand.

The dirt road leads to a tall chain-link fence with barbed wire on top. Piled up behind the fence are countless rusty cars. The road comes up to a sliding gate with a large padlock on it.

Aiden points to a *Beware of Dog* sign. "Is that something we need to be worried about?"

"What, Daisy? She's a sweetheart. She knows me."

Aiden's sour face shows he's not convinced.

My friend Ezra is nowhere to be seen.

"Ezra? Hello?" I call out. No response.

We do a complete circle around the fence perimeter but come across no one and find no other entrances. The junkyard office is next to the front gate, so we peek in the windows, hoping to see something. A desk with piles of papers and old coffee cups rests against the far wall, but no Ezra.

Aiden turns to me. "He doesn't seem to be around. Do you know where this car is that he offered you?"

"Yeah, he keeps it in there." I point to the middle of the junkyard at a rusting metal garage with a large rolling door. The door is closed.

"Well, let's get in there." Aiden picks up a large rock and smashes it through one of the exterior windows of the junkyard office.

"Hey! I don't want to destroy the place."

"See those?" Aiden points to tire tracks going into the junkyard.

"Yeah?"

"Those tracks are weeks old. Maybe months. See how the imprint is no longer well formed? Also, in the office, you can see a thick layer of dust over everything. Nobody's been into or out of this place in a while."

I nod but say nothing, worried about what that may mean.

Aiden punches out the remaining glass with his fist balled into his shirt sleeve. He reaches in and unlocks the window. After opening it, he climbs in, and I follow behind.

As Aiden pointed out, the interior of the office is clearly unoccupied and has been for some time. And it's not only the dust. The air is stale. The whole place feels abandoned.

The front room of the office is much the same. A vintage bright-red vinyl sofa looks pink under a thick layer of dust. Old engine parts and car magazines are strewn about haphazardly.

A small back room off the office serves as Ezra's bedroom. An unmade bed sits in the corner. Spread throughout the room are piles of dirty laundry. The same musty smell permeates everything. I shoot Aiden a worried look, and he looks back with tight lips and arms crossed.

"Doesn't look like he's been here for a while." Aiden looks around the room. "If he left, let's hope he didn't take his car."

"This junkyard was his whole life. I don't know where he'd go."

"You're assuming he left of his own accord. I've heard rumors of slave camps around here. Slavers go around, rounding up survivors."

I glare at Aiden. "You're not making me feel better."

"Sorry. I know he's your friend. Just trying to be prepared for the worst."

"Let's keep looking."

We leave his bedroom to head to the yard. Aiden slowly opens the door from the main office, and we make our way out, glancing back and forth. Neither of us makes a sound. I've given up on calling out for Ezra since it's clear he isn't around.

We make our way to the metal garage in the middle of the yard. I reach down and pull up the large rolling door.

Sitting near the back of the building is a '67 Chevy Camaro. It's painted black with two white stripes down the hood. I have to admit it looks pretty cool.

"Well, he didn't take the car. There she is." I gesture toward the Camaro.

Aiden does a catcall whistle. "Nice! Maybe not the best gas mileage, but hell, if the car runs, I ain't complaining."

We both walk toward it when it hits us—a smell I've gotten all too familiar with in the last year. The unmistakable scent of decaying flesh.

I scan the room, then reel back from a grizzly sight—human remains. *Ezra.* But the clothes are all tattered, and much of the flesh is gone as if it's been ripped away. It's practically a skeleton.

I gasp and put my hand up to my mouth, horrified. Aiden comes over to me and lays a hand on my shoulder. "I'm so sorry, Zach."

I'm numb, but the need for human contact overwhelms me. So I turn to Aiden and hug him. He's a little taken aback and starts out hesitantly but then wraps his arms around me. I'd only met Ezra a handful of times, but he was the only person I had spoken to in the last year—my lifeline to humanity.

"What happened to him?" I ask.

Aiden sighs. "Honestly, it looks like a wild animal got to him."

And then I get a definitive answer. Not a wild animal. A starving one. Standing between us and the exit is Daisy. She's growling loudly, with slobber dripping out between her bared teeth. She's always been a good-sized German shepherd, but now, she's emaciated. Her bones poke out beneath her skin. Ezra must have died of a heart attack or something, and poor Daisy was left without any food. From the looks of her it's been weeks or even months.

We both freeze. Daisy faces me, about ten feet away.

"*Day*—zee," I call out in a singsong voice, but she growls more and starts barking.

"Real sweetheart," Aiden whispers.

Aiden slowly reaches for his rifle, but I whisper forcefully in his ear. "No! It's not Daisy's fault. She's literally starving. There has to be another way."

"Okay. So what do we do?"

"She's blocking the door. On three, we need to make a break for the car. Okay?"

"Okay. Do we know if it's unlocked?"

I sigh. "We'll know soon enough. You take the driver's side. Okay, one…two…three."

We let go of each other and make a mad dash for the car. Daisy immediately pursues, her paws slipping underneath her as she fights for traction on the slick cement floor. Aiden faces toward the car and has a slight head start on me. Daisy detects this and chases after me, the closest target.

Aiden reaches the driver's side door. *And it's unlocked.* He swings the door wide.

I'm still a few feet from my door when Daisy makes her move and leaps in the air. I turn in time to see her gaping jaws with razor-sharp teeth headed directly for me.

A hub cap flies into view, and I spot Aiden in mid-follow-through. It's a direct hit, striking Daisy in the face. This dazes her enough for me to deflect her momentum and send her flying past me.

She recovers remarkably fast and comes back around. I reach for the passenger side door. And it's locked. Aiden dives into the car and shoves open my door. He drags me into the car by my shirt.

The dog leaps again, this time going for my feet dangling out the door. She clamps her jaws around the loose fabric of my pant leg, missing my actual leg by a fraction of an inch. With the free leg, I kick her hard in the snout. She yelps and releases me.

Aiden hustles me the rest of the way in, using adrenaline and brute strength. As he does so, I hook the door handle with the toe of my shoe and slam the door shut as Daisy comes in for another attack. She smacks hard against the closed door.

We land across the front seats, a tangled mess of arms and legs. We're both overwhelmed by the moment, half laughing, half crying.

"Thanks for saving my life. Again," I whisper to Aiden.

Aiden smiles. "The score is two to one. It's your turn next."

*

AIDEN

After the narrow escape from the dog, we both lie across the front seats, our bodies intertwined. The instant peril, followed by tremendous relief, amplifies every sense and every emotion. The feel of Zach's skin on mine, the sound of our heartbeats, and the heat of his breath sends little tingles throughout my entire body. Our eyes lock, our faces inches apart. Zach bites his lip.

Because my subconscious won't allow me an ounce of joy, Marcus hits my mind, sick and dying. I have no control over the reflex, the waves of guilt and remorse. The shift in body language speaks volumes. Zach pulls away and sits up.

It's for the best. Zach still hopes to find his boyfriend, no matter how slim the odds are. He doesn't need me complicating things. And I'm clearly incapable of feeling normal emotions. Not to mention, I'm leaving the first chance I get. The next working car we find, I'm out of here.

But before I can worry about the future, I need to focus on the present. We're not out of the woods yet. Daisy is prowling around the car, growling and barking. And to top it off, the keys are not in the ignition.

"Look." I point to the empty keyhole.

"Crap."

We both hunt for the keys. Zach checks inside the glove box, and we search above the visors, under the seats, and in the ashtray. Nothing.

Then Zach points to a hook on the wall on the other side of the room. "There." A set of keys dangles from it, a Chevy logo on the chain. Between us and the keys, Daisy paces back and forth, growling.

As a last resort, we have the rifles. But I already know Zach won't like that option. And I'm actually somewhat relieved. The thought of shooting her makes me ill. I'm not sure I could do it. This poor dog is trying to survive, kind of like us.

Instead, Zach removes his backpack and grabs his little toolkit from it. "Give me just a few minutes. These old cars have simple ignition wiring."

"Of course you can hot-wire a car." I laugh.

Zach makes a sheepish smile and shrugs. Why did I ever doubt him? If it's mechanical or electrical, Zach can figure it out. I climb into the back seat so he can shimmy his way under the steering wheel. He lowers the front driver's seat into the fully reclined position, then goes in headfirst and tummy up.

I curse myself for being so shallow. But ever since Zach cleaned himself up, I see a different person. I can't help it. Any more than I can't help the fact that I'm into guys. It just *is*. His shirt lifts as he bends backward into the footwell, exposing his bare midsection. His lean stomach and narrow waist peak out. A small tuft of hair around his belly button trails down into his pants. I fight the urge to reach out and touch it. That would only lead to no good.

"Hey, can you hand me the needle-nose pliers?" Zach holds his hand out expectantly.

I fish through the toolkit and place them in his hand. "Here you go."

"Thanks."

A few minutes pass, and Zach exclaims, "Okay, here goes nothing."

Sparks shoot out from below, and the engine tries to turn over. The battery sounds weak, but at least it has some juice.

"That's progress," I encourage.

He crosses the wires, and the car turns over again. But it still doesn't start.

"This isn't working." Zach peaks up at me. "I need a third hand. It's gonna be a little tight, but I need you to push down the gas pedal when I tell you to. Okay?"

"Okay." With no other obvious way to fit, I get on top of Zach and reach down until my hand touches the pedal. With my body fully pressed against his, that same tingle runs through me. I clear my mind. Force out thoughts of Marcus and try to block everything out. But I can't ignore the heat of his body, the light scent of his sweat mixed with campfire smoke, and soft skin—the way our bodies rub together with every breath. I try to fight off the urges, but it's no use as I start getting hard. I hope he doesn't notice.

Zach shoots me a quizzical look that morphs into recognition, and his face turns beet red. "Um…what's that?"

"Sorry! It just happened." I'm so damn embarrassed. "I can't help it."

Zach laughs nervously. "Uh—I guess I'm sorry, too, then."

That's when something stiff rubs up against me.

Zach clears his throat loudly. "Okay! I need to concentrate. For now, I'm going to ignore everything going on down there."

"That works for me," I blurt out.

We both do our best to ignore it.

In a moment, Zach regains his composure. "Okay, when I say go, push down on the gas. Ready? Go!"

Sparks fly, and the engine turns over. As I push down on the gas pedal, the engine revs. It almost catches. So close.

"One more time," Zach says. "Ready? Go!"

The engine sputters and groans. I press down on the pedal once, then twice. The third time, the engine roars to life. I pulse the pedal a couple more times for good measure. The engine purrs as the RPMs ramp up. It's a wonderful sound.

We both cheer, then hug each other. A hug of comradery and joy. *We did it.*

When we climb out of the footwell, I take the driver's seat, and Zach is happy to be the passenger. We don't talk about the elephant in the room. *Or the boners in the car?* Zach has let it drop, and I'm relieved. That's a conversation I don't feel like having right now, with all its complications.

It takes a bit of honking and inching forward to convince Daisy to let us by, but she finally relents. I drive out of the garage and turn toward the junkyard exit. Zach freaks out a bit as I punch the accelerator, heading toward the outer fence, but the aluminum links are no match for the ton and a half of steel. It might not be the best thing for the paint job, but we're not trying to win any car shows.

I pull the car over outside the junkyard. Daisy follows us out and goes running off into the woods.

"Probably going to find some dinner," I say.

"I'm glad she's free."

Zach looks back at the garage we just left. "It doesn't feel right leaving Ezra like that."

"You're right. It doesn't."

In the nearby woods, we find some fallen twigs and small logs. We drag them back to Ezra's remains and cover up the body.

But coming back turns out to be a blessing in disguise. As Zach prepares the pyre, I spot something I hadn't seen before.

"Hey, Zach, look at that." I point to a circular hatch on the ground toward the back of the garage. It's about the size of a manhole cover.

"That looks like the entrance to a bomb shelter. Ezra never mentioned it."

"He had the car parked right over it. That's why we didn't see it before."

"Let's check it out."

The hatch has a latching mechanism. It's hard to disengage by hand, but kicking it does the trick. I open the hatch and stare into a dark abyss. A metal ladder on the side heads downward.

It descends about twenty feet to a cement floor. With a flashlight in hand, I scan the surroundings. It has all the earmarks of a bomb shelter. A long, narrow room extends back about fifty feet. Shelves stuffed with canned food, weapons, and other supplies line the walls.

Zach climbs down and stands beside me.

"Looks like he didn't die of hunger." I point to the lines of canned food.

Zach's shoulders drop. "He was old. Maybe his heart gave out."

"I guess we should see if there's anything useful."

While Zach tops off our packs with more food, I inspect the pile of weapons.

"Man, he's got some military-grade stuff in here." I point to a pile of hand grenades and landmines. On a whim, I stash a few grenades in the front flap of my backpack.

"Hey, look over here," Zach calls out from the back of the bunker. He's standing next to several five-gallon plastic gas cans. "These are full."

"Nice. That'll get us quite a bit farther."

We haul up everything we want and stash it in the back of the car, sprinkling a little of the extra gas over the logs to be sure the fire burns well.

Zach stands over the pyre, matchbook in hand. He pauses momentarily, then strikes a match and tosses it in. "Goodbye, Ezra. I'll miss you."

Chapter Sixteen

On The Road

AIDEN

After we clear the junkyard, we stop to consult a map from an old atlas that Zach packed.

Interstate 90 is the most direct route by far, but we agree it'll leave us the most exposed. So we stick to smaller highways and backroads. The route will take us through the rest of western Montana, across the Idaho panhandle, and finally into Washington.

If all goes well, we could arrive in Seattle in only a few days. That depends on how clear the roads are and how easy it is to find gas along the way.

We're on the open road, and it feels great. The speed is exhilarating. I love to drive. I'm in my element. And this Camaro has horsepower to spare. I'd like to see a carjacker try to overtake me with this baby. Scratch that. I'd rather we not see anybody. But if we do, I'm ready.

As we drive along, I keep my eyes out for cars by the side of the road, but only if the cars aren't too trashed. We're checking for extra gas, but secretly, I'm also looking for unlocked cars and keys. I've found nothing yet.

Unfortunately, the Camaro only has an eight-track player. I've been aching to hear my mixtape, but Zach finds a Credence Clearwater Revival eight-track cassette in the glove box. So we race over the open plains of Montana, with the sounds of "Proud Mary" and "Fortunate Son" blaring over the speakers.

Zach's window is down, and he's letting his hand get buffeted by the wind. He looks over. "So, what did you want to do with your life? Like, before all this."

"I wanted to study molecular biology. Thought I could cure cancer."

"Wow. That's quite a goal."

"Yeah, well. Curing cancer wasn't going to happen. It turns out I wasn't particularly good at school. Too distracted."

"Distracted by what?" Zach asks.

"By parties and boys, mostly."

Zach lets out a little laugh. "Ha, I can relate. When I was touring the U-Dub campus, the boy selection looked pretty comprehensive."

"Was your boyfriend planning on going there too?"

"Oh, Felix? No. He was staying on Vashon. That's part of why we broke up."

"Oh?" My head spins a little. *Broke up?*

"Yeah. It was my choice. We were high school sweethearts, and I'd be going to college. I kinda always knew it wasn't going to be forever."

This is a genuine surprise for me. I had worked up this scenario where Zach and his boyfriend were these star-crossed lovers trying to get back to each other. Things are rearranging rapidly in my brain, and my stomach does a little flutter. *What the heck was that?*

"He was my first love though. And I still care for him." Zach lets out a shallow sigh. "He took it pretty hard. But it needed to happen. Still, it all feels a little insignificant considering the world now."

"It's not like you knew the world was about to end. You did what you thought was right at the time you did it."

Zach looks at me with a melancholy smile. "Yeah. I suppose so. It's all just so damn sad."

Talking with Zach is comforting, and I want to open up to him.

"When Marcus died—" I choke on my words, trying to get the sentence out. "I'm sorry. I can't."

Zach reaches over and puts his hand on my knee. "It's okay. Tell me when you're ready."

His compassion is palpable. It gives me a little glowing feeling. But also, a pang of guilt. When it was a faraway idea, leaving Zach seemed easy and made sense. But each car we stop at could be the one that takes me away. And now the idea is harder to swallow.

"Let's talk about nice things, huh?" Zach smiles. "What's your favorite pizza?"

That's such a *Zach* question. I laugh. "Pepperoni mushroom. No contest."

"Not bad, not bad. That's a classic. But can't beat pineapple and anchovies."

I make a horking sound. "Seriously?"

"Hey, don't knock the sweet, salty, briny until you've tried it."

"You're ridiculous." I laugh.

"Maybe a little." Zach smiles.

"Favorite sport?"

"A tie between downhill skiing and sailing. My family's sailboat is moored in Seattle. Without the ferries running, it's the closest you can get to Vashon Island by car. That's how I figured I'd get back home."

I immediately think the coastline may not exist as he remembers it. But so many things have to go right between now and then, even to have to worry about that.

"I hope you find them," I say.

"The odds aren't great. But if there's any chance at all… Either way, I just have to know." Zach stares blankly at the road ahead.

None of my family survived, but I don't bring it up. Nowadays, that's the default assumption with new people you meet. But Zach still hopes to find them, and I'd rather not crush his dreams with the world's harsh realities. These are things he'll gradually learn the farther we travel. And who knows? He might get lucky with his family.

"Water polo," I say, trying to fight through the melancholy.

"What about it?"

"That's my favorite sport. I played in high school."

"Wow, you must be quite the swimmer."

I laugh. "Yeah, well, maybe not anymore."

"Water polo was one of my favorite Olympic sports to watch." Zach has a mischievous smile. "Lots of good eye candy."

"You aren't wrong." I smile back. "Diving's my favorite in that regard."

"Oh? You have a crush on Tom Daley?"

"I might have a little crush on him, yes. Who doesn't?"

We both laugh.

He leans his head back on the seat. "I probably miss Thanksgiving the most."

"Big turkey fan?" I joke.

"Mashed potatoes." Zach laughs. "No, just the family. I miss them."

"Yeah, me too." I think back to a time that feels like a different life. "My family ditched the turkey and made a big plate of green chili carnitas and tamales."

Zach gasps. "Oh my god, that sounds so much better than dry turkey!" He shoots me daggers with his eyes. "Now, I'm hungry, dang it. Thanks."

I laugh. "Sorry. I think maybe we have some canned corned beef hash in the back."

Zach groans.

We keep going back and forth about all the other things we miss. It's nice, and it makes the time go by. I enjoy talking with Zach. He's clever and funny but never in a mean way. For having such a rough life over the last year, he sure has a positive spin on things.

It's getting late in the afternoon when we approach the outskirts of Helena. The highway we chose goes along the southern edge. The larger the town, the more likely we are to run into Infected, people with guns, or blocked roads. So I always try to stick to the outskirts.

Of the few buildings we see, most have their windows smashed, or they're burned-out husks. We pass by a gas station that is charred and still smoking. Zach shakes his head. "You know, in Elk Springs, this whole Great Collapse was theoretical for me. But it's all gone, isn't it?"

"Most of it, yes. Some groups like the one I came from are trying to rebuild. But we can't build up too much until we can fight the Infection."

"That's what you're transporting, right? Something that can help fight the Infection?"

Why did I bring that up? As usual, Zach's intuition is spot-on. But he's too smart for his own good. Even knowing about it puts him and my mission in greater jeopardy. If he were ever caught, they'd find some way to get it out of him. And what I'm doing is too important.

"Zach, once this is done, I'll tell you everything. But for now, the less you know, the better off you'll be."

Zach doesn't say anything but stares at the road ahead, slightly sighing.

I'm not ready to tell Zach the true details of my mission. Only a handful of people in the world know there's a cure for the Infection stored deep within the emergency medical bunker at UW in Seattle. But they need the vials I'm carrying to make that cure viable. Within my little aluminum box is the power to save all of humanity. And also the power to destroy it. It wouldn't take much to mutate the weaponized pathogen to get around people's immunity. And then it becomes the ultimate weapon.

The only other person who knows this is the director of our bunker, Sophia Hughes. Except Connor—back from the dead—seems to have figured it out too.

*

ZACH

Aiden is going to have some secrets. And I have to be okay with that. But when you team up with somebody, you are putting part of your life into their hands. And having them keep things from you feels—well—scary.

I'm willing to live with that feeling for now. After all, without Aiden, I'd still be stuck in Elk Springs. In the worst case, the FLA would have captured or even killed me.

Not to mention, I really like Aiden's company. After being on my own for so long and having my wits and decisions be the only thing keeping me alive, it's so comforting to have somebody else. I'm safe around him. And safe is something I haven't felt in a long time.

Aiden's in the driver's seat, with a look of concentration. The way his brows knit looks so handsome. He's so in control, good at whatever he does.

I can't stop thinking about earlier, his body on mine as I hotwired the car. It was so damn hot I could hardly stand it. Regardless of what's happening in that brain, his body is clearly into me. I smile.

"What?" Aiden asks, seeing me staring.

"Nothing. I'm glad you want to drive."

"I love driving. I freak out when someone else does. I'm a total backseat driver."

I smile. "Glad it worked out."

We're making good progress on the road. We fill up with one of the five-gallon gas cans and stop at a few abandoned cars to siphon gas. Most of them are already dry, but we find a Honda Accord in a ditch with some gas left. Aiden even finds the keys for it and starts the car up. He's been hoping to find us a car with better gas mileage. But the car is too deep in the ditch to get out, so we move on.

We've got about an hour before sunset when we roll into Missoula. It's a bigger city than Helena, and there's no easy way to get around it without going miles out of our way.

"I hate going through towns," Aiden says, biting the inside of his cheek. "It's unpredictable. Keep an eye out for anything strange, okay?"

"Okay." I dart my eyes back and forth, expecting something to spring out at any moment.

But the city is empty. Not a soul to be seen. As we drive along residential streets, the houses all appear abandoned, with smashed windows and overgrown yards. Some are burned down to the ground. Most of them have a large *X* spray-painted on them, likely the tag of some looter who's already cleaned out the house.

A couple of times, we drive up to a road blocked by cars, forcing us to double back. At one point, we have to motor over ten lawns to get past a pileup that stretched across the entire street. Despite all the cars around, Aiden doesn't want us to stop and check any out. In the city, the risks of stopping outweigh the benefits.

We're almost out of town when I spot a man in the middle of an intersection. Aiden is looking the other way and doesn't see him approaching.

"Watch out!" I point toward the man, who's now running straight at the car.

Aiden swerves, narrowly avoiding him. The car spins out and comes to a full stop on the other side of the intersection. The engine cuts out.

The man wears nothing but underwear. He's got long, ratty hair and a big gray beard. The bulging veins in his neck mark him as one of the Infected. He's screaming at the top of his lungs as he runs toward us.

"GO! GO!" I yell.

"Car's dead!"

"Shit." I reach for the ignition wires under the dash as Aiden frantically pushes all the manual door locks just before the man is on us.

He starts smashing his fists on the driver-side window. After several manic strikes, the window cracks but still holds. It won't last for long though.

Sparks fly between the wires as I touch them together. "Give it some gas!"

The engine comes to life, and Aiden floors it. The man desperately attempts to grab the car but bounces off and lands hard on the ground. I keep my eye on him as we speed away.

Aiden was right to avoid towns. They aren't safe. The world is a changed place.

I shake my head. "Let's get the hell outta here."

Chapter Seventeen

Ghosts of the Past

ZACH

We're a few miles north of Missoula on a small, forested highway. The shadows are getting long, and soon, we'll need the car headlights, so we search for a good place to stop for the night. Driving at night makes us an easy target. Better to only travel during the daylight.

We take a small dirt road that runs off the main highway. After about a mile, we're in the foothills. Out of sight from the main road, we find a big clearing surrounded by woods. By the time we set up camp and eat a simple meal of warmed canned chili, the sun has set, and the sky has turned a deep purple.

I turn to Aiden. The flickers of the campfire illuminate his face. He's so handsome, and again my mind goes to earlier with him pressed against me in the car.

"You're staring again." Aiden says, looking my way.

"Sorry. Just love the glow of the fire." I'm glad he can't see my blushing in the flickering light. "We made good time today."

"Yeah, not bad. That car is fun to drive."

"By tomorrow, we should be in Idaho. We might even pass Cedar Grove."

Aiden looks at me questioningly. "What's Cedar Grove?"

"You've never heard of Cedar Grove?" My mouth gapes open.

Aiden shakes his head.

"It's only the best amusement park in the entire Northwest. Well, maybe the only one, actually."

Aiden laughs. "Well, that explains why I've never heard of it then. What's so special about it?"

"I've just got a lot of memories. It was my first roller coaster." I smile wistfully. "And my first kiss."

Now I have his attention.

"Do tell." Aiden smiles.

"It was Felix, of course. We'd been friends for as long as I can remember. We were thirteen. Both our parents surprised us with a trip to Cedar Grove. We'd done all the roller coasters, so I asked him what we should do next. He pointed to this dark ride called Earthquake. It's not exactly the tunnel of love, but everybody knew that was the make-out ride at Cedar Grove."

Aiden laughs. "I can see where this is going."

"Heh. Yeah. Well, at the time, I had a huge crush on Felix, and I'd been doing a lot of imagining us making out. He didn't know, of course. And I was certain he would freak out if he did.

"I was sure I liked guys. After my massive crush on Tom Holland in *Spider-Man*, it was hard to deny it. It's just that Felix was also my best friend. And I didn't know how to deal with the fact that I was obsessed with kissing my best friend.

"We rode in the car together. He was flinching at every noise, and his knuckles were turning white, holding on to the safety bar. I wanted so badly to reach out and hug him. And then I got my wish. At this one jump scare, our car swerved sharply, and he jumped into my arms. We looked at each other and both laughed. But our eyes were locked together, and we stopped laughing. There was a look on his face I'd never seen before. So I kissed him."

Aiden smiles in the firelight. But something else flashes in his expression. Maybe the slightest hint of jealousy.

"At first, he didn't kiss back. I was sure I'd ruined our friendship. But he didn't pull away either. We still had our arms wrapped around each other. And then he kissed me back. That was it. I knew he felt the same way. We were boyfriends. We rode the Earthquake about five more times, to be sure."

Aiden lets loose a heartfelt laugh.

"We kept it a secret for a while. Until we were both ready to come out to our families. But from that moment, we were inseparable."

"Wow. That's really sweet." Aiden smiles.

"Yeah. It's a nice memory. But even then, it was indicative of our relationship. I had to initiate everything. Felix was always so timid. In the end, that was our downfall. We probably should have broken up earlier, but again, it was me who had to initiate that."

Aiden nods and stares into the fire, looking very contemplative.

I sigh. "Anyway, enough about Felix."

By now, twilight is over, and the stars have come out. I lean my chair back to get a better view. "I'll never get used to how bright the stars are now."

Aiden looks up in wonder. "Yeah, without city lights, we can see a billion of them."

"I get now why they call it the Milky Way."

Before the Great Collapse, there was still a certain amount of light pollution, even in the middle of nowhere. But with all the power grids out, there's no light whatsoever. It's hard to understand the difference until you experience it. On a cloudy night, the darkness is absolute. You can't even make out your hand right in front of your face.

But it's breathtaking on a night like tonight, with a clear, moonless sky. The middle of the galaxy and the radiating arms spreading out from its center are plain to see. And our tiny planet is one of a billion-billion little orbs spinning its way around. It's enough to make me laugh at my insignificant problems.

The stars provide enough light to illuminate Aiden's face. He's looking upward, still with a look of deep contemplation.

"Kinda puts things into perspective, huh?" I ask.

"Yeah, it kinda does."

"Before all this, I had a lot of my life planned out. I was going to finish college. Go work at Google. Fall in love and marry the man of my dreams. Buy a house and maybe have surrogate kids with some lesbian friends. Retire to the Mediterranean and travel the rest of my life."

"That's well planned out." Aiden laughs. "Sounds like a nice life."

"But now, I don't even know what the next month will bring. If life's all about survival, finding the next meal, what's the point?"

Aiden looks over at me, his eyes tired and sad. "You're kinda hitting me at a rough time to get too philosophical. You might not like my answers."

I reach over and put my hand on his arm. "Hey, I'm here if you want to talk about stuff. Tell me what's going on."

*

AIDEN

When Zach puts his hand on my arm, my gut reaction is to pull away. To bury the pain and clam up again. These are things he doesn't need to know. He shouldn't know. The less he knows, the better.

But his touch sends a wave of warmth through me. And the look on his face is so tender and earnest. I've bottled up these feelings, this guilt, for so long. And here's a kind soul who's reaching out, who seems to care.

Zach senses this. "Go ahead. You can tell me."

I take a deep breath and gaze into his eyes. "Nobody knows the entire story. But here goes. You remember the bunker I made it to?"

Zach nods.

"Well, after Connor brought me and Marcus back, they recruited me into the couriers. I didn't really want to do it, but it's why they took us in. So I couldn't really say no. A special forces soldier trained me and taught me how to defend myself. How to survive. It turns out I was good at it. But nobody was better than Connor. We spent a lot of time together training. He was good-looking and friendly to me. I never thought he liked me more than a friend. But Marcus was still jealous."

Zach glances over. "I know the feeling. Felix got jealous too."

I nod. "Connor and I drifted apart after that. Well, that mission I told you about where I thought Connor died? What I didn't say was Marcus was furious. I told him there was nothing to worry about. I didn't see Connor that way. I wanted to learn from him in the field. Learn from the best. But I left on the mission before Marcus and I really resolved it. We left on bad terms, and that's one of my greatest regrets."

I tell Zach about how Marcus was sick when I returned from that horrible mission. For the first time, I repeat Marcus's dying words out loud. "Connor. I know—"

Zach's eyes are glossy when I finish. "I'm so sorry about Marcus. And that you only got to see him at the very end."

I nod, wiping away my tears.

"What do you think Marcus was trying to say?" Zach asks in barely a whisper.

But I can't answer. I can barely meet Zach's gaze. It's been so long since I've dug into these thoughts that other buried memories start bubbling to the surface. Why *did* Marcus say Connor's name? I thought Connor was dead at the time, but now I know he wasn't. What does that mean? Did Marcus suspect what had happened between Connor and me on that trip? There's no way Marcus could have known. Still, the guilt of it rips at me.

Zach looks into my eyes, searching for answers. As his gaze pierces into me, my face gives me away.

"There's something else, isn't there?" he asks.

My heart wrenches. Why does Zach always figure this stuff out? I turn my head, not able to look at him.

"Something else happened with you and Connor." Zach takes my hand. "Tell me."

I breathe deeply, thinking back on a memory I've locked so tightly in my mind, so securely, I can scarcely remember it. But when I say the first words, the details come flooding back. "It was the night before Connor fell off the bridge. We'd been driving all day and finally stopped for the night. We set up camp and made a small campfire.

"When Connor was around other people, he always seemed to put on a show. But he was a lot less intimidating when I was with him one-on-one. That night, we talked about being couriers and what a challenge it was. He said he was impressed by me, which was a huge compliment because I really looked up to him. He told me there were few people he trusted more in the field than me."

I skip the part where Connor tells me his conspiracy theories about the Collective and his thinly veiled attempt to recruit me. I can't tell Zach I'm carrying XT58. I have too many conflicting thoughts about what role the Collective did or didn't play. This is more than I can get into right now.

"I hardly noticed it, but before long, we were sitting next to each other, huddled by the fire, trying to keep warm." I take a deep breath. "And that's when he kissed me. It was so unexpected that it took me a moment to register what was happening. But then I pushed him away and told him no, and that it wasn't what I wanted."

Zach watches with rapt attention, frown deepening.

"But that didn't stop him. He pulled me back in. My immediate reaction should have been to jump up and get some distance between us. But I didn't. I let it happen. He kept kissing me. I hate to say it, but I got caught up in it. Then he reached for my pants and started unbuttoning them. That's what snapped me back to reality. And all I could think of was Marcus and how right he had been. He begged me not to go, but I didn't listen.

"So I tried to get away, but Connor pulled me back again. The sudden forcefulness scared the crap out of me. For a moment, there was something in his eyes. I was genuinely frightened of him."

I pause for a moment, not sure I can continue. These memories were buried so deeply that dredging them up makes the hurt feel fresh again. Tears are welling up.

But Zach is watching quietly, with such intense and caring eyes. "Keep going. I'm listening."

"I yelled 'no' and pushed him away. He grabbed my wrists again, so hard it gave me bruises. This massive surge of adrenaline gave me the strength to get free. I jumped up, ready to defend myself. I didn't know how he'd react. I thought he might come at me again. This man I'd known for months turned into a different person.

"He got up and stormed off to his tent. His face was so filled with hatred. I'll never forget that look."

Zach's eyes are glossy.

I say quietly, "You're the first person I've told that to." And then my tears really start flowing. I'm sobbing.

Zach comes over and puts his arm around me, rubbing my back. "Go ahead and cry. Let it all out."

"I'm sorry, Zach," I say between sobs. "This was too much for me to unload on you."

"Aiden, it's too much for you to *hold in*. You need to let these things out."

"I can't believe I betrayed Marcus."

Zach grabs me by the shoulders and looks into my eyes. "No! Listen. You didn't betray Marcus. Connor pushed you, and he went too far. Once you said 'no' and he didn't stop, that was assault."

"But I didn't stop him at first. I let it happen."

"You didn't let it happen. You fought back. It wasn't something you asked for or wanted. A shock like that can take time to process. Don't confuse your moment's hesitation as anything else. You did the right thing. It was Connor's fault. And *only* his."

Zach's words are comforting. But I'm not sure I'm ready to forgive myself yet. Zach wasn't there. He didn't feel what I felt.

Chapter Eighteen

Not In Kansas Anymore

ZACH

We sit by the fire until the logs have turned to embers. Aiden's eyes look heavy, and his shoulders slump.

His story weighs on me, but I'm glad to help him. Glad to let him get his trauma out in the open. Wounds can only heal if they have room to breathe. A lot of things make more sense now. The fear I saw in his eyes at the campfire last night when we got close. The names he calls in his dreams. The way he's always pulling away. All these terrible things he's been through mixed up together, along with Marcus's death. And Aiden's been holding it all in.

"I think I need to go to bed," Aiden says quietly.

"Yeah. Some rest will do you good."

It's early yet, but the evening was so emotionally draining. The extra sleep will be good for both of us.

It's a warm night, and the stars are too spectacular to ignore, so we sleep outside our tents. I convince Aiden to put our bedrolls next to each other for safety's sake. In reality, I want to keep an eye on him to be sure he's okay. He doesn't object.

We're in our own sleeping bags, but as I lie there, I wish we were together in one. I want to comfort him and hold him close. But Aiden has opened up to me, and I don't want to take advantage of him in a vulnerable state.

Sleep doesn't come easy with everything on my mind. Aiden's soft, rhythmic breathing breaks the quiet of the evening. As I stare up into the vastness of space, my mind travels far, pondering life and existence. Aiden stirs in his sleep, rolls his body toward mine, and hooks his arm around me. A tingle goes through me as the entire length of his body presses against mine.

"Oh, hi," I say under my breath with a barely audible laugh. His breathing is deep and consistent, and he's still sound asleep. Without disturbing him, I turn on my side with my back to his front and nuzzle in. I want this moment to last forever.

We wake up together when the sun comes streaming over the foothills. Aiden yanks his arm away and looks a little startled.

"Sorry." His face turns various shades of crimson. It's adorable.

"It's okay. I don't mind." I send him a warm smile.

His expression softens with the hint of a smile. He's okay with the affection. That little gesture sends warmth through my body.

It doesn't take us long to get packed and head out. We don't say much, but Aiden's mood seems lighter. It's barely perceptible but undeniable.

We've left the vast open plains of central Montana and into densely forested mountains. The farther we get away from Missoula, the fewer cars show up along the side of the road. It's been a while since we've found much gasoline, so we stop at almost every car to siphon. We find a few gallons, but we're using gas faster than we find it. We've already gone through most of the backup gas cans. What this Camaro gains from sheer coolness is lost in lousy mileage.

After a couple of hours of driving, we pass a sign.

Idaho Panhandle National Forest.

"Guess we're not in Kansas anymore, Toto," I say.

Aiden gives a sidelong glance at me and lets out a little chuckle. "Let's hope we don't run into any flying monkeys."

"Or wicked witches."

For miles, we've been driving along a river valley with hills on both sides of us. But then the hills to the left drop away, and we're on the bank of a vast lake. Beyond the lake, snowcapped mountains rise far off in the distance.

The cars on the side of the road have gone from sparse to nonexistent. For the first part of our journey, we couldn't go a mile without running into old burned-out vehicles or a pileup we had to steer around. But it's been at least an hour since we've seen anything.

"Hey, Aiden. Where do you think all the cars went?"

"I've been wondering that myself. It's like somebody's cleared them all away."

We keep driving along the lake's perimeter until a sign for Sandpoint, Idaho, goes speeding by.

Aiden sighs. "Going through towns sucks. But our gas situation is getting critical. We're going to have to risk it."

I lean over and check the gauge. It's well below a quarter tank, and we used our last backup tank about an hour ago. "Yeah. I'd guess we can only make it another forty-ish miles before running out, and I'd hate to get stuck in the middle of northern Idaho."

When we get to Sandpoint, we drive down one of the major arterial roads. There's not a single car to be seen.

"Okay, now this is just plain strange." Aiden's brow wrinkles. "Somebody has deliberately removed every car. What on earth for?"

"No idea. But this whole town is giving me the creeps." The hair on my neck stands up.

Out the side window, the streets are empty, with nothing for blocks in all directions. An old Victorian house comes into view. It's a classic painted lady in hues of lavender, blue, and green. And in the driveway, an old Oldsmobile sits up on cinder blocks.

"Check that out." I point ahead to the car. "Guess they couldn't tow that one away. Think it might have some gas?"

"Hmm, it's worth a try."

Aiden parks the car, and we hop out. He works on the siphon while I keep watch, looking up and down the street. The house probably dates to the early 1900s. The lawn is overgrown, the paint is peeling, and pieces of its filigree are falling off.

My stomach twists as a curtain moves on the second floor. An old woman with long gray hair and a scowl on her face peers out at me. I make eye contact, and she immediately shuts the blinds.

"There was a woman up there." I point to the window.

Aiden's forehead creases as he looks back and forth down the street. "I've got a bad feeling about this. Let's get going."

"Yeah, I'm with ya."

We hop back in the car and head to the highway as fast as possible.

"Do you think that car was a trap?" I ask.

"If I were going to set up a trap, that's exactly how I'd do it."

We get back on the highway and speed out of town. There's no sign of any pursuit, but I keep my attention focused just in case. The road is empty, and after about five miles, my nerves settle down.

We've made it another twenty miles, and still no cars. The gas gauge is a hair away from empty when I spot an old gas station by the side of the road. The pumps look straight from the 1950s, all red with an analog readout. A glass globe on top reads *Gasoline* in flowing script.

"Hey, Aiden, pull in here."

"Got an idea?" Aiden slows the car down.

"Yeah, maybe I can jury-rig one of these old pumps. They're strictly mechanical, so I might be able to bypass the fuel pump."

"We're running out of options. Only a few miles left in this tank. Let's give it a shot."

Aiden pulls the car in and parks it at the side of the gas station, where it's not as easy to spot from the road. I reach into the back seat and grab my trusty toolkit out of my backpack.

Aiden opens the driver's side door and hops out. "I'm gonna scout around a bit. Let me know if you need any help."

"Will do."

With the toolkit in hand, I head over to the pump. It doesn't take long to get the faceplate off. Just a few screws are holding it in. The face is a little rusty, but I pry it off with the flat end of a screwdriver. Once it's open, the whole mechanism looks straightforward. The gas line from the underground tank flows into a fuel pump. Shouldn't be hard to override. I'm getting the gas line detached when Aiden shouts.

"Get down! Someone's coming!" He frantically gestures for me to duck as he heads for cover behind our car.

Looking around, there's nowhere to go, and I'm pretty exposed. So I ball myself up and scrunch behind the gas pump.

The throaty sound of an engine comes from down the road. I crook my head around the pump to get a peek. It's a large pickup truck with extra-large tires and that damn FLA flag we've seen before.

Crap. CRAP.

But they don't slow down. They go past the gas station. Maybe we'll be okay.

The truck is almost out of sight when it stops suddenly, tires shrieking and smoke rising from them. The truck does a three-point turn and heads back. I have a tiny sliver of hope they didn't see us and will continue down the road. But that hope evaporates when they stop right in front of our car.

My anxiety builds. I have only seconds to get control of it before I'm useless. With my eyes shut tight, I breathe deep and clear my mind. But in my mind, I'm surprised to see Aiden there. His calming touch. His gentle voice. How he helped me the last time. My panic has ebbed, and I open my eyes to face my fears.

Four tough-looking people pile out of the truck, each with a rifle. A guy in a camouflage vest and an orange hat yells. "Hot damn, this is the car all right. Just like that old hag said."

I'm sickened as he shoots out the two front tires with a handgun.

A woman with short-cropped blond hair, wearing all-black military fatigues, yells at the gunman, "Jesus, Wayne, put that damn thing away. Remember, we need 'em alive."

"Why can't we just kill 'em, Tyra?"

"The boss said so, that's why. Also, keep your eye out for a small silver box."

I'm entirely exposed in my current spot. If one of them so much as turns their head to the left, they'll see me. Aiden is hiding behind the car. It will only take a moment for them to find him. Our backpacks, propped in the back seats, poke up for all to see.

Aiden makes eye contact with me, his gaze a mixture of sadness and resolve. The box he carries is important to him. Maybe as important as his own life. My chest tightens as I imagine what he might do.

So I know what I must do. I make a couple of quick hand signals to him. First, I point at myself, then show my fingers running. Then, I point to him and mime his hands on a backpack. Aiden's eyes turn wide, and his mouth gapes open. He shakes his head vigorously and mouths *no*.

I nod *yes* to him with a solemn expression. This is what I have to do. The thugs are moments away from discovering Aiden, and the moment they see him, they'll kill him. This is my last chance.

I jump up from my hiding spot and start running toward the forest, away from the men and our car where Aiden is hiding, yelling and making as much noise as I can.

Chapter Nineteen

Searching

AIDEN

When Zach jumps up from his hiding spot, it hits me like a punch in the gut. One second, I'm ready to fight for my life, expecting to likely die for that goddamn box. The next second, I'm fearing for Zach's life. *How could he do that?* This isn't his fight. It's not his sacrifice to make. This is *precisely* why I only work alone. But I've let my personal feelings get in the way, and Zach is paying the price.

Zach is steps away from the forest when he yells out to get the group's attention. They all turn and start running after him. The man named Wayne holds up his rifle, pointing directly at Zach. I'm about to jump up, but Tyra knocks his gun down as it discharges.

"Alive!" Tyra yells. "No shooting!"

Tyra and Wayne run after Zach into the forest. The other two men hang back, but they're looking intently in the direction everybody ran. As sick as it makes me feel, Zach has given me a slim opportunity.

I slide along the side of the car and peek over the edge. Both men are still turned away. With a soft hand, I open the back door and pull the backpacks out. The metal latches on the outsides of the pack hit against each other, making a clinking sound. Stopping in my tracks, I wait for the men to turn. I consider the rifle attached to the back of my pack. Using it is my last resort, a line I've never had to cross. And a one-way trip I don't want to take.

But the men don't turn. They're too distracted to notice. Carefully, I sling a backpack over each shoulder and make my way into the woods behind the gas station.

Moving quietly but swiftly through the forest, I calculate my next move. It's dangerous, but if I head in the same direction as Zach, I could be some kind of help. I pause for a moment and listen. The faint sound of yelling comes from the south, so I head in that direction.

My mind is a jumble of emotions. I curse myself for getting into this situation. We knew the woman back in town was a trap. I should have been more careful. I'm so angry with Zach for doing this. It wasn't his sacrifice to make. But I'm also surprised by how much my heart is aching.

I head toward the shouting, but it's becoming less frequent. And soon, it stops altogether. I continue south, the last direction the voices came from. But I tack slightly east, which will eventually lead me back to the road.

Then voices break the silence, far closer than I expected. They're no more than a hundred feet away, so I get low and listen.

"Well, you said don't shoot him," Wayne shouts. "So it's your own goddamn fault!"

"If you would stop running through the forest like a fucking rhinoceros, he might not have gotten away."

Zach got away.

Tyra continues, "Goddamnit! Connor will have our heads when he hears we fucked this up."

And there it is. Somehow, until they spoke his name out loud, a part of me thought I was mistaken. Maybe it *wasn't* Connor I saw outside the bank. Maybe he truly was dead.

Now, it's become real. The guilt I've carried about his death sheds off me like the dead skin of a snake. Not entirely. There's still a scar there. But my guilt is replaced by anger. And by something else. A sense of dread spreads through me. The conspiracy theories Connor told me were unsettling. If he's fully bought into them, he's not an enemy to be taken lightly.

"Why are we taking orders from that stuck-up piece of shit anyway?" Wayne asks.

"Because that stuck-up piece of shit gave you the gun you're holding and the bourbon you threw up last night. And he's got a lot more when we deliver these bastards. *Alive.*"

"Okay, fine. I guess I can put up with his bullshit for a bit longer."

The voices in the woods continue, but I'm no longer listening. My head is swimming with thoughts. I imagine Zach alone in the woods and me with all his supplies. He won't last long by himself without help. But how can I possibly find him?

Wayne and Tyra are now on the move. Based on the direction of their voices, they're headed back north. It won't take them long to return to their truck and start canvasing the road.

I lie unmoving for several minutes, waiting for them to be out of earshot. After I no longer hear them, I get up from the forest floor. The going is slow, especially with two backpacks. The thought of dropping one enters my mind for a second, but I shove it away. I'm not ready to give up on Zach. Not by a long shot.

But one thing has become painfully clear. It's too dangerous for Zach to travel with me. If I find him again and return his supplies, I'll have to take the next opportunity to send him off on his own. That'll give him the best possible chance to make it. Even though it's the right thing to do, the thought fills me with an unexpected sadness.

After hiking for a while, I come up parallel to the highway. I keep it within sight but stay far back enough so no one can spot me from the road. My hunch is that Zach is continuing on our current heading. I hope he has the sense to keep off the road, too, but I'm keeping my eyes open just in case. And maybe I'll get lucky and run into him. But the hours pass by with no sign of him. There's also no sign of our pursuers on the road, which is surprising, but I'm glad about it.

I stop once to rest and eat. I'm wracked by guilt, thinking about Zach going without. But there's nothing to do except press on and hope for the best. A few times, I risk a shout-out, calling Zach's name. But there's no response.

I plod on until it's too dark to continue. A clearing in the forest is large enough to set up a tent. I won't risk a fire with the FLA breathing down my neck.

Throughout the night, I toss and turn in my sleeping bag. Images of

Zach enter my mind. His gentle smile. His thoughtful eyes. And then the image of him being captured hits me, and it tears me up inside.

I must have fallen asleep at some point because I wake up when the morning sun hits my tent. I have a stale granola bar for breakfast, then head out. The going is slow again. My shoulders rub raw against the weight of the two backpack straps. I'm not sure I can make it much longer.

It's then that I glimpse something ahead in the forest. Some kind of man-made structure. It's tall and wooden, like an old water tower. As I get closer, the structure looks bigger and more complex. A crisscross of wooden beams forms an extensive structure. Maybe an old railroad bridge?

But it's bending and curving more than any bridge should be. Then I figure it out, laughing at myself. It's a wooden roller coaster. I think back to our conversation from the other night. Zach told me about the amusement park around here, where he had his first kiss on the dark ride. This must be Cedar Grove.

And then it hits me. This is where Zach would go. He'd try to meet me at the one common place we talked about together. It's still a long shot, but it fills me with hope. Suddenly energized, I pick up my pace.

Before I get to the coaster, I run into a chain-link fence. It must be the perimeter of the park. Barbed wire lines the top, pointing outward to stop precisely what I'm trying to do. Get in. So, climbing it is out of the question. I walk along it, looking for an opening.

After a short while, I approach a service entrance. A closed gate in the fence, but not locked. I go through it, keeping my eyes and ears open for danger and any signs that Zach came through here.

Walking along the cobblestone promenade, all the familiar sights of a theme park surround me, but everything is abandoned, run-down, and covered with overgrown vegetation. Ride entrances, cotton candy stalls, and large sculptures in elaborate gardens stretch out in every direction. An old, broken-down carousel has horses and carriages with peeling paint and weeds growing up through it.

I pass by a ride with a sculpture of a velociraptor, its claws menacing and its mouth gaping open. A sign beside it says *Raptor* in red lettering with deep claw scratches. Behind it sits a large metal coaster painted dark purple. Vines crawl up the steel structure, eating the coaster whole.

A kiosk in the middle of a walkway has the title *Park Map*. It's faded from the sun and barely legible, but I can still make out some details. A little arrow points to my current location. I scan the ride names and find one called Earthquake, the ride Zach mentioned. It's not far.

A knot forms on my insides as I approach. Zach is either here, or this is a dead end. No gray area. It's a medium-size building, with a track heading out one door and going in another. Old rusty ride vehicles that look like sporty convertibles queue up on the track. The outside of the building depicts an earthquake scene from San Francisco, with bridges collapsing and people running in terror. A large *Earthquake* marquee covers the front.

There's no sign of Zach.

I call out loud enough to be heard in the immediate area but not so loud as to attract outside attention. "Zach. You around, Zach?"

Nothing.

I reach for a flashlight from a backpack. Maybe he's taking shelter inside.

The all too familiar click of a gun being cocked comes from behind me.

"Now you just hold on there. Keep your hands where I can see them."

It's the voice of elderly woman. She talks slowly and has the slightest drawl. I put my hands up as she instructs.

"Now turn around. Slowly."

I turn to see a woman in blue jeans and an oil-stained shirt with the name *Jo* embroidered on it. Her long brown hair is speckled with gray and drawn back into a ponytail. She's got a cocked rifle pointed right at me.

"I'm looking for a friend I lost. I don't mean any harm."

The woman eyes me suspiciously and keeps her gun aimed at my chest.

Behind me, rusty hinges groan in protest as the entrance to the dark ride opens. A familiar voice calls out. "Jo, it's okay. He's a friend."

Jo lowers her gun immediately, and I turn toward the voice. I drop both packs, run over, and give Zach an enormous bear hug, holding back tears of joy.

Chapter Twenty

Like a Dream

ZACH

I was so worried I'd never see Aiden again. But I hoped he would remember Cedar Grove. Remember my story about it. The one conceivable place that would make sense to meet around here. And he remembered. He found me. And now he's in my arms.

He didn't hesitate. He just ran to me, and now the warmth of his body radiates as his arms hold me close, pressing me against him. His hands are trembling as he whispers into my ear, "I'm so glad I found you."

I laugh from pure joy and whisper back, "Me too. I thought I might not see you again."

He takes a deep breath and draws me in closer. This is the first time Aiden's shown me this much deliberate affection. I don't want this feeling to end.

Jo clears her throat loudly.

"Oh, sorry, Jo." I pull out of the hug, my face burning. "Jo, this is Aiden. He's the friend I told you about."

"Pleasure to meet you." Jo raises a hand in a wave.

"Likewise." Aiden returns the wave.

"When I got here yesterday, I bumped into her. She was part of the maintenance team, and she's been living here since the Great Collapse." I smile at Jo. "We—ah—kinda hit it off. Shared love of the place."

Jo beams. "Can't think of a place I'd rather be at the end of the world." She raises her head and looks around, smiling.

Aiden studies Jo as if sizing her up. "How'd you keep people out? Seems like the militias have an iron grip on the area."

"Ah-ha!" Jo yells. She takes a little remote control out of her pocket and presses a button. Faint sparking noises come from various directions. "Not bad, huh?"

Aiden looks confused, so I explain.

"The whole park is surrounded by a barbed-wire fence, and Jo electrified it. She also rigged up cameras. Luckily, she saw me, so she met me at the gate before I touched it."

"Yeah, little Zach looked harmless," Jo says, smiling. "After he told me how he loved the place, I had to let him in. He told me you might be coming, so we kept the fence off today."

"It's a brilliant setup, Jo," Aiden says. "How do you power everything?"

"See there?" Jo points at the roof of a nearby building. Banks of solar panels cover every square inch. "We were converting the park to solar to save on electricity. But I added a bunch more I stole off rich people's houses." Jo laughs a big laugh, apparently thrilled with herself. She's like a little kid in an old woman's body. "They charge our backup batteries, plus I only power the parts of the park I use."

I turn to Aiden. "Jo's a fellow tinkerer. I told her all about my setup in Elk Springs."

"Oh, yes, brilliant." Jo nods to herself. "I particularly liked the Wilsons. It's the little touches that matter."

"Exactly. That's how I feel."

Aiden has an amused look at our banter. It occurs to me this is the first time he's ever seen me talk to anybody other than him.

"You two must be hungry," Jo says.

"Heck, yeah." My stomach literally grumbles at the mention of food.

Jo leads us to one of the park restaurants. We weave through various brick pathways and overgrown shrubs. On the way, Aiden and I talk among ourselves.

"She's quite a character." Aiden laughs, then quietly says, "Are you sure we can trust her?"

"I think so. She's wicked smart, holed up here on her own, living her dream in this park."

Aiden nods and looks around. "This setup she has. With the fence. You think that's enough to make it safe here?"

"I'm not sure. She's made it work so far. The park is very remote. It's forest for miles in nearly every direction. But I also get the sense that people simply leave her alone."

"Hmm. Yeah, maybe." Aiden nods but doesn't look entirely convinced.

"Oh, but I haven't told you the best part yet. She's got a car battery jump starter she's going to let us have. It still works, and she can charge it up using solar power. Plus, she knows a place where there's a car."

Aiden's eyes narrow. "That all sounds great, but she's just gonna let us have it?"

"Well, not exactly. She wants me to get the Earthquake ride working again. That's what I was working on when you got here."

Aiden lets out a chuckle. "This lady's getting more and more interesting. Speaking of 'when you got here,' I haven't heard *how* you got here. How'd you escape?"

"Oh, yeah. Well, when I first ran into the forest, I was scared shitless. Especially after that first gunshot. But after they stopped shooting, I had a moment to think. They weren't exactly the sharpest tools in the shed. So I stopped, picked up a big rock, and threw it far in the opposite direction from where I was running. That was all it took to get them off course."

Aiden has a big smile. "You're amazing."

I smile and feel a flush across my face. "Anyway, after I couldn't hear them anymore, I went straight to the road. I knew it was risky, but I figured if a car came, I could duck into the woods. Cedar Grove was the only place I thought we might find each other, so I wanted to make sure I beat you. I ran the entire way."

"That's like twenty miles. How did you do that?"

"I guess I never told you; I was really into running in my previous life. I finished second in my age group in the Seattle Marathon."

Aiden puts his arm around me and smiles. "You never fail to surprise me, Zach."

And my cheeks burn again. I'm not used to Aiden being this friendly and extra flirty with me. And I'm enjoying it. Like, a lot. Maybe the atmosphere of Cedar Grove is getting to him. Maybe it's the near miss of losing each other.

"So I got here yesterday afternoon. Jo saw me through her cameras and stopped me before I got to the fence. I told her how much I loved Cedar Grove, and the Earthquake ride in particular, and she immediately took to me. We started fixing up the ride yesterday. You know the rest."

We arrive at a themed restaurant called Pirate's Den. It's all done up like an old Caribbean tavern, a place you might expect to see a roving band of pirates drinking rum and starting bar brawls. Long aisles of wooden tables run the length of the room. Nets, seashells, anchors, and other nautical items cover the walls, while treasure chests filled with gems and gold doubloons pile up in nearly every corner.

Jo takes us behind the front counter and into the kitchen. Here, the pirate theme ends. The bright, clean industrial kitchen has stainless steel counters, stoves, fryers, and a walk-in refrigerator. Most notably, the power is on. Fluorescent light fills the room.

Jo ducks into the walk-in freezer and is gone for a moment. Then she comes out with a few boxes of frozen goods under her arm. She fires up one of the deep firers and makes us a meal fit for a carnival. We have fish and chips, corn dogs, fried cheese sticks, and funnel cake. I can't remember the last time I ate anything like this.

"Where did all this food come from, Jo?" Aiden asks.

"It was all here. If these fridges stay closed, they keep stuff frozen for a while. And it only took me a few days to reroute the power from the backup batteries to power the fridges." She smiles proudly. "I've been eating nothing but carnival food for a year."

We all laugh.

It is delicious and fiercely nostalgic. But my stomach aches a bit after my second corn dog. My body is used to eating a lot more simply.

Before bedtime, we both get a nice hot shower, thanks to electricity and well water. Jo's got a good deal going for herself here. But it also makes me a bit worried. I'm afraid it'll only be a matter of time before somebody figures out what she's got and tries to take it from her, kind of like what happened to me back at Elk Springs. Being smart can only get you so far. You need luck, too, and that can run out at any moment.

Aiden and I sleep in dormitory bunks designed for kids who live and work here the whole summer. We sleep in shifts, so somebody is alert the whole time. I take the first shift, and Aiden takes the second.

While he's sleeping, I can't help but stare at him. When he's awake, Aiden looks like he's carrying the weight of the world on his shoulders. He always looks so serious and stressed. But now, he looks so peaceful. I'd love to know him when he's done with whatever this damn mission is he's on. I'd like to know the happy-go-lucky Aiden. The Aiden I caught a brief glimpse of today, walking around the park.

The next morning, we wake up to a real honest-to-goodness cup of coffee. Jo has brewed some in the kitchen. It's been at least a year since I had one.

"Jo's made a cup of joe." She keeps repeating the joke, and we laugh every time. It's actually pretty funny.

She also made us microwave breakfast sandwiches. The kind that looks like little croissants with eggs, cheese, and a sausage patty. I really don't know how people used to live off this stuff. This entire experience feels very surreal. Like this is a little bubble in the world that the Great Collapse didn't reach.

After breakfast, I get to work on the Earthquake ride again. Aiden comes in and helps too. Jo has most of the electrical work done on the ride. She really gets electricity, especially considering all she did with the solar power and electric fence. I help with some of the mechanical issues.

Many ride vehicles need minor repairs to their wheels or drive mechanisms. Several of them are flat-out broken, and we clear those away. Aiden also runs through the entire course of the ride, ensuring all the scenery is in working order and secured, especially the ones that move near the cars.

It takes the better part of the day, but we have the ride in working order by midafternoon. Jo, Aiden, and I stand outside it. Jo has the biggest grin on her face.

She puts her hand over the green start button on the control panel. "Just wanted to say thanks. I couldn't have done it without you guys." With that, she presses the button, and the entire ride comes to life. The cars move along the track, banging through the swinging doors.

"You first, Jo." I hold out a hand to the closest car, moving along the track.

Her eyes light up, and she runs over and hops in the car.

"You guys coming?" Jo says, looking up at us.

"We'll catch the next one," I say.

I jump in the next car and pat the seat, shooting a sly smile at Aiden.

He returns the smile, his cheeks now rosy, and gets in beside me.

*

AIDEN

The car we're riding in is modeled after an old red convertible, complete with a fake steering wheel. Zach and I scrunch up together. I put my arm around him, and he nuzzles into me. The feel of his body pressing against mine sends tingles through me.

Conflicting emotions fight inside me. Any time Zach enters my mind, all I want to do is hold him close and protect him from harm. I nearly lost him, and the thought of that is tearing me up inside. But with him in my arms, so adorable and content, I can only think of wanting to kiss him. It overwhelms me.

It's a little strange that this ride has emotional significance to Zach. Like maybe I'm trouncing on sacred memories. But life is too damn short to get hung up on things like that, so I let it slip from my mind.

The car careens through the swinging doors, and we're in the first scene—a normal-looking living room. A fake window looks out to the Golden Gate Bridge. An animatronic brother and sister sit around the TV. Suddenly, the whole room shakes. China in a display cabinet rattles, and pictures fall off the wall.

We move on to the next scene and are on a freeway. Another car is beside us. A large crack forms in the roadway, and the car falls into it.

Then our car turns into a tunnel. Large iron support beams hold it up. As we go under a beam, it cracks in the middle and starts falling toward us. The headlights of a bus head directly for us. It's about to hit head-on when our car swerves away at the last second.

The force pushes Zach further into me, and my entire body tingles. This must be the exact moment in the ride when he kissed Felix. The whole thing is a little surreal. I take my eyes off the ride to look over at Zach. He's gazing at me with these soft and longing eyes. I can't resist anymore. It's too overwhelming. My brain tells me this is a bad idea, but every other part of me disagrees. So I give in to the moment.

I lean over and kiss him.

His lips are soft and wonderful. The touch makes my heart flutter. We come apart for a moment.

"Is this okay?" I ask gently.

"*Yes*," Zach says with certainty and a little laugh.

Our lips join again but with more urgency this time. Our mouths open slightly, and I delicately explore with my tongue. But I take my time to savor the feeling. I lightly brush my tongue against his, and a pulse of electricity runs through me.

The world melts away, and only Zach and I are here. The heat of his breath, his soft lips, and the scent that is uniquely his fill my senses. This wave of emotion overtakes me, and I'm filled with euphoria. I never want this to end.

Then our kiss intensifies. Our lips separate and join again, both of us needing to kiss deeper and further, with a want and desire that's been building for days. I grab the back of his head and pull us in closer. Zach's soft moan through my lips drives me wild.

All around us, the Golden Gate Bridge sways back and forth, and the suspension cables snap. But we ignore it all, lost in bliss.

The car turns and goes through the exit doors of the ride, and we find ourselves in the late afternoon daylight. Only then do we separate, both breathing deeply.

Jo greets us, positively beaming. "You guys look like you had a fun time."

"We did!" Zach says, recovering quickly and returning the smile. "Thanks so much for the work you did to get it running."

"Thank *you*, Zach and Aiden!"

I put my arm around Zach as we return to the Pirate's Den. I give him another little kiss. He smiles and practically starts skipping along the path.

I have to admit, I'm very conflicted. This day with Zach has been like a dream. Maybe it's the surrealism of the theme park creating this powerful nostalgia. If I squint my eyes, I can almost imagine the world is back to normal. I miss it and would love for it to last forever.

But the other part of me knows what I must do. This really is like a dream, and we'll have to wake up from it sooner rather than later. The realities of the world will come crashing down on us. Every day I spend with Zach is another day I put him in mortal danger.

I may end up regretting that kiss. But for now, for this moment, I let my worry slide away, and I am blissfully happy with Zach by my side.

Chapter Twenty-One

Waking Up

ZACH

When Aiden kissed me, I could hardly believe it. And *wow*. I've never been kissed with so much intensity and so much longing. Those powerful feelings almost scared me. I've wanted that since I first saw him stumble into Elk Springs, and here it is. But now what? What does this mean for us? Are we boyfriends? How do relationships work in a dangerous world when we're on the run together?

Aiden's affection continues throughout the evening with the occasional gentle touch, a small kiss on the cheek, and even the looks he gives me. But as the evening gets later, we don't talk about the kiss and what it means. I want to, but I'm afraid to press the matter. Marcus still weighs on Aiden's mind, and when I've pressed him before, it just pushed him away.

But since he kissed me, maybe things are different now. Maybe he's ready to open up. Or perhaps the kiss meant nothing to him, and now he regrets it. It's not hard to imagine with all the uncertainty in our lives. I'm so confused.

Later that evening, in the dormitory, Jo comes in with the battery jump starter. True to her word, she gives it to us in exchange for our help. I have a slight pang of guilt that maybe it's not a fair trade, but it's what Jo truly wants. We spend the evening organizing our backpacks. Jo also re-stocks some of our supplies. I try to turn her down, but she insists.

The following day, we head out at first light. Jo travels with us for the first part of the journey. She says it would be too hard to explain where the car is. We all head out of the park and down a wooded gravel trail for about a mile. We then meet up with a two-lane road and turn left on that. After a while, we reach a small bridge spanning a dried-out stream.

Jo takes a turn off the road and goes down the embankment. Underneath the bridge, sitting in the middle of the dry stream bed is an old Toyota Corolla. From the body style, I'd guess it's from the mid-2000s.

Jo takes a set of keys out of her pocket and throws them at Aiden. "Hey, whenever you get done doing whatever it is you guys need to do, come visit me again some time, will you?"

"We will." I run over and give Jo a big hug. She's a little shocked initially but warms up to the hug and grins from ear to ear. Aiden joins in.

"I can't even begin to thank you enough, Jo. You're a good person," Aiden says.

Jo blushes a bit. "Okay, gotta run before this gets too gushy."

"Can we give you a ride back to the park?" I ask.

"Nah, I'll enjoy the walk. Plus, it wouldn't be safe for you guys. Make sure you stay off the freeways and main highways."

"We will," Aiden says with a nod.

And with that, Jo heads back up the embankment and disappears out of sight.

*

AIDEN

As expected, the car battery is dead. But we hook up the jump starter to the battery terminals, and immediately, the dashboard in the car comes to life with LED lights and little electronic dings. I press the starter, and the motor turns over. But it doesn't start.

"Give it a moment to juice up," Zach says.

I wait for about a minute and try again. I press the ignition button, and this time, the little engine comes to life, purring like a kitten.

We both cheer and exchange a hug, grinning.

The car has around three-quarters of a tank of gas left. These Corollas sip gas, too, so it's entirely possible this could get us all the way to Seattle.

But the best feature of the car by far? The tape player in the dash. I've held on to my mixtape this whole time. I pop it in, and the base starts pumping.

Harder, Better, Faster, Stronger…

Zach looks at me with a broad grin. "Nice. I love Daft Punk."

Of course, he does. Zach is awesome.

"This is my own mix. I made it," I say.

"Really." Zach's eyes are wide.

"Yeah, I used to be a DJ."

"DJs are so sexy."

"Stop it. Now you're just teasing." I wave off Zach's comment.

"No really. I always loved seeing them up in their booth, so completely into what they were doing. All mysterious and aloof. And super sexy."

"Yeah, yeah. Let's get going."

I carefully drive the car along the creek bed until we reach a dirt road. That quickly meets up with the paved road, and we're on our way.

Consulting the map, we take a lot of roundabout ways to avoid the main highways, heeding Jo's advice. Despite that, we're making great time.

We don't speak a lot as we cruise along. And the farther we get from Cedar Grove, the more the real world weighs on me. We still haven't talked about that kiss, and I'm regretting it more and more as the pressing need to set off on my own dominates my mind. It seems Zach can sense that something is up. He keeps sending pensive glances my way.

Abandoned cars are showing up along the side of the road again. Now that we have the battery jumper, little is stopping me from finding my own car and turning Zach lose. But how am I going to break it to him? The second he sees me messing with another car, he'll be on to me. Then we'll be in a huge discussion about it. He's got to understand why I have to do this, and if he can't, then so be it. My mission is that important. But I ache from the worry. I'll wait a bit longer.

Soon, the outskirts of Spokane spread out to the south. We steer well clear of the city, but we still pass by a few buildings. Once we get past Spokane, the going is even faster. Soon the trees disappear, and the land flattens out. Eastern Washington has miles of farmland. The highways go in straight lines for fifty miles at a time because there's no reason they need to turn.

The silence is thick, and Zach looks gloomier by the minute.

"Hey, let's play a driving game," I say.

"Okay, like what?"

"It's called 'how far away is that?'"

"Wow, sounds riveting," Zach deadpans.

"It's fun, honestly. And you can only play on super flat roads like this, so it's a special game. We spot a point on the horizon, and we both guess how far away it is."

"Pretty much what I expected. Riveting."

"Hey. It's more fun than it sounds. Okay, I'll pick a spot, and we both guess. See that windmill up there? How far?"

Zach sizes up the target. "Uhhh…one and a half miles."

"No way. That's more like two and a half."

"Well, let's see. Speed this car up." Zach slaps the dash.

I reset the trip odometer, and we both watch tenths of miles tick away. By the time it reads 1.0, we still have a way to go.

1.3 miles.

1.5 miles and still not there.

1.6 miles.

Zach cries out. "Lame. Is this Price Is Right rules? Like, no under-bidding?"

"No, just straight-up the nearest guess wins."

"Okay, I'm still in it." Zach rubs his hands together.

The odometer is at 2.0, and the windmill is rapidly approaching.

"Come on, windmill. Get here." He shakes his fists.

Just before we pass it, the odometer ticks to 2.1 miles, and Zach lets out a big groan. "Fine, you win. I want a rematch."

I laugh. "See? It's fun."

"Shush. Rematch."

We keep playing that for a while. It kills time and takes the tension out of the air. It works so well that we're driving up to the Columbia River before I know it.

The road we're on comes right up to the massive gorge. We're on the edge of a high desert plateau that drops a thousand feet to the vast Columbia River. The land is barren, without a tree to be seen for miles. Only sagebrush and rocks dot the desolate landscape. The massive river runs through the middle of the gorge and is nearly a mile across. I pull the car over at a good vantage point, and we both get out. I walk over to the edge with binoculars from my backpack.

The river heads north and south for miles. Off to the south, a bridge spans it where Interstate 90 crosses. I've been worried about this part of our journey for a while. There are only a few ways to cross the Columbia River, and this is the primary route. If militia were guarding anywhere, this would be the spot to do it, at a choke point.

I focus the binoculars on the bridge, scanning the entire span. It looks clear. I don't see any sign of people or cars. And then I spot it—the slightest bit of motion on the west bank near the bridge. A man dressed head to toe in combat gear, carrying an assault rifle, emerges from behind a large boulder. I scan the area and see camouflage netting. Behind it, there are several military vehicles.

I hang my head low. "Shit."

"What's wrong?"

"The bridge is guarded. See for yourself. Look on the west bank."

I hand the binoculars to Zach and point to where the men are.

"Yeah, that looks bad." Zach nods. "Are they FLA?"

"I'm not sure. But it doesn't matter. We want to avoid anybody with guns."

"What are our other options?"

"The next closest bridge is nearly an hour's drive south, and that would take us over a hundred miles out of our way. But I don't see any other way."

"Well, let's get to it." Zach has a determined look on his face.

We hop into the car and start driving. I have to backtrack a few miles to a road that heads south and doesn't expose us. We continue south, avoiding highways and taking back roads. A few times, I have to drive on poorly maintained dirt roads, stressing the off-road capabilities of the Corolla. But the topography is not cooperating, and soon, we hit a massive ridge a few hundred feet high that blocks our progress. Our only option is to take a road that funnels us back to the main highway, running alongside the river.

Once we get there, my worst fears are confirmed. The ridge and the river form a natural pinch-point, and it's swarming with guards.

Zach looks on in disgust. "What the heck do we do now?"

I consult the map. "We've got two options. Backtrack along this ridge for fifty miles or so, then go downriver until we find a bridge that isn't guarded. We may have to go as far as Portland, where there are lots of crossings. Or follow the river north until we get to less populated areas. We may have to go all the way to Canada. Either way, we're going hundreds of miles out of our way, and we'll have to find some more gas."

"What about a boat?"

"We can keep our eyes out for one, I guess. But that would mean ditching the car. And this damn river is over a mile wide, so we'd be exposed the whole time we cross it."

Zach nods slowly, eyes downcast.

"It's getting kinda late," I say. "Let's find a place to set up camp, and we'll think about what we want to do tomorrow."

Secretly, I worry that *every* bridge will be guarded, and taking the vials across is too risky. But there's another option I'm not telling Zach. It's the moment I've been dreading for days, but the time has come. About ten miles south of the I-90 bridge, the Wanapum Dam spans the river. Though there's no way to *drive* across it, a person could walk across. But it's dangerous. I'm sure it's guarded, so getting across will require stealth and probably life-or-death choices.

This is a risk I'm willing to take for myself.

But I can't take Zach.

Chapter Twenty-Two

Tough Choices

ZACH

We head back north, looking for a good campsite. The area around the Columbia River Gorge is arid. No trees or vegetation anywhere—just a vast canyon desertscape with a massive river running down the middle. But we finally find a little overlook with a view of a dam that crosses the river. A rocky knoll provides cover from the road where we can park the car and set up camp.

Aiden's been acting strange since we left Cedar Grove. He seems distant. Distracted. I've noticed he chews his lip when something is bothering him. And I guess it turns out that worry was the Columbia River.

Crossing a river is something you'd take for granted before the Great Collapse. A pretty view for a couple of minutes on an otherwise boring drive. But now the river is a barrier. I imagine how an explorer might have felt hundreds of years ago, seeing a massive river lying in their path.

I keep looking at the dam. "What do you think about trying to cross there?"

"It doesn't have a road," Aiden says quickly. "We couldn't drive across."

"We could walk across. Bring the battery charger. Hope for the best."

Aiden shakes his head. "With as much work as it was getting this car, I'd rather not ditch it if we don't have to."

He seems set on not considering the dam, so I let it drop.

We go without fire and eat a cold dinner. Jo had packed us some sandwiches, complete with homemade bread. It's the first time I've eaten bread in ages, and I didn't know a sandwich could taste this good. Aiden sits in his chair, lost in thought. He's been saying almost nothing and barely looking at me.

Our time at Cedar Grove almost feels like a dream now. The kiss with Aiden was magical. But we haven't talked about it at all since then. And the longer we wait, the stranger it feels. I'm starting to think maybe it *was* a dream.

After dinner, I find a pleasant spot to admire the vista. I sit on the ground with my back up against a sloping rock. I have a stunning 180-degree view of the entire river gorge. After a while, Aiden comes over and stands next to me.

"Hey, is this seat taken?" He points to the patch of dirt to my left.

"Well, I was kinda saving it for somebody. But you seem like a nice guy. Go ahead."

Aiden sits and puts his arm around me, filling me with warmth. Maybe the magic from Cedar Grove hasn't entirely left.

"I wish we could have met at a different time." Aiden stares ahead. "Under different circumstances."

"We've got to make the most of what we have in the time we have it."

"You're pretty wise, Zach. You know that? Like a Baby Yoda."

"Grogu!" I smile and smack Aiden's shoulder. "But thanks."

We sit together and watch the scene unfold before us. The sunset is spectacular. Clouds on the horizon turn vivid colors of red, orange, and yellow. The golden light shimmers off the flowing river.

When the sun finally drops below the horizon, we head off to bed. The temperature dips pretty low, so we both have full sleeping bags and tents. No sleeping under the stars tonight. Aiden heads to his own tent. I half expect an invitation to join him. Or, at the very least, a goodnight kiss. But I get neither, and my heart breaks a little.

I lie awake for a while, wracked with worry. Wondering if Aiden regrets our kiss. Wondering what tomorrow will bring. Wondering what will happen when we get to Seattle. We have yet to talk about that as well. I'll want to go to Vashon Island to find my family, and Aiden has his own business to complete. I hope we can do both of them together.

After lying awake for a long time with my racing thoughts, my mind finally quiets, and I fall into a restless sleep.

*

AIDEN

I wrote a note when Zach was watching the sunset, then slipped it into his jacket along with the car keys.

Zach,

Let me start by saying how much you've meant to me. I've kept you at arm's length, not because I don't care but because I care too much. My mission is more important than my own life. That's a choice I made. But it's not a choice I can make for you. If I told you, I knew you'd follow me. And I can't have you dying for my cause.

I don't regret our kiss. You're the best thing that's happened to me in a long time. I hope you understand and can find it in your heart to forgive me. And I hope we meet again under better circumstances. I've left you the car keys. You should go to Portland. That will be the safest route. Without me, it will be way less dangerous. I know you can make it. I wish you the best.

Aiden

PS: If we both make it through this, I'll wait for you every Sunday in Volunteer Park in Seattle at the Black Sun statue at noon.

At about three in the morning, when I'm sure Zach is fast asleep, I break down my tent and pack up. With a deep sigh, I take one last look, then turn toward the dam. I picked our campsite to be within walking distance. The dam is less than a mile away.

I don't want to leave him, but I have to. Thinking about it tears me up inside. This is the right thing to do. I'm sure of it. Zach's life has already been at risk multiple times. When he tried to sacrifice himself at the gas station, my heart felt like it would rip in two. I simply can't take the thought of him being hurt, especially on my account.

Running is easy at first. We camped up on a slope, so it's all downhill. I half walk and half jog through the arid land and sagebrush. Soon, I get to the highway, which I cross, then turn south. The dark outline of the dam is before me.

The whole time I run, thoughts of Zach fill my mind. His tender smile. His soft lips. His kindness and patience in everything he's done for me. Imagining him waking up and reading my note makes me profoundly sad, thinking about the pain it will cause him, all because of me.

I'm about halfway to the dam when the aching in my chest starts. This pain is familiar. It's an emotional pain, but it hits me so hard that I can actually feel it radiating from my center. The force of it nearly knocks me over. Each step I take is heavier than the next. I'm finding it hard to keep moving forward. I'm doing the right thing, but I can't figure out why it feels so wrong. This makes no sense. *What's wrong with me? Why can't I do this? I'm stronger than this.*

That's when it hits me. The realization lands on me like a ton of bricks. I'm not doing this to protect *Zach*. I'm doing this to protect *myself*. This whole time, I insulated myself from my true feelings. But the wall I built around my emotions is crumbling, and it's hitting me hard and raw. I care deeply about Zach, and the idea of leaving him is tearing me apart.

I convinced myself that leaving him was inevitable. I've been doing this the whole time: when I left him in Elk Springs, when I kept looking for cars to head off on my own, and now. I keep making the same mistake.

Walking forward becomes impossible. My body won't allow it. I can't leave him. Whatever our fates, we need to face them together. I turn around and start heading back to camp. The weight that held my feet down lifts, and my walk becomes a run. I need to get back before he wakes. Before he finds my note.

Headlights shine down the road. Two sets of them heading toward me. I hit the ground, hiding behind some sagebrush, hoping they won't see me in the darkness. Hoping they'll pass by without noticing the figure lying by the side of the road. But before they reach me, the cars turn off the road.

They're headed down the road to our campsite. They're headed right to where Zach lies asleep, unaware of the danger headed his way. The danger *I* put him in. *Again.*

I jump up, sprint toward the camp, and grab my rifle out of my backpack. I turn off the safety. No matter what the cost, I am ready to defend Zach. I won't let anyone hurt him.

Not while I'm still alive.

Chapter Twenty-Three

Fracture

ZACH

I'm woken up by a noise outside. It's the sound of tires on gravel. A vehicle is approaching. In a panic, I grab the rifle next to my sleeping bag and jump out of my tent.

"Aiden!" I call but get no response. Where his tent once stood, there's only a smattering of footsteps in the dirt. No backpack. No Aiden.

My heart drops into my stomach.

But our car is still here. I reach into my jacket pocket and find the car keys. He must have slipped them in when I wasn't looking. And there's a note. But I have no time to read it. A truck pulls up beside our car. The headlights blind me. The sound of doors opening and guns cocking fills the campsite. A voice shouts out from behind the lights.

"Drop the gun, or we drop you!"

*

AIDEN

It takes an agonizingly long time to get back to camp. Each second that ticks by feels like an eternity. I run around the knoll where we set up our tents to find the campsite in shambles. Zach's tent and sleeping bag are ripped up and his belongings scattered. He's gone.

Zach is gone.

I crumple to my knees and start weeping. I failed him. Out of my own misguided need to protect myself, I sacrificed Zach.

The sound of tires on gravel nearby snaps me out of my misery. I jump up and run around the knoll. A few hundred feet away, two trucks and our little Corolla head down the road. I *just* missed them. Thirty seconds earlier, and I might have stopped them. But there's still a chance.

I race after the vehicles, staying low and trying to keep out of sight. The vehicles move slowly on the gravel road, and I'm almost able to catch up to them. But then they make it to the highway and turn to the south and start to speed away. Even if it's hopeless, I'll run for as long as I can. I'll run all night if I have to.

Then, the vehicles slow down and take the next right turn into Wanapum Dam. My spirit soars. I might catch them. My lungs burn as I sprint, but I welcome the pain. I deserve the pain. It's nothing compared to what Zach will feel soon if I don't rescue him.

As I run up the drive, the Corolla and trucks are ahead of me. They park at a building connected to the dam. Four people get out, armed with rifles. A fifth person has a bag over their head. From the body and clothing, I can tell it's Zach.

He's alive.

Up to this point, I've been going on pure instinct and adrenaline. My plan has only been to catch up. But running into this group and fighting them all isn't an option. They'll kill Zach immediately. It's me and the vials they want. Once they see me, he'll be of no more use to them.

So I stop, take cover behind a boulder, and watch. One man shoves Zach, and he almost falls over. Rage courses through me. All I can think of is protecting Zach. I have to fight back the urge to run right into them.

They enter the building attached to the dam. Once they are out of sight, I take deep breaths to calm myself down. My anger, fear, and fatigue slip away, replaced by a steely resolve.

Staying low to the ground, I head up to the door they entered. This will take all my training in stealth and arm-to-arm combat. But I'm ready. I have to do this for Zach. I reach for the doorknob, ready for my fate.

Locked. Fuck.

Chapter Twenty-Four

The Dam

ZACH

I see nothing. The bag over my head rubs against my face. It's tied so tightly that it constricts my airflow. My hands are bound behind my back with a plastic zip tie. It's digging into the skin around my wrists.

Hands from behind shove me forward. I nearly trip but get my feet under me enough to keep me from smashing my face on the floor. My captors lead me from room to room, going down flights of stairs along the way. Earlier, I heard loud flowing water. I must be at the dam.

I don't understand what happened. Aiden was gone when I woke up. Did they already capture him? But how could they have done that without me hearing? Aiden must have left on his own. Left me again.

Our footsteps echo in what sounds like a cavernous room. A shove to my chest sends me backward, falling hard into a chair. A cutting pain hits my ankles as my feet are bound, followed by a zipping sound of plastic ties mercilessly tightened. The left tie goes under my pant leg and digs into my skin.

I sit there for what feels like forever, but my sense of time is distorted with the bag over my head. Then, footsteps approach, and out of nowhere, my gut explodes as a fist hits me hard in the stomach.

"That's for the gas station, punk."

That voice. I recognize it from when I was fleeing into the forest near Cedar Grove. It's the idiot who tried to shoot me at the gas station. Wayne was his name. Despite the pain in my gut, I smirk, thinking about how easy it was to trick him. Maybe I can trick him again.

I project so he can hear me through the mask. "Hey, Wayne. You should hear what Tyra and the guys were calling you. No-Brain Wayne."

There's laughter from several people. Another voice says, "You gonna let him get away with that, No-Brain?"

"Why, you little fucker!"

Another punch to the gut. Harder this time. Enough to make me lose my breath. I gasp for air. But it was worth it.

"Besides, you're the stupid one," Wayne sneers. "Camping out in the open like that. We're the FLA. We've got spies everywhere."

"Jesus, Wayne! Don't tell him that," Tyra shouts.

Another set of footsteps approaches, and a new voice yells out. "Shut up, you idiots. I said don't talk to him."

I recognize it—the strange accent I heard way back in Elk Springs.

It's Connor.

"Take that off," Connor says.

The drawstring around my neck loosens, and they rip off the hood. A flashlight blinds me. I blink rapidly, my eyes watering. Details emerge as I adjust to the light. A man I don't recognize with a gray goatee is holding the flashlight. Next to him, and towering above, looms Connor. His platinum-blond hair and handsome, icy features are unmistakable. Wayne and Tyra from the gas station stand at his side.

I'm in an enormous room with giant circular machines running down the middle. These must be the turbines for the dam. None of them appear to be functioning. Dim candlelight illuminates the room.

"Now, what do we have here?" Connor paces back and forth, looking me over. "Are you Aiden's latest boy toy, then?"

"Better than being his latest rejection," I hiss back at him.

Connor lets out a little laugh. "Quite the little smart-ass we have here."

He walks over and whispers into my ear, "No, my dear. Aiden's latest rejection would be you." He takes a piece of folded paper from Wayne. It's the note that was in my pocket.

"I heard he wrote you a sweet love note." Connor unfolds it. "You're practically love birds. But he left you like he leaves everyone. He left me, too, you know. Left me for dead, hanging on the edge of a bridge while he ran off with the vials. Sound familiar?"

I grit my teeth but say nothing.

Connor reads the note out loud, dripping with sarcastic passion. Hearing Aiden's words is hard. Knowing for sure that he left me is worse than anything these people could do.

I try to make sense of it. Aiden left the car with me. He was trying to save me. He was wrong and misguided and should have asked me what I wanted. But he was doing it from a place of love.

But my heart shouts back, hurt and angry and sad. Even with his best intentions, how could he leave? I could never have done that.

When Connor finishes reading, he throws the note on the ground, then paces back and forth, shooting glances my way. "Well, Aiden must have liked you a lot. That's good. It means he'll probably do anything to get you back." Then he turns on his heel and stares directly at me. "But did he trust you enough to tell you what he's carrying? I imagine not."

Emotions are simmering up, but I fight to keep them hidden. Aiden *hasn't* told me what he's carrying, and it's been a particular thing that has bothered me. An ever-constant reminder that complications fill our lives to the point that we can't be honest with each other.

Connor picks up on my hesitation. "No? Well, I guess he doesn't trust you *that* much then." He lets out a single nasal laugh.

He paces back and forth again. "Aiden is carrying a weaponized version of the Infection. One that could be altered to control people. Or altered to kill everyone. Even immune people."

"You're full of shit," I spit back. He's clearly trying to get under my skin.

"I wish I was. You know that grand and noble Scientific Collective that Aiden is an errand boy for? They created the Infection. It's called XT58. It was built to control people. Did a pretty shit job though, since it mostly killed them. But they're trying to fix their mistake. And Aiden is knowingly helping them."

I shake my head. Now I'm sure Connor is lying. Aiden would never do that.

"You know, he could be responsible for the death of the rest of humanity. He's been using you this whole time." Connor shoots me an icy smile. "Why do you think he left you? You're a decoy. He used you so he could sneak past us. But it won't work."

He puts his face up to mine. "Tell me where he is, and I'll let you go. I'm on your side."

Connor makes me sick. He's responsible for all our misery. I spit into his face. He lurches back, then calmly wipes the spit away. His eyes seethe with rage.

He balls his hand into a fist and cracks the knuckles. "You're going to regret that."

*

AIDEN

Of course, they locked the door behind them. That would have been too easy. No other doors lead into the building, and fencing with razor wire blocks all access to the dam. No going through that way.

Downriver, a small boathouse sits near the base of the dam, a wooden structure built into a dock that runs along the riverbank. If I can find a boat, maybe there's a way to get into the dam from the water. I scamper down an embankment to check it out. A quick test of the door to the boathouse confirms it's locked. No surprise there. But the front of the structure is open to the water. With a little gymnastics, I climb around the edge of the building and slip in.

A small power boat bobs in the water, tied up on the dock. It has

Police printed on its side and a flasher and siren mounted on top. No keys, of course. A small rowboat sits next to the police boat. It looks perfect for heading out on the water undetected. I hop in and push it out into the river.

It's dark on the water, with dawn still at least an hour off. The dam looms large on my left as I paddle along it, looking for some way to get in. But I'm met only with fifty feet of concrete heading nearly straight up.

As I continue, the rushing sound of water gets louder. In the middle of the dam is a large ramp with water racing down it. This must be where excess water spills over from the upriver side of the dam. Concrete shoulders run along each side of the ramp, guiding the water. They appear wide enough to walk up; this might be my ticket to getting in. I navigate the boat to the edge of the dam and tie it up.

I stow my backpack under a seat in the rowboat, then grab the handgun from the front flap and tuck it into the back of my pants. The grenades I took from Ezra's bunker are also in the front flap. I take a few and clip them to my belt. You never know.

The ramp starts nearly flat, so it's easy to climb, though a torrent of water rushes next to me. The farther I go, the steeper it gets. Before long, I'm crawling on my hands and knees along the ramp's shoulder. From below, it didn't seem quite this steep. But as I get higher, it's more like I'm scaling the face of a cliff.

Near the top, the slope of the ramp is practically vertical. Clinging to the concrete edges takes all my strength. Hand over hand, leg over leg, I inch closer. The swiftly cascading water beside me punctuates just how steep the ramp is. A peek downward sends my head reeling. I must be fifty feet high. A drop from this height would not end well. My pulse, already fast from the exertion, jumps up another notch.

Finally, I reach the top edge and heave myself up and over. *Wow, that's a long way down.* Here, the ramp flows through the structure of the dam, and I continue on to see if there's a way inside. And not a moment too soon. An armed guard above me, patrolling the top of the dam, shines a flashlight in various directions. I scamper under cover of the dam mere seconds before the beam scans the area where I just stood.

Inside, a metal catwalk spans above the spillway ramp. It's slick from the splashing water below it, so I carefully climb onto it. On either side of the catwalk, steel doors lead inside. I head to the door to my right.

If this is locked, I'm screwed.

To my relief, the doorknob turns, and I slip through. Inside, a metal staircase descends into darkness.

"Hello?" A gruff male voice far below me calls out. "Who's up there?"

A flashlight turns on, its erratic glow creating dancing shadows. I catch glimpses of a man running up, each footfall making a booming echo.

Shit.

There's nowhere to hide.

I crouch at the landing, waiting to pounce. As the man rounds the corner of the stairs below me, I leap over the railing and drop fifteen feet, landing hard on him and knocking his gun away. The element of surprise is enough to give me the upper hand. In seconds, I have him in an air-constricting headlock. He grasps at my arm and flails his legs, trying to get free. But I've practiced this move far too many times, and soon, he succumbs to the lack of oxygen.

I grab his gun and hurry down the remaining flights and come to a door. The muffled sounds of voices come from beyond. Cupping my hand,

I listen. Several people are talking, but one voice booms above the rest. *Connor.*

I open the door and close it gently behind me. I'm in a massively long room, illuminated by candlelight. This must be the turbine room.

Inside, the voices are more distinct. Among Connor's voice are others I don't recognize. And then, Zach's voice lifts above the rest. A wave of relief flows through me. I found him, and he's alive.

I get low to the ground and slink closer, using the massive turbines as cover. Peering around one, I see what I'm up against. And it's not good. Zach is strapped to a chair. Connor, two men, and one woman hover around him, all armed. One I could handle. Two is pushing it. Taking on four people would be suicide.

What I need is a distraction.

Chapter Twenty-Five

A Distraction

ZACH

After I spit into Connor's face, the look in his eyes sends chills through my whole body. He glares down with those icy blue eyes. Then he strikes me hard on the cheek with his fist. My vision flashes white, and my ears ring. A hot pain shoots out from where his fist landed.

He's coming back for another hit when the sound of an explosion comes from my left. Vibrations rock the room, and bits of dust kick up from the ground. Everyone looks up, surprised. I crack a smile. It's got to be Aiden.

Another explosion, but this one is closer. Tiny bits of concrete fall off the walls and ceiling, covering everything in a cloud of fine dust.

Connor points to Wayne and then to me. "You. Watch him. The rest of you are with me." He runs off toward the explosions with the other two in tow.

Wayne stares at me with a sadistic grin on his face. "Well, well, well. Isn't this interesting?" He walks toward me. My constraints bind tightly as I try desperately to get free.

As he approaches, he clenches his fists. "What's the matter? You don't have anything to say now that it's just you and me, smart ass?"

I fight against the plastic ties. Digging deep, I use all the force buried inside me, trying to break free. But it's useless. The binds are too strong.

Wayne puts his face right up to mine, then plants his tongue on my cheek. "You taste good." His breath is stale with whiskey and chewing tobacco.

Good god. This can't be happening. With his head next to mine, I lurch forward and smack my skull hard against his. He staggers back with a look of shock covering his face.

"Oh, you're gonna pay for that, you little shit!" He comes racing at me, a pistol in his raised hand, ready to strike. I reel back, waiting for the impact. It's going to hurt like a sonofabitch. He's inches away before his gun flies out of his hand, clattering harmlessly on the ground. A hand reaches around, covering his mouth as an arm travels around his neck. Eyes wide, Wayne flails his arms and legs. His face goes purple as he fights for air, then collapses in a heap on the floor.

Aiden stands behind him. Conflicting emotions consume me. I've never been so happy and furious at the same time. He's a bastard. But the bastard came to rescue me.

"Aiden, thank god," I squeak, overcome with relief.

Aiden runs up and cups his hands against my cheeks. "Are you hurt?"

"A little banged up, but I'll live."

"I'm so glad I found you. Let's get you out of this chair." He cuts my bonds with a knife, and relief follows, but also pain. The zip tie around my left leg cut a deep gash into my skin, and I'm bleeding from it.

As soon as I'm free, I punch Aiden hard in the shoulder, and he yelps.

"That's for leaving me."

And then I hug him like I never want to let him go. "And this is for saving me," I whisper in his ear.

"I'm so sorry, Zach. I have a lot more apologizing to do. But for now, we have to go."

We end our embrace, and Aiden runs for the exit opposite the explosions. "C'mon, we gotta run."

My left leg howls with pain, but I try to ignore it and hobble along behind him. The note Aiden wrote me sits on the ground, dropped by Connor. Part of me wants to leave it behind and forget this dark moment. But I grab it anyway and stash it in my pocket. Some things are too significant to forget.

"Connor and the others went that way, right?" Aiden points to the far side of the room, and I nod.

"Good." He continues in the other direction. "Follow me."

We run to a metal door at the right side of the turbine room. As we get to it, the door on the far side opens, and Connor comes in with the others. Connor looks up, and his face twists with rage.

"Stop them!"

Aiden pauses for a moment to glance back. The expression on his face is complex, to say the least. Anger mixed with sorrow. "Let's go," he says quietly.

Tyra and the man with the gray goatee head toward us, drawing their guns. The moment they do, we run out the door and slam it behind us. The brutal impact of bullets against the door sends concussive blasts through the stairwell.

We sprint up the stairs, three steps at a time. As we open the door at the top, the downstairs door opens. Aiden grabs the last grenade off his belt, pulls the pin, and sends it clattering down the metal stairway.

"Fire in the hole," Aiden yells. It says so much about Aiden that he warns the very people trying to kill us. He trained to survive in this terrible world but still has a gentle heart.

"Go back!" voices from below yell as the door shuts.

We jump out of the top door and slam it shut as the grenade detonates, sending vibrations through everything.

"That'll buy is a little time but not much," Aiden says.

We're on a metal catwalk spanning a rushing torrent of water. It extends to our left and slopes downward in what looks like a massive water slide, angling steeply at first, then gradually at the end.

"Okay, this is our stop." Aiden gestures to the water below us.

"You're kidding, right?" My voice cracks as I gape at the harrowing descent.

"I'm afraid not. There's a boat at the bottom."

"Is it safe?"

"This is the spillway for the dam. Wildlife pass through it all the time. If it's safe for salmon, it should be safe for us."

"Let's go together." I look at Aiden with pleading eyes.

"Okay, take my hand."

Hand in hand, we jump from the catwalk into the spillway, and the current sweeps us off our feet. The water pushes us along, sending us over a curved edge and down the length of the slide. It's not as smooth as a water slide, but not as bad as I feared. My pants take most of the beating on the rough cement. The descent is fast at first, but it levels out gradually until I plunge into the cold waters of the Columbia, with Aiden still by my side, holding my hand.

When we surface, Aiden swims to a small rowboat moored next to the spillway, and I follow. He hoists himself up into the boat first, then lends me a hand and heaves me over the edge. We both tumble into the bottom of the boat, our bodies intertwined and our faces inches apart. I'm still a mix of emotions, and anger and hurt courses through me, but rising above it all is this overwhelming desire to hold him close and never let go.

Aiden has a pained expression. "Zach, I'm so sorry. As soon as I left, I knew it was a mistake. I came back to get you, but they had already—"

I put a finger over his mouth. "I'll want a full explanation later, but right now, this is what I need."

And then I kiss him.

As our lips join, it's filled with all the intensity of the moment. Rough and angry but also yearning and grateful. As we press our bodies together, I run my hands through his wet hair. I forget the world around me for a few seconds, and I am lost in the moment, lost in Aiden's grasp.

We pull away from each other almost simultaneously as our gaze turns to the dam looming above. The tenuous nature of our situation comes snapping back, and reality sets in.

"Wow," Aiden whispers.

"Yeah." I give a hushed laugh.

"I don't expect you to forgive me yet." Aiden looks at me with vulnerable eyes.

"We'll talk. But right now, let's get the hell out of here."

"Agreed." Aiden sits up and grabs the oars.

I'll set my hurt aside until we are safe. He thought he was protecting me. That much I understand, but he can't make decisions for me. He needs to understand that before we can move forward. I *hope* I can forgive him and learn to trust him again.

Aiden rows the boat downstream, away from the dam, as fast as possible but quietly. It's not a moment too soon. On top of the dam, flashlights shine around in all directions. But we've made it far enough, just a dark spot in the middle of the massive Columbia River.

Aiden stops rowing and lets the current carry us. He talks in a whisper. "Let's coast for a bit. Keep things quiet."

"Where are we going?" I ask in a hushed tone.

"I want us to get farther downriver before we head to the west shore."

"How on earth did you find me?"

"I got to the camp right when they captured you. I ran after you the whole way. When they drove to the dam, I saw exactly where they took you."

I shudder at the memories of them binding my arms and throwing the bag over my head. But Aiden returned to rescue me. I *want* to forgive him, though these conflicting feelings continue to churn in my gut.

"If you'd been there, we might have *both* been captured," I say, almost talking to myself. "Or worse."

"That's still no excuse for leaving you." Aiden looks down, avoiding my gaze.

I sigh. "But thank you for coming back." I smile slightly. His face lightens a bit at the sight of it.

"Zach, I'll always come for you. No matter what." The earnestness in his eyes gives me hope that we can get past this.

"I mean, you practically blew up a dam to get me." I chuckle. "Those were Ezra's grenades?"

Aiden nods. "I knew they'd come in handy eventually. I've never used one before. It was kinda fun."

"And this boat?"

"I found it tied to the dock next to the dam. I rowed out until I found a spot I could climb up. Didn't take long to find you. Connor's voice projects."

"You're just like James Bond."

"Does that make you a Bond girl?" Aiden says with a tentative smile.

"Bond boy, thank you very much."

We both laugh under our breath. I'm happy to joke with him again, but my laughter is bit hollow with my hurt right under the surface.

Aiden looks up and down the river. "We should be far enough away. I'm going to row us to the west shore."

He takes the oars and quietly nudges us westward. Soon, the boat scrapes the bottom, and he hops out and drags it ashore. He grabs the backpack he stowed in the boat and slings it over his shoulders. "We're down to one backpack now, so we'll have to share everything from here on out."

Together, we push the boat out into the water as far as we can, watching it for a moment to be sure the current has picked it up. If anybody finds it, we want it far from where we landed.

Aiden points up to the foothills in front of us. "We need to get into those hills before the sun rises. I'm afraid we're going to be on foot for a while."

I nod. Blood has seeped into my sock from where the zip tie cut into my left leg. I'll wait until we're out of sight from the river before I mention it, but it hurts like a bitch.

And with that, we make our way into the foothills of the Columbia River Gorge.

Chapter Twenty-Six

The Journey Continues

AIDEN

We make our way through the desertscape. Towering layered rock walls in shades of brown and gold lie before us. Scrub brush and wild grasses growing in tufts are the only foliage, so our only cover is the land itself. Luckily, the trail we are on runs into a small canyon, and after about fifteen minutes of hiking, we can no longer see the river behind us. More importantly, no one can see us.

The trail gets steeper as we make our way to the first plateau of the gorge. We're both breathing heavily, and Zach is lagging behind. I slow the pace. Neither of us slept much last night. The entire experience has been physically and mentally draining, but we need to get farther away from the dam before we rest.

I can't help but smile as Zach follows with a look of determination. He hasn't forgiven me for abandoning him. Nor should he. After I rescued him, many emotions flew around in the heat of the moment. He'll need more time to process them all. Heck, even I will. I have more I want to discuss.

Wind whistles along the limestone as we crest the top of the first plateau. We're exposed again. Luckily, dawn is still a ways off, with the sky going from black to deep purple. The dam is to the north and too far to make out any details. I don't see any lights or other obvious activity.

We'd be easy to spot on the wide-open plateau. The second canyon wall is ahead of us, about a mile away, so I pick up the pace.

Zach is struggling and favoring his left leg. "Sorry, Zach. Once we make it to those canyons, we can slow down. Are you okay?"

"My leg is a little banged up. But I can push through. Let's keep going."

In a short while, we make it to the next canyon. The sky is lighter now, and dawn can't be too far off. We find a large rock formation jutting out of the ground, which provides excellent cover. We stop to rest.

"Let's have a look at that leg," I say.

Zach lifts his pant leg up and winces. It's a ghastly sight, with his entire sock saturated in blood and a few small beads of red dripping down his shoe.

"Oh, wow. That looks worse than I thought." I grab some medical supplies from my backpack.

The gash is deep and wraps around much of his ankle. As I remove the blood-soaked sock, Zach lets out a little yelp. But he puts his hand over his mouth to muffle any further noises.

Seeing him in pain is making my heart a little achy. *Wow*. I forgot what it was like to care for somebody. To open myself up. All I want to do is wrap him in my arms and protect him from harm. It hurts to see him like this.

I use a little of our limited water supply to wash out the wound, then wrap some gauze around it, which immediately starts turning red. I wrap it with an ace bandage to encourage clotting.

Zach sucks air in through clenched teeth. "It's okay. I can take it. Make it tight."

We only rest for a few more minutes. I hand Zach a protein bar and take one for myself as well. "We'll need the energy."

The trail gets steep again as we approach the second plateau. It takes nearly an hour to get to the top. Once there, the sun has risen, and we're met with golden, rolling hills as far as the eye can see. Dried patches of sagebrush cover the landscape, and snowcapped mountains line the horizon.

The dirt trail we're on cuts through the landscape. Before the Great Collapse, this would have been a great mountain biking trail. But it doesn't appear as if anyone has been on it for months. The wind has blown away all the footprints and tire tracks long ago.

I turn to Zach to see how he's doing. He looks okay but still has a visible limp on his left side. "How's the leg feeling?"

"Better since we cleaned it up. But it still stings a bit."

"In a few miles, we can look for a place to stop and take a long rest."

"Sounds good. What trail are we on?"

I grab the map from the backpack. "It's called the Palouse to Cascades Trail. It runs across most of Washington State."

I show Zach the map, pointing to where we are. "I'm thinking we're going to have to stay on it for a while. It meets up with I-90 in about twenty miles. We can try to find a car again, but we've lost the jump starter."

Zach nods and lets out a sigh.

We've been hiking for about an hour when we come to a small stream that cuts right into the arid landscape. I'm guessing it's only seasonal and stops flowing after the spring runoff. But fortune is smiling on us.

A small grove of dried-out trees and sagebrush provide some shade and cover. We're both exhausted, so we take an extended rest and set up camp. We even risk a small fire. With it, I boil some water for a more thorough cleaning of Zach's cut.

He sits, propped up by his arms with his feet forward, while I tend to the wound. The bleeding has stopped. There's some dirt ground into the wound, and I wash it out with warm water. Zach winces in pain as I scrub. The edges of the cut are red and puffy. I try to be gentle so it doesn't hurt too much.

Once we set up camp and have a bite to eat, Zach and I sit under the shade of the tree. This is the right time to clear the air.

"Zach, I want to talk about last night. About leaving you."

Zach's shoulders slump, but he says nothing.

"It was an important moment for me. And I need you to understand it."

He nods and lets out a sigh. "Okay."

"When I left, I did it because I thought I was protecting you. But the farther I got, the worse it felt. Every step got harder than the next. I couldn't leave you. I turned back to the camp to rip up that note. Tell you how I feel. But then I saw headlights headed your way. I started sprinting back, but when I got there, you were gone."

"When I realized you had left me, I was devastated." Zach chokes out the words. "I didn't understand."

"I'm so sorry for putting you through that, Zach." My voice croaks, and my eyes get glossy. "When Marcus died, I shut down my emotions. Since then, I've let no one in. But I *do* have feelings for you. That's what I realized last night as I was walking away. I was doing it to protect *myself*, not you. So I wouldn't have to face those feelings. To not be afraid of losing someone again. Of losing *you*." A tear streaks down my cheek. "I like you, Zach. A lot. And I'm sorry I left you. I hope you can forgive me."

"I like you too." A smile cracks through Zach's sad face. "Hearing you say all that helps. But it'll take some time. And you have to promise me one thing."

"Name it."

"Trying to protect me came from a good place. But next time you make a big decision like that, you need to include me in it. You need to trust me. Okay?"

I smile and let out a sad laugh. "I promise."

Zach scoots in closer to me until our legs touch. He gently puts his hand on my knee and looks into my eyes. Our lips join, and we kiss, tender and filled with kindness and hope. But then Zach pulls away, puts his hands around his legs, and sighs.

Hopefully that kiss is the start of healing and he can find a way to forgive me.

*

ZACH

I sit there with Aiden beside me, lost in my thoughts. He professed his feelings for me, which filled me with joy. After all, this is what I've wanted since I first saw Aiden stroll into Elk Springs. But I'm still hurt. And my joy is tapered by his choice to leave. This little nagging worry is now firmly planted in the back of my mind. No matter how much we trust each other, a part of me will always be worried that he'll up and leave me.

We also continue to guard our secrets. I still know very little about his mission or the Scientific Collective. I consider saying that total honesty is a requirement for my forgiveness. But I'm not ready to talk about what actually happened with my uncle, so that would be hypocritical. Maybe this world is too complicated for total honesty.

Connor said some horrible things about Aiden. He said them to provoke me. That much, I know. But is there a sliver of the truth in there somewhere? What would it take to make someone like Connor become the way he is? He wasn't born that way. Something changed him. Everybody thinks they're justified in their actions from their own point of view. So what is his point of view?

We spend the remainder of the day resting. I need the break after all I've been through in the last twenty-four hours, and I'm sure Aiden does too.

After a simple dinner, Aiden leans against a rock with a pensive expression, watching the sun getting low in the sky. When I approach, he smiles tentatively and looks at me with hope. His soft and caring eyes melt my defenses, and I sit down and wrap my arm around him.

As the sky dims, the warmth of his body protects me from the chill of the evening. The sunset is spectacular, with unobstructed views west. Streaks of high cirrus clouds turn shades of yellow, orange, and purple as the sun tucks behind the horizon.

With one of the backpacks gone, we only have the remaining tent and sleeping bag, which Aiden set up earlier. He grabs the emergency blanket from our first aid supplies.

"Zach, you can have the tent." He starts to unfold the blanket.

"Don't be ridiculous. You'll freeze out here. We can share."

Aiden's face lights up, and he tries to suppress a smile. "Are you sure?"

"Of course, I'm sure. We like each other, right?" I smile at him, and he smiles back with hope in his eyes.

We snuggle up in the sleeping bag. It's a chilly night, so we keep our clothes on, and that's probably for the best. As I lie there with Aiden's arms wrapped around me, my hurt starts to ebb. Tonight, I feel safe with Aiden by my side.

*

We wake at first light before the sun crests over the horizon. After quickly breaking camp, we hit the road. The hiking is easy, and I'm well-rested after our long downtime yesterday. But I'm more aware of the slight pain in my leg the longer we hike. The wound has stopped bleeding entirely, but parts of the skin around the cut are red and inflamed.

A little past midday, we approach a sizable hill. The path leads into a man-made ravine that appears blasted out with dynamite. The walls of the ravine rise higher until they're fifteen feet tall. We approach the entrance of a dark tunnel framed in cement, with an inscription on the side.

Boylston Tunnel

Est. 1872

In the tunnel, darkness greats us. I shoot Aiden a side-eye. "That looks ominous."

"Just an old railroad tunnel. Should be a straight shot through."

I shade my eyes from the sun and peer in. "I can't even see to the other end."

"We'll be fine."

I'm not so sure. I stand at the edge of the tunnel in the stagnant air. But Aiden is already starting in and gesturing me forward. He pulls the flashlight out and shines it into the darkness. The narrow cone of light does little to illuminate the tunnel, revealing just a few steps in front.

Outside, the heat of the noonday sun is quite warm, but the temperature inside is at least twenty degrees lower. I wrap my arms around myself. Graffiti litters the walls. Mostly standard fare, like people's names in hearts, tags, and crude pictures of genitalia. One piece stands out.

Here lies death.

The hair rises on my neck. Aiden is already ahead of me, so I run to catch up and loop my arm around his. "This place gives me the creeps."

Aiden plants a little kiss on my forehead. "It's okay. We're in this together."

We've walked a good distance into the tunnel, with the entrance now a tiny pinprick of light. A slight breeze brushes against my skin, but it carries the smell of decay and rot.

Goosebumps cover my whole body. "Oh god, I hope that's not what I think it is."

A few more steps, and I get my answer. Aiden shines the light over a group of decaying bodies. They're around a burned-out campfire. Old, tattered sleeping bags lie about. A rush of panic hits me. I back up to the tunnel's edge, and my legs give way as I land hard on the ground.

Aiden runs over to me. "Are you okay?"

I'm not sure I am. It's the same paralyzing fear I had when I saw my uncle staggering up the driveway. The same one that didn't let me leave the house until I was nearly out of food.

But unlike before, Aiden is here. He puts his arms around me and rubs a hand on my back. "It's gonna be okay, Zach."

I'm shivering and can barely talk. "I—what—if they're Infected?"

"They've been gone a long time. They can't hurt you now. Plus, you're immune, remember?"

The first part may be true. They may not be capable of hurting me. As for being immune, I don't know. I consider telling Aiden about my uncle, that I couldn't even help him as he lay dying on the porch, begging to be let in. But what will he think of me? The thought of Aiden being disgusted by my cowardice and cruelty is unbearable.

Aiden must sense that I'm unsettled. He reaches into the pack and grabs a medical mask. "Here, let's put this on you."

The mask covers my nose and mouth, and Aiden helps me secure the straps.

"Wanna try getting up?" His tenderness and patience fill me with resolve. I want to be strong for him. He helps me to my feet, and even with his guidance, I wobble a little, but he's there to steady me.

He takes my hand and whispers in my ear, "Close your eyes. I'll guide you through."

With my eyes clamped shut, I let him steer me, putting all my trust in him. The tug of his hand pulls me forward as he gives the occasional adjustment in direction or warning about a stray rock. The smell gets more intense. Almost unbearable. I hold back heaving in my throat.

Aiden whispers in my ear again. "Zach. I'm going to pick you up. Okay?"

"For real? Can you lift me?"

"Yeah, I got you."

Aiden puts an arm around my back and another behind my knees and sweeps me up. I was ten years old the last time someone carried me like this. I sprained my ankle on a hiking trip, and my dad carried me five miles through the forest. It's comforting, feeling Aiden's breathing and his heartbeat as I nuzzle my head into his chest. I clutch onto him tightly.

"It's gonna get a little hairy here. Keep those eyes closed," Aiden whispers.

He doesn't have to tell me. My eyes are shut tight. Aiden does some serious jumps but clutches me tight through it all. The smell is worse than ever. I can't imagine what Aiden is witnessing.

In a few minutes, things improve. And soon, the musty scent of the tunnel replaces the stench of rot.

"Okay, Zach, I'm gonna set you down now. You can open your eyes."

I open them to see the tunnel exit just ahead. We've made it to the other side. Aiden gently lowers me to the ground.

"Thanks." My eyes are downcast, avoiding his gaze. "Sorry I was such a wimp back there."

"It's okay. It can be hard sometimes." His caring and genuine expression eases my anxiety. There's no judgment or condescension. Aiden is a good person. He's not perfect, but neither am I. And while a shadow of hurt for his leaving remains, at this moment, I know I can find some way to forgive him.

Chapter Twenty-Seven

Mending

AIDEN

As we leave the tunnel, I shudder at what we just went through. I don't want Zach to know how bad it was. The first bodies we encountered were lying haphazardly around a fire. But the deeper we got into the tunnel, the more it was clear we had stumbled into a mass grave. Bodies were piled on top of each other ten high. At times, the path through the carnage was so narrow I had to turn to avoid us touching them. The worst moment was when I saw a body moving under a pile of dead, trying to reach out and grab me. I had to jump to avoid it. I shake off the thought as best as I can. But some things can leave a permanent mark on your memory. And I worry this is one of those things.

We return to the flat desertscape that spans in all directions with the slightest hint of snowcapped mountains to the west. The Cascades. That's where we're headed. We'll eventually have to go up and over Snoqualmie Pass to get to Seattle.

Though we make good time on the flat trail, Zach hobbles along, getting slower by the minute. We pause to rest, and I take a moment to inspect his wound. A scab has formed all around the cut, but the redness has increased, and there's a bit of swelling. When I press the area, Zach winces. And when I release my finger, a noticeable white indentation remains before the blood flows back.

"How does it look?" Zach asks.

"It's swollen. It might be a little infected. How's it feeling?"

"It's been better. But I'm managing."

"We're not far from Ellensburg. I don't love going through cities, but we may need to scavenge a drugstore for antibiotics."

"You think it'll be safe?" Zach's brow crinkles with worry.

"We'll have to be careful. But let's take it easy on your leg and search for a place to camp for the night. We'll head to Ellensburg tomorrow when we're fresh."

We continue down the trail until we find a small grove of trees with cover from the sun. I lay the sleeping bag on soft sandy soil in the shade and have Zach rest while I set up camp. Then I lie down next to him.

We both lounge with our heads propped on our arms, looking into each other's eyes. Even travel weary and his hair a complete mess, I still find Zach irresistible. He looks at me with a soft smile. I care for him so much; it makes me ache inside that I've caused him pain. I'd do anything to make it up to him.

"Thanks for the help at the tunnel," Zach says. "And for rescuing me back at the dam. I was so upset that I might not have thanked you properly. You risked your life to save me, and for that, I'm grateful."

"Zach, I'll do anything to keep you safe. You have to know how deeply I care." My emotions are building, and I choke out the words. "I'm so sorry for leaving. But no matter how stupid I am, I'll always come back for you. No matter what."

Zach's smile widens, and he puts his hand on my shoulder. "Aiden?"

"Yes?" I say, chin trembling.

"I forgive you."

Relief. "You do?"

"Does this answer your question?" Zach scoots over and wraps his arm around me. As our bodies press together, I can barely contain my joy.

Then he kisses me.

Our mouths open, and Zach explores with his tongue as tingles spread from head to toe. But we go slow, with near misses and the occasional light contact, like a game of cat and mouse. With each touch of the tongue, a wave of pleasure.

Zach runs his hand down my chest and then along my back, sending shivers through me. The light moan from my lips makes his kisses more insistent. I follow Zach's lead and explore his body with my hand, across his lean shoulders, down his rib cage, and back up to his chest. His muscles flex instinctively, and I squeeze them, feeling their shape.

Craving his bare skin, I start to untuck his shirt. Then I pause. "Is this okay?" I want this so much, but Zach has to be ready.

"It is *so* okay. You have no idea how long I've been thinking about this."

I laugh from pure happiness.

I slip my hand under his shirt and along his side. He shudders at my touch and lets out a little giggle.

"Does that tickle?" I smile.

"A little." He shudders again and laughs. "It's been a while. Everything's a little extra sensitive."

I move my hand from his side, exploring his abs, then continuing upward. Zach's skin is soft and warm. My touch is a gentle caress, like he's something precious I could break.

I go to my knees and guide Zach to do the same so we face each other. I take off his shirt, and he does the same to me. For a moment, I take in his half-naked body. His chest is smooth and lean. I run my fingers along it, and he shivers again. I lightly pinch his nipple, and he lets out a gasp.

The hunger in his eyes ignites a burning desire as he brushes his fingers along my chest. Little ripples of delight pulse through me with his hands on my skin. It's been a while for me too.

We join in a hungry kiss, with passion building in each of us. With my hands free to do what they want, I reach for his ass. Zach grabs my ass, too, and we press our bodies together, kissing deeply. We strip off the rest of our clothes with a ferocious intensity. I stop for a moment to take him in. He's beautiful. The heat of his breath, the softness of his skin, and the scent of his salty sweat consumes my senses.

We tumble to the ground, kissing and grinding together. It's building me up so fast that I have to pull back, nearly losing control.

"Whew, that was close," I say, gasping.

"Um, hmm."

Zach's eyes burn with passion, and I'm overcome with desire. I go slow to be sure he's comfortable and happy, and based on the sounds he makes, I'm hitting the mark. When it's his turn, he does the same, sending waves of pleasure running through me. The longer we go, the more I'm immersed in overwhelming bliss. I don't want this moment to end. Both of us close to the edge, we press together again. With each touch, each glance, and each sound Zach makes, I'm more connected to him. I'm so vulnerable in his grasp as we open ourselves completely.

As the final waves course through every inch of me, there's so much more to it than the physical sensation. I've opened my heart a crack, and Zach is forcing his way in. It's so intense that it scares me.

Afterward, lying in each other's arms, we continue to kiss and touch. I want to hold him forever, whisk him away from this terrible world, wrap ourselves up, and hide where no one can find us. We lie there, exchanging giggles, pawing at each other, with the occasional peck on the lips. Neither of us wants it to end.

Finally, Zach smiles and breaks the silence. "That was amazing."

I smile back. "Yes. Yes, it was."

*

ZACH

I lie there with Aiden in my arms, basking in the afterglow of what we shared. It's been a long time since I've felt these strong emotions for another person. It takes a lot to open myself up this much to him. And while the slightest bit of me fears being hurt, right now, I am blissfully content.

We take it easy for the remainder of the day, saving our energy for what tomorrow may bring. We spend time in each other's arms, kissing softly, whispering loving words, and enjoying each other's company. It's a joyous evening, and I hope there'll be many more like this.

When it's time for bed, we snuggle up in the tent and sleeping bag. The evening is warm, so we keep the rain fly off. Aiden lies beside me, his naked body illuminated by the moon. His body is beautiful. Broad, muscular shoulders. Defined arms. The little V shape that starts in his lower abdomen and runs down to his inner thighs, outlining his hips. I turn on my side, facing away, and he presses up against me, cradling me gently. Just as we did last night, but this time there's nothing between us. I'm in bliss.

Halfway through the night, I wake up with something hard pressed against me. Aiden's breathing is deep and rhythmic. I nuzzle into him, and he wakes up enough to start nuzzling back. So I start grinding, and he makes these soft moaning noises that drive me wild.

"You're a bad boy," he whispers in my ear.

"Um-hmm."

After a little more fun, we kiss and cuddle until we fall asleep in each other's arms. Nothing further disturbs us that night.

*

The next morning, we hit the trail, well-rested and ready for the day. As we continue down the trail, I look over at Aiden, and he looks back. My cheeks warm, and I smile bashfully, thinking about what we shared yesterday. He blushes a bit too. I want more of that. More of him. And now, nothing is stopping us.

I'm in such high spirits that I overextend myself as we push on through most of the morning. As a result, I'm paying the price with my leg. A dull ache has replaced any sharp pains, but the ache is constant. An ever-present reminder that my leg still needs to heal.

A few hours after leaving camp, Aiden points into the distance. "See that dark line up there?"

"Yep."

"That's Interstate 90. We made it back to the freeway. Let's keep our eyes open."

"What are we looking for?"

"Hopefully a car we can scavenge. But keep your eyes out for dangers too. Connor will still be looking for us. Really, it's best if we don't run into anybody."

My muscles tense at the mention of Connor. I hope I never run into him again.

The freeway cuts into a valley between two hills. Up ahead, the trail we're on goes over the freeway on an old railroad bridge converted to a pedestrian overpass. When we get to the bridge, Aiden scans the freeway with the binoculars.

"Well, I do see a few cars." Aiden points westward down the freeway.

When I squint my eyes, several dark specks are visible where he is pointing. "Do you think we should chance it?"

"I'd like to at least try."

I'm wracked with worry at the thought of being that exposed on the freeway, but I agree anyway. If we hit the car jackpot and find one we can drive, we could be in Seattle in a matter of hours. The prospect of that is too attractive to ignore.

So we scamper down an embankment toward the freeway. An access road runs alongside it. It's close enough to see everything on the freeway, but it's less exposed than walking right on I-90. The wide-open plains of central Washington have few places to hide.

The cars didn't seem too far from our vantage on the railroad bridge. But it seems to take forever. What was once a couple of specks on the horizon slowly take shape. As we get closer, it's clear there was a large pileup.

It's a real mess. An overturned semitruck stretches across the freeway. Several cars are intertangled in the wreckage. *Cars* is a generous description. More like twisted masses of steel and glass. The wreck blocks all the westbound lanes from the middle barrier past the shoulder, which is fortunate because quite a few abandoned cars are lined up behind the wreckage.

Walking among the vehicles is a ghastly affair. Many of them have the fully decayed remains of their former owners. I've seen enough rotting corpses recently, so I steer clear of these cars and let Aiden inspect them. I take the empty ones.

Of all the cars I check, only two still have keys. And in both cases, the batteries are dead. All the cars are newer models, too, meaning hotwiring or compression starting them is not an option.

A large smashing sound startles me. Aiden stands by a car with the rear side window freshly missing, holding his rifle backward.

"Warn me before you do that next time! I almost pissed my pants," I shout with a slight laugh.

"Sorry. Will do."

Aiden reaches into the broken window, opens the back door, and enters the car. I shudder as he reaches over a figure in the front seat. It's too much for me, so I avert my eyes. A second later, the door slams shut.

"No luck. Dead battery."

We finish searching the remaining cars with the same result. This must have happened long ago. Every battery is dead. If we hadn't lost the battery jump starter, we'd be driving along the freeway at this moment, headed for home.

"Well, I guess we should keep going," Aiden says. "Let me scout the freeway real quick." He scales the overturned semi by climbing the under-carriage and hoists himself up to the top.

Through the binoculars, he checks the road. "Well, I don't see any abandoned cars nearby. Oh, wait. Maybe I see one."

He reaches out and points. Far off, a glint of metal catches the sun. But then that glint of metal moves.

"Shit! A car is coming this way," Aiden yells. "Quick, hide!"

At the same instant, something moves in one of the cars Aiden checked. Out of the open door a large man lumbers, clothes tattered, veins bulging. Infected.

He sees Aiden first and starts running toward him.

"Aiden, watch out!"

As I shout, the Infected man turns toward me. He looks at me with those vacant eyes and starts racing my way.

Chapter Twenty-Eight

Ellensburg

AIDEN

So many terrible things are unfolding at once, like I'm watching a horror movie on fast-forward. The glint of light on the horizon has become two pickup trucks, the sound of their throaty engines faintly audible.

Then Zach cries out, and I turn to see an Infected man heading toward him. I aim my rifle at the Infected, knowing the gunshot will immediately advertise our presence to the trucks. But it doesn't matter. I have to protect Zach.

I've got the man in the sights of my rifle, but then Zach jumps into an empty SUV. The Infected gets there seconds later and pounds his fists on the window, but Zach is safe.

Zach is safe.

I let out a massive sigh of relief.

"Hey, fucker! Over here!" I wave my hands to get the Infected's attention. He turns quickly and starts my way.

I sprint to the other end of the semi, then jump off. I land hard on the roof of a nearby car, rolling into the fall and smashing my shoulder on the pavement. The impact makes me shout in pain.

I run down the rows of cars with the Infected in pursuit. The last thing I want is to bring him back to Zach, but Zach opens the door and shouts at me to get in. I try to wave him off, but it's useless. So I sprint over and jump in, me in the back seat and Zach in the front. The Infected is outside, pounding on the windows.

"Shit. I hope this doesn't give us away," I say.

Zach nods, his face wracked with worry.

The sound of engines gets louder as I take in the uncomfortably familiar sight of pickup trucks bearing the FLA flag. They're driving east on the opposite side of the freeway. One comes to a stop across the median from us. A man sits outside on the edge of the passenger seat window. He has a rifle in his hand.

"Get down," I hiss under my breath, and we both get low in the car.

Muffled shouts call out from across the freeway. "Look, Wayne. Target practice."

A bullet strikes the rear window sending an explosion of glass shrapnel throughout the cargo area. I cover my mouth to keep from crying out.

"Wayne, you aim like my grandma. And she's dead."

The Infected heads toward the opening in the broken window. *Fuck.*

FUCK.

"We may have to make a run for it," I whisper to Zach.

The Infected peers in through the window. He puts his hands on either side of the frame and starts crawling in. I shift quickly to the other side of the car, about to open the door, when—BAM!

"Woohoo! Got 'em!"

The Infected slumps halfway inside the car, still alive, but probably not for long. Luckily, the shot was low. If it were a headshot, we'd be covered in blood.

We both sit motionless in stunned silence. The Infected lets out a blood-curdling cry as he writhes, the last bit of life leaving him. I chance a peek over the edge of the window at Wayne holding his gun up and cheering.

Then the truck accelerates with a throaty rumble as it speeds away down the freeway. We both let out a long breath. The good news is we're alive, and they didn't spot us. The bad news is this road is being watched.

When the sound of the trucks has long passed, we get out of the SUV. Zach runs into my arms, and we hug tightly. The more I let Zach into my heart, the more painful moments like this become. Up until now, my emotions were dulled and muted. It was much easier to cope. Now, when he's in danger, I'm overwhelmed with fear.

"We better get going," I finally whisper into his ear.

"Okay."

This time, I scan the road east and west with the binoculars, looking for moving cars. Nothing to the west. To the east, the trucks are off in the distance, traveling farther away.

"Okay, I think we're safe to go." I wave for Zach to follow me.

"So the FLA is patrolling this road?"

"I'm afraid so."

"That probably means no cars, huh?" Zach looks visibly anxious.

"It would be risky."

We return to the trail, out of sight of the freeway. Zach has slowed a bit, visibly limping, and I give us regular breaks. After several more hours, I'm more concerned about Zach's leg. Without antibiotics, a person can die from a cut if it gets badly infected.

We're heading to the good-sized town of Ellensburg. Under normal circumstances, I'd go entirely around it to avoid any chance of encounters, but it's the last town we'll pass for a long time. So, we need to risk it. We'll watch for hospitals and drugstores and hope for the best. Assuming looters haven't taken everything already. And assuming it isn't crawling with Infected.

As we walk, the occasional building appears alongside the trail. First, it's only light industrial buildings, like corrugated metal warehouses and junk yards. But soon, we see churches, stores, and homes. The trail leads us directly into the middle of town. I slow our pace, and we stop to listen more often. The rule for cities: avoid anything moving at all costs.

So far, the town is eerily quiet.

The trail ends unceremoniously, butting up to a city street. The map shows the trail picking back up again on the west side of town. We're on our own, navigating the streets. Cars are everywhere, but most of them are obviously ruined—smashed up, with slashed tires, or burned to a crisp. The few intact ones don't have any keys and are too modern to hot-wire.

Zach points to a blue sign up ahead with an *H* and an arrow pointing left. "Look, a hospital. Should we check that out?"

"Yeah, let's do it. But don't get your hopes up. Hospitals are usually the first things looted in a town."

We turn left and continue for a few blocks but soon realize this hospital will be useless to us. The *Ellensburg Regional Hospital* sign still stands, but behind it are the charred remains of several buildings. The fire even spread to the surrounding neighborhood.

Zach laughs. "So I'm guessing that's a no."

I laugh back. "Yeah, that's a no." I'm glad he still has a sense of humor, despite obviously being in pain.

We continue down a main arterial. I haven't seen a single drugstore yet, nothing either way as we pass each cross street. Finally, on our right, several blocks down, a sign with a big red *S* dominates the view.

"Perfect," I say, pointing toward it.

"Safeway?"

"Yep. People forget about the drugstores inside supermarkets. And they're secured from the rest of the store, so there's a chance of it being untouched."

The Safeway is in terrible shape. All the windows are smashed, and a car has crashed into it, collapsing the front facade. We carefully step over broken glass and loose bricks and head into the store.

Almost all the shelves are bare, picked over by looters long ago. We go up and down each aisle, grabbing anything we think will be valuable. A few cans of dog food. Some baby formula. Not great, but they have calories. That's about all that's left.

When we get to the pharmacy, I'm happy to see the metal security door rolled down. A small keyhole sticks out of the bottom right side. Zach shines his flashlight on it, scrutinizing it.

"Well, looks like somebody already tried to force the lock. But let me give it a go, anyway."

"Of course you pick locks. Why didn't I guess that?" I laugh.

"I've been known to dabble."

"You just keep the surprises coming, don't you?"

Zach shoots a mischievous smile back at me and removes the small set of tools from the pack. "Life on Vashon Island was boring. I had lots of free time."

"So you became a thief?"

"Hey, picking locks comes in handy. Once people on the island knew about it, they'd call me before they called a locksmith. My currency was chocolate bars."

I laugh. "Well, I'm fresh out."

"I'll take other forms of payment," Zach says, dripping with innuendo, and I shoot him back a sultry look.

He turns his attention to the lock, inserting two delicate-looking tools into the keyhole. For a moment, I watch him work. I love that look of concentration he gets when he's got a problem to solve. His face scrunches up, and his lips purse. It's so adorable. I still have so much to learn about this guy. I keep finding out new things about him all the time.

Giving Zach some space to work undistracted, I search more of the aisles. Around the pharmacy area, some shelves even have a few items left. I find a couple of bottles of children's ibuprofen and stash them in the bag.

Then I come up to a section I hoped would still be stocked. Family planning. A couple of boxes of condoms and three bottles of lube have yet to be looted. I smile, and my cheeks get a little warm. This is precisely what I was looking for. If Zach and I decide to take things to the next level, I want to be ready.

Some might think during the apocalypse, it's easy to say *screw it* and not care about safe sex anymore. But they'd be wrong. Without health care, you have to be *more* worried about that kind of shit. Not less.

As I reach for my backpack, a strange sensation comes over me. That charged energy when somebody enters a room. I turn to see a small girl down the aisle, staring at me. She can't be any older than five or six. Honestly, she gives me the creeps as goosebumps cover my arms. It's like I'm watching *The Shining*.

She stares at me, unblinking, with a blank expression on her face.

"Hey, little girl." I speak in soft tones to not startle her. "Are your parents around?"

She turns around and runs.

Shit.

I grab my rifle off my pack and run after her. I don't know what to do when I catch her, but she can't be allowed to tell anyone we're here.

"Zach!" I call out in a hushed yell. But he's too far to hear me, so I continue after the girl.

She runs out of the front of the Safeway and darts left. When I get to the store entrance, I pause for a second. Standing to my left, about twenty feet away, the girl stares at me like she did earlier.

Down on one knee, I gesture her over. "Come here. I don't mean any harm."

She takes a few cautious steps forward. She's just out of reach.

"I'm lost," she says. Her face is still blank. No expression.

"When was the last time you saw your parents?"

"My parents are dead." She frowns.

"I'm sorry to hear that. Come back into the store and tell me about it. I'll give you a treat." If I can get her back into the store, maybe I can keep her occupied long enough to warn Zach and get us the hell out of here.

I put my hand out to her, palm upward. The second I do, she takes off running again. She gets to the edge of the Safeway and turns left.

I give up. I'm not going to chase this girl all around town. I have to get Zach and clear out as fast as we can. But when I turn around, a man is behind me, holding a rifle at my head.

"Drop it!" he yells.

He's made a serious tactical error though. He's standing too close. He'll never expect what I'm about to do, so I have the element of surprise. In a flash, I close the distance between us and swat away the barrel of his rifle with the barrel of mine. His gun goes off, but it shoots harmlessly to my left. In the same motion, I smash him in the head with the butt of my rifle, and he crumples to the ground.

Never saw it coming.

But neither did I. A sharp pain stabs in the back of my skull, and a blinding flash of white envelops my vision. I'm only vaguely aware of my body crumpling to the ground.

Then darkness.

Chapter Twenty-Nine

From Bad to Worse

ZACH

Picking a lock takes a steady hand and concentration. The trick is to turn the lock enough to put tension on the pins. Then you insert a small pick and push up each of the pins until you hear the slightest click. Once you've done that to all the pins—voilà—the lock turns, and that's just what I do.

I remove the lock from the rolling door and slide it open.

"Aiden. I got it."

But my excitement quickly turns to disappointment. Inside are nothing but empty shelves. Someone beat us to it and cleaned out the pharmacy entirely. Not so much as a bottle of aspirin.

"Aiden. It's a bust."

No answer. Hmm.

"Aiden?" I turn around and see no sign of him. But the aisles are too high to see all the way across. I head along the back of the store, looking down each aisle as I pass, calling his name.

"Aiden?"

"Aiden."

Down the next aisle, his backpack rests on the floor, leaning against a shelf. My chest tightens as I approach it. Still no sign of him. When I get to the backpack, the rifle is missing.

"Aiden!" I call out. Okay, I'm getting freaked out now.

The sound of a gunshot outside sends my pulse through the roof. I sling the backpack over my shoulders and grab the .45 out of the front pocket, all while running to the entrance. I'm just in time to see Aiden struck in the back of the head with the butt of a rifle. He falls to the ground, his attacker standing above him.

I cover my mouth to keep from screaming.

The man is tall and muscular, with short dark hair, and he's wearing a flannel shirt and jeans. In one hand, he holds the rifle he struck Aiden with.

"Drop the rifle, or I'll shoot!" I yell as I point my gun at him.

His body tenses, and he raises his arms above his head but doesn't drop the rifle. He stares at me, hard and angry, like a killer.

I fire a warning shot. "I said drop it!"

He finally drops the rifle. "You're making a big mistake," he says in a deep, gravelly voice.

"Put your hands behind your head and start walking slowly. Count out five hundred paces and don't turn around."

"You're dead boy. We're gonna hunt you down and kill you."

I fire another shot, closer this time. "Start walking! I mean it!"

He puts his hands behind his head and finally starts moving. Once he's a short distance away, I run over to Aiden. I relax when his chest moves. He's still breathing.

I slap his face. "Aiden, wake up!"

But he doesn't respond.

I run over to an abandoned grocery cart and pull it over. Using strength aided by adrenaline, I hoist Aiden up and place him in the cart. I also gather all the rifles on the ground, and stash them in the cart beside Aiden's limp body.

The man is probably a hundred paces away. He looks back, then starts running away from me. But that's okay. I don't plan to be anywhere near here when he returns with reinforcements.

I push the cart as fast as it will go, and it clatters hard against the uneven surface of the road. I take a side street next to the Safeway, then zigzag left and right at each intersection to throw off any potential pursuers. The pain from my left ankle radiates up my leg. I need to find a place to rest and also let Aiden recover.

A cheap single-story motel appears in front of me, with peeling paint and overgrown hedges. Grass sprouts up through every crack in the pavement, and half the windows are smashed. A fenced pool is thick with green algae.

I try the door of one of the guest rooms. It's locked, but the knob is flimsy. I channel all the strength inside me. Screaming, I kick with every ounce of energy I have left. Splinters shoot from the frame, and the door swings open, banging hard against the wall.

I push the cart in and slam the door behind me. The air is horribly musty, but I'm way beyond caring. I roll the cart next to a bed, gently tip it over, and shimmy Aiden onto it. His breathing is slow and steady. Then, I bar the door with the cart, wedging it under the doorknob. I'm unsure what else to do, so I simply crawl into bed next to Aiden and fall into a tortured sleep.

All my dreams are of Aiden, and he's always leaving me. It's either by choice or by force, but he keeps leaving. My empty bed in the bank. His missing tent by the dam. The abandoned backpack in the grocery store. Each time, Aiden is in the distance, just out of reach. I run to him, but he floats away faster than I can catch him. I scream at him, but he doesn't hear. He keeps floating farther away.

I wake up to my own screaming. I try to open my eyes, only to realize they are already open. The room is pitch black. Night has descended. My throat is dry and sticky with mucus, and my stomach grumbles. But I'm too exhausted to care. Beside me, Aiden's rhythmic breathing continues. It's best to let him rest. I drop my head on the musty bedspread and drift back to sleep.

When I wake again, sunlight streams in, casting the entire room in a sickly yellow hue, but next to me, the bed is empty. I dart my eyes around the room, and I'm relieved to see Aiden standing and peeking out the motel window.

"Aiden! You're okay!"

"Shhhhh." He puts his index finger to his mouth, but then he shoots me a smile and gestures me over. When I'm next to him, he kisses me.

"Thanks for saving me," he says in a hushed voice. "I assume that's what happened, but I don't remember much."

"No problem." I beam.

"I want to hear all about it, but first check this out." He points out the window. On the road in front of the motel dozens of armed people march in unison.

Following behind the gunmen, a group of people trudge down the middle of the street, their expressions neutral and their shoulders slumped, hands hanging downward and swaying as they move.

More people fill the street, all shuffling their feet, moving from right to left, all with the same blank stares. There must be at least a hundred of them. It's by far the most people I've seen in one place out in the open.

"What the hell?" I say.

"Must be one of the slave camps I've heard about. They used that girl to lure me out of the store."

At the rear of the ghastly procession, ten people wear steel collars around their necks, each guided by a captor holding on to an attached chain.

Trailing them is the man I chased away with the gun.

"That's the one who attacked you. In the plaid." I point toward him.

"He looks tough. I'm impressed."

"I let the gun do the talking."

Aiden lets out a soft laugh and kisses my forehead. "If it weren't for you, I'd probably be walking with them as we speak."

When the macabre parade has passed, we both let out a long breath.

"And *that* is why I don't like going through cities," Aiden says.

"I'm starting to agree with you."

"The only good news is I'm guessing they've managed to clear out most of the Infected. That's probably why we haven't run into any." Aiden turns to me. "Still, I think we better hightail it outta here before they find us again. How's the leg?"

"Been better, but I agree. We should get going. How's the head?"

Aiden touches the spot where the gunman hit him and winces. "I'll live."

As we wait for the people to disappear well out of sight, I fill Aiden in with the details of the attack and how I rescued him. He smiles broadly as I recount what happened, wearing an expression I can only describe as pride.

Once the street is clear, we quietly open the door, slip out of the shabby motel, and never look back.

*

AIDEN

Both of us are *so done* with Ellensburg. All we want is get the hell out of this town and its bizarre residents. Zach is limping badly on that left leg. But neither of us wants to spend another second in this town. We'll take our chances finding antibiotics elsewhere. Cle Elum is the next good-sized town. Hopefully, we'll have more luck there.

We stay quiet while we snake our way through abandoned neighborhoods. Only talking enough to discuss which way to go. We meet up with the Palouse to Cascades Trail again. Once we're on it, we go as quickly as possible to leave Ellensburg behind us.

As we continue down the trail, farmland stretches into infinity in every direction. Being this exposed isn't great, but at least it's unlikely somebody would be out here. We make it another few miles before the shadows get long. Zach's shoulders are slumping, and he's looking worn out. We cross the Yakima River. A lush forest runs all along it, giving us an excellent place to camp away from prying eyes.

We find a day-use picnic site nestled into the trees. It has a wooden shelter with picnic tables underneath, well water from a pump, and vaulted outhouses. Overall, a nice find. Much better than the desert landscapes we've camped in the last couple nights.

We both strip naked and wade into the chilly river water to wash off the mud and grime from ourselves and our clothes. Once we're done, we dry off and lay our clothes out to catch the last rays of the fading sunlight.

Zach's been a trouper. I'd guess he's been operating on adrenaline and willpower for the last few days. But he looks spent now that the crisis is over and we're resting.

I set up the tent and let him rest in it while I make us dinner. The site has metal BBQ stations. I risk a small fire so we can have a warm meal. When I bring it to Zach, he cracks a smile, but it doesn't reach his eyes. He looks exhausted.

"Thanks." He tries to sound cheerful, but it comes out flat.

"No problem. You get some good rest tonight." I smile and try to hide my worry.

We sleep together in the tent again, but Zach is restless all night. We both sleep poorly. Toward the middle of the night, he's radiating heat. Sweat beads up on his brow. I press the back of my hand to his forehead and feel a fever. He's already half awake, but I give him a little shake.

"Here, take these." I hand him a few ibuprofen pills.

He swallows them without question. In a while, his fever subsides, so we get a few hours of sleep before sunrise.

In the morning, we wake to dark clouds. It's a change of pace from our relentless sun, but rain won't be welcome today, especially with Zach feeling worse by the hour.

His wound looks more infected than ever, with pronounced red streaks heading up the leg. Pushing him like this tears me up, but things could get dire if we don't get some antibiotics soon. Cle Elum, the next town, is still a twenty-mile hike.

Going for antibiotics by myself is an option. But a forty-mile round-trip hike would take me all day and into tomorrow. Leaving him alone for that long is a bad idea, so I convince him to at least try part of the trip. I won't be gone for so long if we can make it halfway.

It's slow going. We've been at it for a few hours, and Zach looks more pitiful with every step. His fever has returned, and the ibuprofen isn't doing much this time. Anything he eats makes him nauseous.

And then the rain starts. It's just a little sprinkle, so we press on, hoping it will end soon.

I'll try anything to take his mind off of how he feels. "Hey, Zach, let's sing a Beatles song, whacha think? 'Here Comes the Sun'?"

Zach sighs but manages a little laugh. "Clever. Okay. Let's try."

I start with the melody. *"Here comes the sun—"*

I sing the next verse, and Zach joins in with harmony. *"Here comes the sun—"*

But as we get into the rest of the verse, Zach trails off.

I turn around as he collapses in a heap on the ground. As if on cue, the skies open up and start pouring rain.

I run to his side. "Zach! Can you hear me?"

He doesn't answer. He's still breathing, but his forehead radiates heat.

The rain comes down in a torrent. This is nothing less than Mother Nature giving us the middle finger. My backpack is getting soaked, so even setting up a tent for him would mean he'd be lying in wetness.

With no other choice, I hoist him into my arms and start heading down the trail. Maybe if I can find some shelter, I can at least get him out of the rain where he can rest and get dry. I'm wracked with guilt. I can't believe I pushed him this hard. He went downhill so quickly. If I'd known how bad it would get, I would have set him up with the tent, then tried to run the entire way. I might have made it in time.

Zach's eyes flutter open, and he makes a little groaning sound. Then they close again.

"Hang in there, Zach."

The rain is relentless. My shoes fill with water, and blisters form on my feet. My shoulders and back are aching. But I have to press on. I ignore the pain. Nothing would feel worse than losing Zach.

It's been at least an hour, and there's no good shelter anywhere. Even under the trees, the water still pelts us. My endurance is waning. Carrying him is getting too hard. The muscles in my shoulders and legs quiver, nearing failure.

Then, off to the left, a thin trail of smoke rises from the forest. With no options left, I take a leap of faith and turn into the woods. After a few minutes, I get to a short chain-link fence, which is easy to get over, more designed to keep animals in than people out, I'd guess. Just a bit farther, we get to a clearing where a farmhouse sits, nestled among the trees. It looks well taken care of. A wrap-around porch covers the front, and smoke rises from its chimney. Dim firelight flickers in the window.

I approach the house, hoping someone will take mercy on us. This thin sliver of hope is all I have left at this point. I'm almost to the door when the sound of a shotgun being cocked rings out.

"Now hold it right there!"

Chapter Thirty

Homestead

ZACH

My entire body is numb. When I collapsed, I had no choice in the matter. My mind shut things down.

Now, I'm drifting between a dream state and a semiconscious fog. I'm roughly aware of a big man in overalls approaching from behind us. My vision is blurry, so I can only make out vague shapes. But blurry or not, the man clearly has a gun. I try to cry out to warn Aiden, but no sound comes out.

There's no sense of time or space. My body floats in blackness. An occasional thought comes into my mind, then hurries away. It's as if my brain is trying to remember things, but I don't have the energy to sustain them. Aiden flashes before me. Then my parents. Then Elk Springs. All brief moments, breaking up the monotonous void.

Finally, I'm vaguely aware of my surroundings. Above me are worn timbers. Rough burlap rubs against my skin. The smell of hay and barnyard animals fills my nostrils. Off to the side is the man in overalls I saw earlier. He's facing a tool bench with his back turned to me.

Aiden lies still on the ground, not moving an inch. I try to cry out, but again, no sound comes out. Aiden needs my help. I need to get up. What has this man done to him?

I try to move but I'm constricted somehow. My hands and feet are tied down. I fight against my bonds, but it's no use. In my mind, I scream, but only a low guttural noise comes out.

The man turns around. He's large in stature and girth, wearing blue-jean overalls over a white cotton shirt. A mask covers his face, with a long gray beard poking out from underneath. He says something, but the words make no sense. My mind hears only gibberish. He walks over to me with a hypodermic needle in his hand. I thrash around, but he holds my chest down with his forearm. There's a pinprick on my shoulder.

Then my consciousness quickly slips away.

*

When I wake up, I'm lying in a comfortable bed. Soft white sheets surround me. The bed frame is wrought iron, adorned with broad sweeping curves. A patchwork quilt covers me. My head is still foggy, but I'm feeling far better than I did before.

Is this a dream? The smell of bacon wafts in the air. I don't smell in my dreams, so I must be awake. This must be real.

Looking around, I'm in a bedroom. Lime-green plaster walls contrast against white wood trim. The floor is hardwood, but the bed sits on an old, worn rug. The sun streaks in through the windows, which are covered with sheer white curtains.

I kick off the quilt and sheets covering me. I'm dressed in pajamas that are not my own. Someone has cleaned me up. My arms are clean, and I smell fresh, like soap.

The wound on my leg is much better. Red streaks are no longer visible, and the swelling is down. The scab looks clean.

But there is no sign of Aiden. The memory of seeing him lying on the floor sends a wave of panic through me. What if the man killed Aiden, but he chose to save me? Maybe he plans to make me a slave. Maybe Aiden was too much to handle, and the man only needed one of us.

A noise comes from outside the bedroom door. As I move to get out of bed, every motion creates a creaking noise from the metal box spring beneath me. Gently, I step off the bed and tiptoe to the door. An old brass doorknob is cold to the touch. I turn it until there's a quiet click of the door unlatching.

Through a small crack in the door is the kitchen of an old farmhouse. Butcher-block countertops rest on painted white cabinets. There's a stove and a refrigerator that looks fifty years old.

The big man I saw in the barn is at the countertop with his back turned toward me. He's wearing those same overalls, and a long gray ponytail goes well past his shoulders. He's hovering over the stove. I'm hit with another waft of bacon, and my stomach gurgles. I'm ravenous.

He's probably given me more of whatever was in that needle earlier to keep me sedated. Maybe it wore off quicker than he expected. This may be my only chance to escape before he realizes I've regained consciousness. I have to take advantage of his mistake.

I creak the door open and tiptoe into the room. A cast iron pan rests on the kitchen table. I grab it and raise it over my head, sneaking up behind him. A quick whack on the head should be enough to give me a head start.

"Zach! What are you doing?" A familiar voice calls out from my right. I spin around as Aiden jumps up from a chair he was sitting in.

He's okay.

Aiden is okay.

The man in overalls turns, sees me, and snatches the cast iron pan out of my hand.

"I'll take *that.*" His voice is gentle and singsongy. Not what I was expecting from this big, lumbering man. He sets the pan down on the counter, away from my reach.

In the meantime, Aiden crosses the room and wraps me up in a big hug. I hug him back. The swing of emotions in such a short time makes me lightheaded.

"I don't understand. What's happening?" With arms still around him, I pull away to look into Aiden's face. He's got a broad grin, and his eyes are bright.

"Everything is okay, Zach. This is Curtis. He saved your life." He gestures to the big man, who also has a grin on his face. Curtis makes a friendly wave. His eyes look a little damp.

"But I thought— I mean I was bound up— You were on the floor—" I trail off. My head is fuzzy, and my legs are getting a little weak.

Aiden keeps me from falling. "Whoa! Let's get you seated."

He guides me into a nearby chair. He drags another one up next to me and sits down.

"First, let's get some food into you. Your body is weak. I'll answer all your questions over breakfast." Aiden's kind eyes gaze into mine. I'm confused, but seeing him calms me. I trust him and know I'll always be safe with him. I care so much for Aiden.

In no time, Curtis sets a plate of food in front of me. Crispy bacon, scrambled eggs, hash browns, and toast with jam. I shovel food into my mouth like I haven't eaten in forever.

"Slow down, Zach," Curtis says in a soft tone. "You'll make yourself sick." He sets a plate down in front of Aiden and one for himself.

Between bites of food, Aiden starts his story. "Okay, from the beginning. We were hiking along in the rain, and you weren't looking so great. Then you collapsed."

"I have a fuzzy recollection of that."

"Well, I picked you up and started down the trail. I knew I had to get you someplace dry. By complete chance, I found this place. It was the smoke from the fireplace."

Curtis cuts in, smiling, "I hadn't had a fire for weeks. Been too warm. Luckily, it was a chilly day, or you guys might not have found me."

I nod. "I remember us going up to the farmhouse. It's all hazy though."

Aiden continues, "Anyway, I ran up to this house. Curtis was there, holding a shotgun. It's hard to blame him. I would have, too, if total strangers came running up."

Curtis smiles and shrugs.

"I told him about everything that happened. That you had this infected cut, and we haven't been able to find any antibiotics. He could tell you were in terrible shape. Curtis has connections around here. People he can trade supplies with. We were able to get antibiotics."

"But I remember a barn, and I was bound up."

Curtis nods. "Well, I refuse to turn away people in need. The world may have gone to hell, but I still have my morals. But with the Infection, I had to be sure you guys weren't contagious. So I quarantined you in the barn for the first few days."

My jaw drops open. "Days! How long have I been out?"

"You've been out for a week, Zach. It was touch and go for a bit there. The bacteria from the cut spread from your leg into your bloodstream." Aiden puts his hand on my shoulder. "We had to bind you up. Sorry about that. You were thrashing around so much we were worried you'd hurt yourself or fall off the bed."

"But I saw you on the ground, Aiden. I thought you were dead." The memory gives me a chill.

"That must have been the first day when I fell asleep, exhausted. I carried you for miles through the pouring rain."

Emotion overcomes me, and I wrap my arms around Aiden. "Thank you. I owe you my life." I turn to Curtis. "And I owe you my life too."

"You don't owe me anything." Curtis waves away the notion. "Except your thanks."

"I don't know how to thank you enough. And I'm sorry I tried to hit you with a frying pan," I say, cringing.

"Aww, I've had a lot worse done to me," Curtis says.

We all laugh.

*

For the rest of the morning and into the afternoon, I do nothing but rest and eat. Curtis is a natural host, attending to my every need. Aiden apparently didn't sleep well while I was recovering, so he's taking a well-deserved nap.

By midafternoon, my head is no longer foggy, and my strength is returning. I relax on an overstuffed couch set up next to the fire. Sitting in it feels like a big warm hug. Curtis heads over from the kitchen.

"Zach, is there anything else I can get you?"

"I wouldn't mind a little fresh air and a stretch of the legs."

"Well, I'd love to give you a tour of the farm. If you feel up to it."

"That sounds perfect."

Curtis leads me outside. Next to the farmhouse is the barn, bordered by a fence. Goats, sheep, and cows, basking in the afternoon sunlight.

"This is Homestead Farm." Curtis looks around with hands raised and a glint in his eye. "I moved here about ten years ago. I was fed up with city life, so I came out here to see if I could live more simply. Off the grid. Turns out I can."

He leads me past the barn and out toward his fields. We approach a large structure covered in white plastic. "This is my greenhouse. Allows me to grow fruits and vegetables year-round."

We enter through a slit on the wall. Inside, we're greeted with row after row of plants in various stages of growth. Some rows are empty, others have small plants, and others bear fruits and vegetables.

"This is incredible. It's like you're custom built to withstand the apocalypse."

Curtis smiles. "Well, this was more about trying to reduce my impact on the planet. But yeah, it had that benefit too."

"How have you stayed safe out here? With militias roving about. And the Infected."

Curtis guides me out of the greenhouse. "Follow me. I'll show you."

He points his finger to the south. "First of all, we're tucked into a bend in the Yakima River. That gives natural protection from three sides." He then moves his hand around to the north. "And that way is nothing but abandoned farmland for miles. No roads. Nobody snooping. And all around is dense forest. Nobody can see it, and we're miles away from the closest paved road. As for the Infected, I have a fence that runs the entire north perimeter of the property. Once they hit it, they just turn around."

"Wow. It's like a little oasis."

"Plus, I still know a few other people around who've survived. They let me know of any trouble brewing. We watch each other's backs around here. And, we do some trading. You can thank that for your bacon this morning."

I smile, remembering how wonderful it tasted. "Yeah, that was a treat. I can't remember the last time I had it."

"I've been trading vegetables, and it's hard to meet demand. If I could grow more, I would. Problem's getting enough water."

"I am pretty good at mechanical things. Show me your setup. Maybe I can help."

"You sure you're up for it?" Curtis scans my face.

"Yeah. I feel great." I send him a broad grin. "Plus, I'll let you do all the work."

Curtis leads me to his irrigation system. It draws from the Yakima

River, and he's got a hand-operated screw pump with a crank on the side.

"Problem is, I gotta pump this water myself each day, and my old back can only take so much work." He shows me by turning the crank. Water flows, but it's slow going and, as he said, lots of work.

"Have you ever heard of a ram pump?" I ask.

"Nope."

"Got any extra PVC pipe lying around?"

"Yeah, lemme show ya what I got."

Curtis leads me over to a shed. It's a treasure trove of building supplies with everything I need. I work with Curtis for a couple of hours. I'm still too weak for heavy work, so I direct Curtis to dig out a trench while I assemble the pump. He's got a lot of strength and energy for a guy his age. I guess that comes from years of working on a farm.

We assemble all the pieces and drop them in the ditch Curtis dug. One end pokes out to the river, and the other extends to the irrigation channel. Curtis watches in amazement as water from the river rushes into the lower chamber, then sputters out on the top.

"Would you look at that? It's working." Curtis studies the contraption we built as if it's some kind of magic.

"Yeah, we're just using the natural power of the flow of the river to create a pressure vessel. That builds up enough pressure to pump water upward."

"Zach, how in the hell did you know how to do this?"

I shrug. "I used to spend a lot of time watching YouTube science channels."

"Thank you so much." He gives me a big bear hug.

I smile warmly. "It's the least I can do."

No matter what Curtis says, I do owe him my life.

*

AIDEN

I must have been out for hours because the shadows are long when I wake. It looks like late afternoon. I peek at the Casio watch Zach gave me, which reads 4:47 p.m. It's the best sleep I've had in months. That's when it hits me. No nightmares.

The last week was rough. Seeing Zach lying unconscious, looking so pale and near to death. It brought floods of memories back. I spent days crying, crying for Zach, but also crying for Marcus.

When Marcus died, it felt as if a part of me died too. But I've spent no time thinking about it. I buried it. There was too much to do. I insisted on getting back out and doing courier work. No one was there to stop me. Things needed to get done. My feelings could wait.

In the last few days, that old wound of Marcus's death reopened. But it never healed properly the first time, and it needed to. It's been raw and exposed, flowing openly and purging emotion I've bottled up for months.

The worst part was watching Zach flail around. Seeing him struggle against his bonds while his body fought off his infection was torture. I was physically and emotionally drained. But then, little by little, he made progress. First, his fever went down, and the thrashing stopped. Then, the swelling in his leg improved. The red streaks receded. His wound scabbed over. As Zach healed, my crying subsided.

After three days in the barn, Curtis let us move to the house. We made Zach more comfortable and got him cleaned up. He was still getting heavy doses of antibiotics, and Curtis thought it best to keep him sedated until yesterday.

And now Zach's back. Someone I care for was on the brink of death and came back.

*

When Zach and Curtis return from the fields, they're covered in mud from head to toe.

"Did you guys wrestle the pigs?" I laugh.

Curtis pats Zach on the back. "*This one* just figured out how to improve the yield of my farm."

Zach beams.

"Somehow, that doesn't surprise me," I say. "If anybody could figure that out, it'd be Zach." I shoot a big smile at Zach, and he blushes.

After Zach gets cleaned up, he joins me, sitting by the fireplace. We snuggle up on the couch, and I put a blanket over both of us.

"This is like a dream," Zach says.

"Yeah, we certainly got lucky."

"Curtis is so nice. And this little farm he has is incredible." Zach waves his hands around.

"It's unbelievable he's been able to just keep on living, almost like nothing happened. I hope he can keep doing it."

"Me too." Zach smiles. "This place is so peaceful. I could see living here."

I nod and smile. "Yeah. So could I."

And why not? The idea of finding a peaceful place where we can settle down and have a normal life. Why is that too much to ask for? But maybe that's a dream for another day. There's work left to do.

Zach seems to sense my thoughts. "But I imagine we need to hit the road soon."

"Yeah." I point my eyes downward. "But we can still wait for a few days for you to regain your strength. I don't want to rush anything."

Curtis comes in carrying three mugs.

"Hey, boys, I thought you might like some hot chocolate." He holds out the mugs.

"Thanks," we say together as we take them eagerly.

The warm mug is comforting in my hands. I blow on the cocoa, then take a sip. It's delicious. Rich, bitter-sweet, and velvety, this doesn't taste like something from a pouch.

"Wow, this is spectacular." I take another sip.

"Thanks. My own recipe. I've perfected it after many years."

Curtis sits in the chair across from us and takes a sip from his own mug. "Now, I wanna ask you boys a question."

"Sure," I reply.

"First, I wanna say I'm so happy to see you two are a couple. I kinda hoped you were, honestly. If I can be so presumptuous, that is."

Zach blushes, then looks at me expectantly. My own cheeks warm. I smile and give him a nod. We've had little time to discuss our relationship and what we mean to each other. But I'm sure some bond exists.

"Yeah, we are," Zach says, smiling.

"Oh good. I'm so glad. Finding someone special, especially now—it's a rare thing. You two should cherish it."

We look into each other's eyes, and I can't help but smile.

"Now I have a favor to ask of you." Curtis takes an envelope out of his pocket. "I know you're headed to Seattle. I hope you can deliver this for me."

Zach leans over and takes the envelope from him. "Of course. This is the *least* I can do."

"A long time ago, I left someone very special back in Seattle. We left on less-than-ideal terms, and I never got to make amends. It's the biggest regret of my life. It would mean a great deal to me if you could get this letter to him. If he's still alive."

A tear goes down Zach's cheek. "Curtis, you saved my life. I promise you I'll see it delivered."

"Thank you." Curtis puts his hands on the arms of the chair and pushes himself up. "Okay. Well. You boys probably have some catching up to do. I'm gonna be out doing some more work on the farm. I'll be gone for at least two or three hours."

"Okay, Curtis. Thanks again for the hot chocolate." I wave to him.

We watch as he walks across the room and opens the door to the outside.

"Two or three hours. I promise. See you boys later." He gives us a nearly undetectable wink, then shuts the door behind him.

Zach and I turn to each other and laugh.

"Was he just giving us alone time?" I ask.

Zach's eyes lock on mine, and he stops laughing. "Race you to the bedroom."

Without another word, we jump up and run to the bedroom, undressing on the way.

Chapter Thirty-One

We Could Be Happy

ZACH

No sooner does the bedroom door shut than we join together, kissing with urgency. Our shirts are off, and I'm running my hands up and down Aiden's bare chest.

I take a moment to soak Aiden in. He's so beautiful. So handsome. And there's something different. He has a lightness to him. A little more life in his eyes. I kiss him more passionately than before.

Aiden unties the string of my pajama bottoms and yanks them down in one swift motion, exposing me. "Well, somebody's excited," he says with a gentle laugh.

I smile at him sheepishly. "We didn't even make it to the bed yet."

"Lead the way."

On the way, we finish stripping. We jump on the bed and press our bodies together, kissing, grinding, and feeling pure joy. I'm so happy to be with him. To share this with him.

We continue for several minutes, passion rising, when Aiden pulls away and hops off the bed. At first, I'm startled by his jumping away so quickly, but he's got a wry smile.

"One sec," he says with a mischievous grin. He goes over to the backpack in the corner of the room and starts rooting through it.

What on earth is he looking for?

My jaw drops when he takes out a pack of condoms and lube. "Where did you get those?" I feel my cheeks flush. I can't say I haven't thought about going further with him. In fact, sometimes, it's all I can think about.

"I picked them up on the way." His face turns ruby red. "Is this okay?"

His shyness and vulnerability make me fall for him even harder, and I want this even more. I bite my lip and nod. This is a big step, but I care for Aiden profoundly and want to share this special moment with him.

We take it slow and gentle, both attentive to the other. The passion and the tenderness in his eyes fill me with wonder. This was always meant to be. With our arms wrapped around each other, I revel in complete ecstasy. Our rhythm steadily increases, and he pulls me down into a passionate kiss. My surroundings drop away, and all my senses are consumed by only Aiden. For a moment, there's only us alone in a world of euphoria.

I collapse onto him, the sweat from our bodies mingling. We lie there, breathing deeply, letting our heart rates ease.

Kissing, tender now, we savor being together. We stay like this for a long while, neither of us wanting to separate. I'm so safe and fulfilled, lying next to him.

This depth of emotion is startling. It takes my breath away. It's been so long since I've felt this way about someone. Or maybe I've never felt this way. I didn't expect this so soon, yet here it is.

I'm in love with Aiden.

*

AIDEN

Zach is so special to me. We lie in bed for a long while, and I can't look away from him. The soft afternoon light illuminates his gentle face and loving eyes. With the walls I've built around me crumbling, the intensity of my feelings for him almost makes me want to cry. It's a little scary, to be honest.

"This place is so peaceful. I could see living here."

Zach's words resonate in my mind. And why not? Have I not done enough to deserve peace and happiness? Maybe I should forget the damn vials and find a place to spend the rest of my life. The rest of my life with Zach, maybe? The idea doesn't seem so farfetched. In fact, I'm finding it hard to imagine a life without him.

But then, reality comes crashing in on me. I *know* what I must do. This box has to be delivered. No matter the risk. The idea of asking Zach to keep taking these risks fills me with dread. But I've been down this road before. I made a promise to him. I have to let him make his own choice.

True to his word, Curtis returns to the house around three hours after he left. And believe me, Zach and I took full advantage of all three hours. We're making up for lost time, after all.

Curtis carries a box filled with vegetables, meats, and other foods. "I thought I'd make us a nice meal for dinner." He sets the box on the counter and starts taking items out, inspecting each one as he does.

"Where did you get all this?" Zach asks.

"Various places. With the greenhouse, I always have some fresh veggies. The meat is salt-cured. I got both that and the cheese from my larder. Plus, fresh cream from the cows."

We all chip in to help cook. We make a lasagna filled with zucchini, ground meats, homemade noodles, and cheese. Curtis bakes it in his country-style wood oven.

The food is delicious. I even have a third helping. When we're done, Curtis makes more of his famous hot chocolate. We all sit around the dining room table with full bellies, sipping from our mugs.

"You know, you boys are welcome to stay here as long as you want." Curtis looks at us over his mug.

"That's a generous offer," I say. "I imagine we'll stay a few more days. But I've got some unfinished business I have to—"

Curtis puts a hand up. "It's okay. I can tell that whatever you're doing is very important. And I'm guessing the less I know, the better."

"That's true. On both counts."

"But know that once you two are done doing whatever you need to do, you're welcome back here. Even if it's just to visit."

Zach and I trade glances, smiling. "Curtis, I promise you, we'll be back."

*

We spend the next few days resting and recovering from our travels. Each day, Zach feels stronger. It's remarkably easy for us to fall into a happy routine. We wake up at dawn every morning and help Curtis around the farm. We feed the animals, tend to the crops, and milk the cows. When evening comes, we gather and make a wonderful meal together. At night, Zach and I explore all the different ways to make each other happy.

In some sense, the days at the farm remind me of our time in Cedar Grove, where everything was cheerful. But Cedar Grove had a fake veneer to it, as if walking around in a dream you knew you'd wake up from. The farm is much more grounded. More sustainable. This is a life I can see for myself.

But despite that happiness, with every day we stay here, the thoughts of my burden become heavier. Soon, I'll have to level with Zach. Make sure he understands the threats we are up against. Let him decide with complete information. The thought of that fills me with dread. What if Zach decides the risks are too great? I'm not sure how I'd react if he chose to stay. Then again, if he stays with me, I'll be a bundle of nerves as we head deeper into danger. I can't put this discussion with him off forever. But maybe just for another day.

On the fourth night since Zach woke up, we've finished a delicious dinner, and we're all sitting around the dining table. Curtis's usually cheerful face turns stony.

"Boys, I have something important to tell you. Earlier today, I visited a trusted friend, and she asked me if I had seen any strangers around."

I freeze. If Curtis told somebody about us, we'd need to leave immediately. With us being hunted, staying isn't a risk I'm willing to take.

Curtis picks up on my nerves. "Now, don't you worry! I didn't say a thing about you two. Margret is somebody I meet from time to time to trade with and get news from around the area."

I settle back, but I'm still on edge. Zach rests his hand on my arm to calm me.

"Anyway, I asked Margret if there's been any news lately. And she tells me some nasty guys are driving around in trucks all around here. Them, and some tall blond guy."

I cringe at the description. Connor.

Curtis continues, "They're causing a lot of trouble. Roughing people up. Supposedly looking for someone. Don't suppose that someone is one of you two?"

I say nothing, but I don't need to. Curtis can read my worries like a book.

"Hmm. That's what I thought. In that case, you two will wanna be extra careful. These guys are nasty, from what I hear. And you'll probably want to leave as soon as you can. They've been going house to house, looking for you. Only a matter of time till they make it here."

Zach and I shoot worried looks at each other. Our time here has been nice, but I knew it would have to end soon. We can't afford to wait with the FLA and Connor hot on our trail.

"Now for the next thing," Curtis says. "You're headed west over Snoqualmie Pass, I assume. Am I right?"

Even though I like Curtis and have no reason not to trust him, talking about specific plans with anybody makes me apprehensive. "I think so. But I want to keep all options open."

"Well, if you're going to make it through the Cascades, you have limited options. Even though it's June, we had a big snowpack last winter. Since that glacier melted, it messed with the jet stream. We had a record winter last year. Snoqualmie Pass is your best bet. Stevens Pass and Cayuse Pass won't be free of snow until August."

I'm getting a sinking feeling. I hate the idea of another pinch point. The last one was at the Columbia River, and we barely made it through that alive. Curtis gets up from the table, roots around in his desk for a bit, then takes out a map. He returns to the table and sets it down in front of us.

"As I see it, you have three options." Curtis points to the map. "You can take Interstate 90. That's by far the easiest option, but it leaves you the most exposed. Right at the pass here, the freeway is a hundred feet or more above that valley. If you run into those thugs, there's nowhere to run."

"Yeah, we'll want to avoid the freeway," I say.

"I agree. That leaves you with Forest Service road 58 here." He points to a small line on the map. It runs near I-90 but charts its own path. "That may be your best bet. But there still may be snow on it. And nobody's plowing those roads anymore."

He moves his finger south on the map. "Or you go through the Snoqualmie Train Tunnel here. It's over two miles long, so you'll need a reliable light source."

Zach shoots me an uncomfortable look. Our last tunnel experience was less than ideal. All the Infected bodies I had to avoid and the jump over haunt my mind. But I shove the memory aside, squeezing the bridge of my nose to relieve the tension. "Yeah, not a whole lotta good options. But thanks for the advice."

Curtis nods.

I point to the map. "Can I keep this?"

"Absolutely."

*

Later that night, Zach and I sit together by the fire. I need Zach to understand the actual risks we face. For the first time, he has a realistic choice. He could choose to stay here. Without me or the vials, it'd be less risky for him. I need to let him decide what he wants to do.

"Zach, we need to talk."

He looks at me, scanning my face. "That sounds ominous."

"You made me promise we'd make important decisions together. Well, in order for you to make those decisions, you need to know the truth. The problem is, the truth is extremely dangerous. Even *knowing* it is dangerous. Before I say more, I need you to understand this."

Zach grabs my hands and looks me in the eye. "I'm ready."

"Okay." I nod slowly. "What I've been carrying. I need to get it to the emergency bunker at the UW. One of our sister stations. They've isolated a key compound of the Infection. Something only they've been able to replicate. All they need are the lab samples I've been carrying. With them, they can synthesize a cure."

Zach's eyes open wide. "Aiden, that's amazing."

"It is. But it's also perilous. If these samples fall into the wrong hands, someone could turn them into a weapon. I need to protect these with my life. I made an oath. And if there comes a time when I have to decide between my life and protecting the vials. Then, well—"

Zach's expression becomes solemn as the weight of my statement settles. "I'm not leaving you, Aiden."

"*Your* life is at risk too. You have a genuine choice, Zach. You could stay here with Curtis. I could come back and get you when it's done."

"I'm *not* leaving you." Zach says it with such intensity it borders on anger. "Honestly, after all we've been through together, I can't believe you're even suggesting this."

"Zach, I'm giving you a choice, like you asked me to."

"I appreciate that, but it's not really a choice. No place is safe. No choice is without risk. And if I have a chance to be with you? Especially if I can make a real difference? There's only one option. Tell me you feel the same way too."

"Yes, of course," I say, but I'm not sure how well I sell it.

"Okay," Zach says, but his eyes are narrow. "We're in this together until the end, no matter what. Right?"

"Right."

I say it instinctively because I'm too afraid to say any differently with the way Zach reacted. I'll stand by his side under all circumstances except one. I will *not* let Zach die for my cause. I care for him more than I can express. A few weeks ago, I wasn't sure I was capable of this level of emotion anymore. And it's come on quicker and more intensely than it ever has before.

If the choice ever came to where us splitting up could save his life, then that's what I'll do, even if it means losing Zach.

Chapter Thirty-Two

No Good Options

ZACH

We wake up before dawn the next day, prepared to leave. Curtis cooks up a wonderful breakfast to send us off. But nobody is in a chatty mood. I stare down at my food for nearly the entire meal. Curtis has been such a good friend, and I'll miss him.

As we finish the last bites, Curtis breaks the silence. "Boys, there's one more thing I need to tell you."

Aiden and I look up. Curtis's eyebrows wrinkle, and his face is strained.

"There's no easy way to say this, so I'll blurt it right out. I'm not long for this world."

My chest tightens. "Don't talk like that. You've got years ahead of you." I search his eyes for reassurance.

"I'm afraid not. Just before the Great Collapse, I was diagnosed with stage four liver cancer. The doctor said I had six months tops. I've beat that by a long shot, but I can tell things are getting worse. At this point, every day is a gift." He lets out a little laugh, but his eyes look glassy.

I reach over and hug him.

"Oh, Curtis, I'm so sorry," Aiden joins in.

"Hey, I've had a good life. And helping you two out has meant a lot to me. I have few regrets."

The tears are flowing freely now, and Aiden looks the same. I've only known Curtis for a few days, but he's one of the kindest and most gentle people I've ever met.

"What I said earlier about you two coming back? I meant it. When you're finished doing whatever it is you need to do, this place can be yours. I'd be happy to know there'd be somebody caring for it."

"We'd like that," I say, and Aiden nods in agreement.

"And please, don't forget to deliver that letter," Curtis says.

I tap the left breast pocket of my jacket, where I've stowed the letter. "I won't forget."

Curtis is generous to a fault. He outfits us with a new backpack to make up for our lost one. He stocks it full of food that will travel well. Cured meat, hard cheeses, and some fruits and vegetables. He also gives me a vial filled with oral antibiotics to ensure I fully recover from my leg wound.

We gather outside as the sun peaks over the horizon. There's no more delaying. Now is the time we must leave. Aiden gives Curtis a big hug, and

I follow suit.

"Thank you so much for everything," I say, burying my face in his shoulder.

"I only did what any other decent person would do."

There's not a dry eye among us.

As we start to walk away, Curtis yells out to us. "Watch out for those nasty folks looking for you. Stay clear of the main roads and freeways. And always watch your back."

"We've been dodging these guys since Montana," Aiden says. "We'll keep our eyes open."

Curtis's face looks grave when he hears this. "Be careful, you two. I couldn't stand the thought of anything happening to you."

"We will," I say, giving Curtis a reassuring nod.

As we head into the forest, on the way to the trail, we both stop to look back. Curtis stands at the edge of the farm, watching us leave. He gives us one last wave, and we wave back. Then we turn and head off into the trees.

*

Hiking along the trail is easier than ever. Perhaps it's because I'm healed and well-rested. Perhaps it's because I'm with the guy I love. And yes, I love him. I'm not ready to say it out loud yet. I don't want to add more pressure on him, but the feeling is unmistakable.

The trail continues along the Yakima River, matching each curve. The river is tranquil, with the smallest current creating swirls and eddies. Farmlands give way to woods as we approach the eastern side of the Cascade foothills.

After a few hours, our trail goes under a freeway overpass. We cross Interstate 90 again. After our last near miss, we approach the intersection with care. We keep our eyes and ears open for cars, ready to jump off the trail should one come.

Just as we pass I-90, a loud rustling comes from the forest. We swing around. Aiden reaches for his rifle. The underbrush moves, and I expect to see either an Infected or the faces of Connor, Wayne, and Tyra running at us with guns blazing.

Instead, a large buck jumps out, so close he almost knocks us over. He stands on the trail, staring us down, looking startled but ready to defend himself. We all stand motionless, each staring into the other's eyes.

The buck moves first, turning and bounding off back into the forest. In an instant, he's gone.

Aiden and I face each other, our eyes wide, mouths open.

"Did we just get spooked by Bambi?" I say with a straight face.

We both crack a smile. And then a rabbit jumps out of the forest, sees us, then scurries back to where it came from, terrified.

"Thumper?" Aiden asks.

And that's it. We both lose it, laughing uncontrollably. I love Aiden's laugh so much. Hearing it makes me laugh harder. At some point, I end up rolling on the grass on the side of the trail, clutching my stomach and gasping for air.

Aiden lands beside me, smiling and giggling. Our giggles trail off, and we lie on the ground facing each other, hands pawing at each other's bodies.

Aiden has a silly grin on his face. "I—um—I like you so much."

Did he almost say *love?*

"Me too."

I go in for a soft kiss. It's gentle and caring. Aiden brushes his hands through my hair as our lips press together, and all I want to do is stay like this forever.

Aiden pulls back and looks into my eyes. "I wish we didn't have to keep going. I could have stayed at the farm with you for the rest of my life."

"I was thinking the same thing. Maybe we'll end up back there." I let out a long sigh. "But for now, we have to finish this."

"Yep." Aiden sits up with his arms clasped around his bent knees. "Let's get it done."

We continue without stopping for the rest of the morning. At around noon, we stop for lunch. We're at the fork of the Yakima and Cle Elum Rivers, sitting on a rocky outcropping near the riverbank. The rivers extend in three directions.

Aiden turns to me as we eat. "I've been thinking about our path through Snoqualmie Pass. I think we should take the Forest Service road. It might be the toughest going, but it gives us the most cover. I for sure don't want to take I-90, and I'm not excited about the tunnel."

The mention of the tunnel makes the hairs on my neck stand up. "Yeah, I agree. I don't want to do that damn tunnel."

"After lunch, we should try to get in about twenty miles, then. Try to get all the way to Keechelus Lake." Aiden points at the map Curtis gave us. "That way, we're close to the pass in the morning, and we have the whole day to get through."

"That sounds like a good plan." I'm not excited about the idea of another twenty miles today, but the going has been easy. I hope my energy level stays high.

We start up again after lunch. The trail no longer follows the river as it has for the last twenty or so miles. Instead, we head alongside the interstate. But it's not too close, and our trail is tucked behind a line of trees.

"I don't love seeing that freeway." I gesture with my head toward it. "Makes me feel exposed."

"Yeah, same here. Let's stay alert."

As we continue along, I keep glancing over, expecting at any moment to see those same damn trucks with their damn flags flapping. Nothing approaches. It must be my imagination, but things keep appearing in the corner of my vision. A slight motion. A splash of color. But each time I turn to look, there's nothing there. "This may sound paranoid, but I'd swear somebody is watching us."

"Just because you're paranoid doesn't mean people aren't out to get you." Aiden smiles.

"Have *you* seen anything strange?"

"Nope. Maybe you *are* just paranoid."

I whack him on the shoulder. "Shut up!"

Aiden laughs.

After a few hours, our trail veers to the left, leaving the interstate behind. I'm glad I no longer have to glance over my shoulder every minute.

Our surroundings have changed distinctly—the forest denser, the trail gaining elevation, and the air a little crisper. An occasional patch of snow appears, hiding in a gully or shady spot. We've moved to the edge of the Cascade Mountains.

"Aiden, what do you plan to do when we're done? When this is all over."

He looks over at me with a scrunched face. "That's a good question. Originally, I imagined I'd stay at the bunker for a while. See if they had any local courier jobs for me there. And at some point, make my way back to the East Coast, I guess."

He takes my hand, and smiles. "But now, I'm not so sure. Are you thinking about what Curtis said? About the farm?"

"Yeah. I was crushed to hear about his cancer. But I can't help but think it's fate's way of telling us we should take it over. To honor him."

"A lot will happen between now and when we need to make that decision. We still need to track down your family, for instance."

"*We?*" I beam at him. The end of our trip isn't something we've talked about. I wasn't sure if he planned to help me.

"Yes, we." He grabs both of my hands and looks me in the eye. "We're in this together. Remember?"

The earnestness of his statement makes me glow. He intends to stay and help me. Before now, I wasn't sure of his plans. My love for him grows with each kind gesture he makes. Each selfless act.

I want to tell him I love him. To scream it out loud to the world. And I'm pretty sure he loves me too. But to say it to him now is too risky. I'd be a mess if he weren't ready to say it back to me. So I'll wait.

Instead, I say *I love you* with the warmth of my smile. The look in my eyes. And he returns that look. That's enough for now.

*

AIDEN

Melting snowdrifts are a common sight now, streaked with dirt. The sudden coldness and increase in the snow make me apprehensive. The more snow we encounter, the more complicated our crossing becomes. Zach's face looks calm and content. Seeing him steadies my nerves a bit. Maybe things won't be so bad.

We trudge across slush and mud along some shady spots on the trail. All the while, the sun is still bright and warm in the clear blue sky. But the difference in temperature between the sunny and shady spots is dramatic. The thin air of the higher altitudes doesn't hold as much warmth. When we're not standing in the sun, it gets downright chilly.

It's early evening when we get to the shores of Keechelus Lake. An old primitive campsite looks ideal for setting up our tent for the night. The lake is beautiful and stretches on for miles.

The Snoqualmie ski area is far off to the north. Ski runs crisscross the otherwise forested hills and white alpine peaks. That's where we'll be tomorrow when we hit the Snoqualmie Pass.

Like the night before we crossed the Columbia River, I'm a bundle of nerves. But the mix of feelings is different. I'm more in control. Zach will be with me this time. And while I fear for our safety, knowing he'll be by my side somehow fills me with more confidence. More hope.

Snow blankets most of the ground here, but we find a nice dry patch to set up our tent. Despite it being a colder evening, we go without a fire tonight. Best not to telegraph our position to any prying eyes the day before we go over the pass.

We eat a cold but delicious meal, care of Curtis. Cured meats, cheeses, and a rustic baguette he baked in his oven last night. The food is a delicacy we haven't experienced since before the Great Collapse.

When we finally go to bed, we snuggle up tight into the one sleeping bag. It's cold enough outside that we're still in our clothes. It's a bit of tor-ture not being able to feel Zach's bare skin against mine.

The next morning, we awaken with the sun lighting up the tent. We have a small, cold breakfast, pack up, and head out. Neither of us are talkative. We're focused on our next objective. Getting through the pass. We continue on the trail to the north. Snow covers it completely now, with the occasional patch of dirt showing the only hint of where to go. Before us, the ski areas loom closer.

Soon, ski lifts dot the hillside on our left, heading up a ridge forming Snoqualmie Pass's southern border. The lifts are in serious disrepair, with several chairs falling down. Snow still covers the ski hill. Before the Great Collapse, this would mean a great spring skiing season. But now, worry consumes me, wondering what the conditions of the Forest Service roads will be.

We come to a left bend in the trail. Farther down, I spot the entrance to the train tunnel. Zach makes a nervous twitch at the sight of it.

"Don't worry," I say. "We're not headed that way. This is where we get off the trail." I guide us up an embankment to the right and onto a road.

Snoqualmie Summit isn't so much a town as it is a patchwork of vacation homes and businesses, all serving the four small ski areas that dot the surrounding hillsides. We go north through the streets, keeping an eagle eye out for any movement. The little town is quiet and empty.

Off to our right is Interstate 90. At the northern edge of Snoqualmie Pass, the massive freeway bends westward, heading through a tight choke point between two mountain peaks.

We take an access road that runs under the freeway, then turn to the west ourselves, onto the Forest Service road. Much of the snow has melted at the top of the summit, where sunlight hits it. There's only an inch or so on the ground, and the going is easy.

But soon, the road descends into a large ravine. Sun has not permeated here as much, and our boots sink several inches into the snow. The ravine acts as a natural collection point of snow falling from the peaks on either side.

From below, the freeway is an impressive sight. There must be at least ten lanes across on both sides. Massive pillars hold it over the deep ravine, looking like the gigantic legs of some ancient creature. It must be a hundred fifty feet above us now. Its shadow casts across the whole valley.

We continue, but soon the snow is up to my knees, and my pants are getting wet. The going is slow; I'm not even sure we're still following a road. The lack of trees in our path is our only clue.

I glance at Zach. He gives me a meager smile. He's doing his best to trudge along. But the snow only gets worse. It's nearly up to my waist, and continuing becomes serious work. Just moving my leg to the next position is an exercise in frustration.

Zach breaks the silence. "I don't think this is going to work."

Even turning to him is a struggle because of the snow. "Yeah, I don't think we can continue this way."

Zach lets out a deep sigh. "The tunnel, huh?"

"I know it's not your favorite idea. If it's any consolation, I'm not excited about it either."

Zach laughs. "I'm not sure if that makes me feel better or worse."

"The point is, I don't think it's going to be fun. But it might be our only option."

Zach nods. "Yeah, I've been psyching myself up for that as soon as the snow was knee-high. Okay, let's turn this ship around."

Going back is easier. Even though we're going uphill, we use the existing path we've already made through the snow. Zach is up front now, and I follow behind him. But then Zach stops and looks back at me with a quizzical expression.

"Is it just me, or does it look like there's an extra set of footprints in the snow here?" Zach says.

I lean down and inspect the prints. "Well, I for sure see our prints. But yeah, right here, it almost looks like another set veers off our path."

Zach starts scanning around with a worried expression.

"But maybe that was just one of us pausing for a moment to look around," I say. "I remember a few times when I did that."

Zach nods but doesn't appear too reassured. "Or, maybe someone *is* following us. Maybe I'm not paranoid."

"Well, let's for sure keep our eyes open."

All told, our detour took a little over two hours. It's about midmorning by the time we get back to the tunnel.

We find a spot to have an early lunch nearby to observe the entrance. As we eat, we lie in the sun, trying to dry our shoes and pants, soaked from our little snow adventure.

There's no sign of life or movement around the tunnel the entire time we sit there.

"Okay, are you ready to do this?" I ask.

Zach shoots me a worried look. "No. But there's no other choice. Let's go."

We head back down to the trail toward the Snoqualmie Train Tunnel.

Chapter Thirty-Three

The Tunnel

ZACH

Aiden and I approach the tunnel side by side. A blast of cool air shoots out, sending goosebumps across my exposed skin. It's like walking into a refrigerator. Before entering, we check our flashlights to ensure they have fresh batteries. Aiden has his rifle at the ready, pointed downward in his folded right hand.

"Here goes nothing," I say as we walk into the darkness.

The tunnel is tall and wide, curved at the top. It starts out heading northward but gradually bends to the left, due west. Soon, light from the entrance disappears. We're in total darkness, save what our flashlights reveal.

The temperature has dropped dramatically, with water dripping from the ceiling. At certain points, the drips are more like a steady downpour, and it's impossible to avoid a few landing on my head, making me flinch every time. Each step risks a twisted ankle as large divots in the path have formed where the water falls into pools.

Once we've completed the bend westward, a tiny pinprick of light is visible far off to the west. The exit to the tunnel.

"Looks like it's a straight shot through. That doesn't look so bad," I say. The sight of our exit gives me the slightest bit of relief.

"Yeah. That's still a long way off though. The whole thing is over two miles, so expect it to take a while."

It doesn't take *a while*. It takes *forever*. We keep on, and the pinprick doesn't seem to get any bigger. The cold is getting to me, and my whole body is shaking. My hands are the worst. The flashlight feels like an icicle. I alternate back and forth, letting one hand warm up in my pocket as the other one shines a light on our path.

Every hundred feet, an indentation in the wall holds old rusted wiring poking out of metal boxes. In one indentation, a dirty, cracked porcelain doll sits against the wall. Its dead eyes stare at me as we pass.

After a half hour, the exit is more defined, with the shape of the tunnel now a crisp arch of daylight. We're getting close. That's when a faint sound comes from behind us.

It's barely audible at first. It could almost be mistaken for the wind blowing through the tunnel. But then it gets louder and more defined. Soon the noise is recognizable. The sound of motors.

We both look back. Two little pinpricks of light curve around the bend, nearly two miles back. They are approaching at great speed. As they get nearer, we can make out the high-pitched sound of revving engines.

Without speaking, both Aiden and I take off at a full run. The sound of the engines gets closer. The whine echoes throughout the tunnel into a deafening crescendo. Aiden fumbles with his rifle as we run.

We're getting closer to the exit. Only fifty feet away now. We're going to make it. Our pursuers are gaining, but our exit is nearby.

Aiden shouts at me over the engines. "When we get outside, jump to our right. We'll try to lose them in the forest."

I nod.

We're nearing the entrance, now only twenty feet away.

But then silhouettes of three people appear from outside, all holding rifles pointed right at us. The silhouette in the middle is taller, and coming from it, that dreaded and unmistakable voice. Connor.

"Drop the gun! Right now!"

Two dirt bikes roll up from behind. The sickening stench of exhaust fills my lungs.

Aiden looks at me and then at the men. He's holding back, worrying about my safety.

"Do what you need to do," I say to him, loud enough to be heard by all.

Aiden's eyes look pained. "I'm sorry." He throws the rifle on the ground near Connor's feet. My heart sinks.

When Aiden's gun hits the ground, the people swarm us. A shove in my back sends me smashing into the ground, face first. My hands blunt my fall but cut against the jagged gravel.

Aiden falls next to me. They take our packs, then bind our arms behind our backs. For a moment, we face each other. In his eyes is a profound sadness. I want to lean into him to tell him I love him. As I start to, hands grab me ruthlessly from behind.

They lift and shove us toward Connor and all the usual suspects. It's the same group that's been chasing us all the way from Elk Springs. Wayne and Tyra are behind us. The man with the gray goatee is on Connor's left, and a bald man with huge muscles covered with tattoos is on Connor's right.

Connor walks up to Aiden with a smug expression. "Aiden, old friend. Surprised to see me?"

Aiden says nothing, only looking at Connor with disgust.

"You two really are predictable." Connor lets out a little laugh. "You had to know I'd have people watching the tunnel. The second you went in, I had you trapped."

"Why are you doing this, Connor?" Aiden's face looks deeply sad.

"I need those vials. We finally get to finish our business on the bridge when you stole my vials and left me for dead."

"You fell off the bridge. I thought you died."

Connor shakes his head, jaw clenched. "You looked right at me, then ran off and left. Denying it is an insult to my intelligence. I had to kill to save your life. Then you left me to die."

"But I saw you fall into the mist near the valley floor, over a hundred feet down. No one could survive that."

Connor raises an eyebrow, a shadow of doubt flashing for a moment. "I didn't fall. My leg got tangled in construction netting below the bridge deck. You really didn't see me?"

"No." Realization dawns on Aiden's face. "*That* was how you survived. But then who did I see—*oh shit*—it was the guy you knocked over the bridge."

Connor pauses for a long moment. His usual cocky assurance looks shaken the slightest bit. A small chink in his armor.

"Connor," Aiden says in a steady voice. "Let us go. It's not too late. Nothing you've done is irredeemable. We used to be friends."

A shallow laugh comes from Connor. "If you knew everything I've done, you wouldn't say that."

"What do you mean?"

Connor almost looks regretful. But then he brushes it off, and the regular Connor reappears. "It doesn't matter. The result is the same. You took vials from me. Now I'm taking vials from you."

"You don't have to do this, Connor," Aiden pleads.

Connor's face darkens. "You more than anyone know that I have to do this. The Collective has to be stopped. I gave you your chance to help me, but you turned it down."

"The Collective is our one chance to *cure* the Infection."

Connor laughs. "Cure it? They just want to alter the damn thing to make it more powerful. With it, they can control the Infected. Build a whole army. You're a pawn, Aiden."

"Is that what you're planning on doing? Building an army?" Aiden shakes his head in disgust.

"I'm going to stop the Collective from playing god. When that's done, *I'll* find the cure."

"But you'd need a lab and the expertise."

"Don't worry about that," Connor snaps. "I've recruited enough scientists to do what I want. Unlike you, they understood their responsibility when they discovered the Collective created the Infection."

"But the Collective didn't create it!" Aiden shouts. "The military did."

My head spins at what Aiden just said.

Wait, what?

"What do you mean, they *created* the Infection?" I ask Aiden. "It's man-made?"

Aiden hangs his head. "It is."

"And you *knew* this?"

"I found out just before I left."

My head is reeling. Connor told me this at the dam, but I dismissed it as a lie. The idea that all this death was caused by something man-made makes me feel ill.

Connor is clearly pleased with our exchange. He gestures to Wayne, who's holding on to the small aluminum box. *Aiden's box.* Aiden struggles with his bonds but gets shoved in the back and falls to his knees.

Connor takes the box and opens it. Inside, packed in molded foam padding, are the three vials of pale green liquid. He holds one up to my face. "This has the power to kill everyone. And the Collective has known it all along. And so has Aiden."

I shake my head. It can't be the truth. Aiden said he was transporting a *cure*. "That isn't the actual Infection, right?"

Aiden lets out a long breath. "To make a cure, they need one thing." Aiden keeps his eyes pegged to the ground. "The original weaponized XT58 created by the military. Not the one out in the wild."

I feel the blood drain from my face, with the swirling green liquid in the vial just inches away. How could Aiden have kept this from me?

Connor sees my fear, and his mouth curves into a smile. "*Wait.* You aren't immune, are you, Zach?"

I say nothing as panic rises.

Now it's Aiden's turn to be shell-shocked as he looks at me in horror. "But—your uncle—You're immune, right?"

He searches my face for an answer, but I can't look at him. I never told Aiden the true story about my uncle, that I left him outside to die. That he never exposed me, and I'm likely not immune.

Connor gives a sad laugh. "Another nice *feature* of this weaponized Infection. It's concentrated enough that if I twisted off the cap of this vial, just breathing it would doom you to a horrific death. Or worse." He shakes his head, then puts the vial back in the case and hands it to Wayne.

"Don't worry. Unlike the Collective, I wouldn't wish *that* death on anyone. But you're too dangerous, Aiden. You've proven that. I can't have you chasing after me and ruining my plans. There's too much at stake. This gives me no pleasure." Connor points to a spot along the wall of the tunnel.

Wayne forces me to the wall and shoves me down on my knees. Aiden lands next to me and looks into my eyes with a sorrowful gaze.

"I'm sorry, Zach."

My whole body is numb. I'm incapable of words.

The sound of a rifle cocking echoes through the tunnel. I clench my eyes closed, unable to watch. There's so much left I have to say to Aiden. There's so much more I want to do. Instead, I wait for eternal nothingness.

A gunshot rings out, and a body hits the ground next to me. It must be Aiden. Another shot. That one is for me. But I feel nothing. My mind has spared me from the pain.

Then another shot, and another.

Huh?

I open my eyes to see Wayne on the ground staring up at me, his eyes staring with an expression of anguish, but he's unmoving. Turning to my left, Tyra and the man with the gray goatee are down too. All shot dead.

Aiden is next to me. *And he's still alive.*

I'm so light I could float away. And Aiden looks how I feel. Surprised, relieved, and terrified, all mixed together.

Connor and the man with the tattoos shoot down the tunnel indiscriminately. The flash of rifle fire breaks through the darkness deep in the tunnel. The next shot hits the tattooed man in the face. He falls into Connor, who reels in disgust. Another gunshot rings out, and Connor turns and runs.

A man walks out of the darkness, holding a rifle—a large man in blue-jean overalls.

Curtis.

He's saved us.

He must have been the one following us this whole time when I thought I was being paranoid. But as he gets closer, he's clutching his side, where a red stain spreads across his overalls.

"Hey, boys. I knew you were going to need help. With those guys hot on your trail, I couldn't stay back and do nothing. I had to watch out for you." He takes a knife out of his pocket and cuts the zip ties binding our hands.

Then he collapses in a heap on the ground.

*

AIDEN

"Curtis!" Zach runs over to him.

While Zach checks on Curtis, I scan the area, trying to absorb everything that happened. Four people lie dead on the ground. All of Connor's mercenaries. But Connor is nowhere to be seen.

I grab the rifle that I dropped earlier and approach the tunnel exit. Peeking my head out, I scan the trail and the surrounding woods. No sign of Connor. Back in the tunnel, Zach is at Curtis's side. And Curtis doesn't look well. His face is pale, and a pool of blood has formed beneath him.

Zach looks up at me. "We need to get some pressure on—"

"No, you don't," Curtis cuts in, straining, using his last bit of energy to talk. "I'll be gone in a minute. I can feel it. Plus, this is a helluva better way to go than sitting around waiting for the cancer to eat me alive."

"Don't talk like that, Curtis. We're going to get you fixed up." Zach's looking frantically at the ever-growing blood stain on Curtis's overalls.

"Just glad I could—ugh—help you two one last time." Each word is a struggle. "The letter. Don't forget—" He trails off. His eyes are open, staring upward. But Curtis is gone.

Zach weeps openly. I'm crying too. I put my arm around him, and he buries his face into my chest. I try to make sense of what just happened. Any of the bodies lying here could have easily been Zach. And if he's really not immune to the Infection, having him anywhere near me is dangerous beyond comprehension. His immunity was a constant for me. I never doubted it. I dread what I must do, and I worry Zach will never forgive me.

After a moment, I whisper into his ear. "Zach, I know you won't want to hear this. But it's time to go."

"We can't just leave him here like this." Zach looks down at Curtis with a pained expression.

"We'll come back for him. But Connor is still out there, and he could be back any minute. He might have reinforcements. We need to leave.

Now."

I pull Zach up. He's clutching Curtis's body, but I tear him away.

Then I take him by the shoulders and look him in the eye. I need to convince him this is the right thing to do. But I'll be breaking the one promise I made to him. The one I knew I couldn't keep if it came to protecting his life. I don't know how he'll react. "Zach, there's something else I need to say. With you not immune, it's too dangerous for you to be around the vials. We'll meet up after I'm done, but I have to finish this alone."

"What?" Zach reels away from me, looking like I slapped him. "You said we'd stay together! You promised me!"

"That was before I knew you weren't immune. You were never exposed by your uncle, were you? Why didn't you tell me?"

Zach looks wretched. "Because I was too damn ashamed, that's why. I let him die alone on the porch. And you kept assuming I was immune. I never said it once. You did!"

"You should have told me."

"Just like you should have told me what was in those vials!"

"I couldn't do that—"

"I'm sick of hearing that!" His face transforms into a twisted mix of sadness and anger. "Do you realize Connor was more truthful to me than you were?"

That hits me like a punch in the gut, and my anger rises. "How can you say that? Connor is a traitor. He tried to kill us. I took an oath to the Collective."

"Didn't you make an oath to me too? When will you trust me enough to let me take my own risks?"

"Look what happened." I gesture to Curtis. "That could easily have been you. It almost *was* you. I couldn't live with myself if you died. And you being near the vials? If I so much as set my backpack down too hard, I might have killed you."

Tears flow down Zach's cheeks, but he grits his teeth in anger, and he's breathing hard. Seeing him like this is tearing me apart.

"I need to finish this on my own. We can arrange to meet—"

"Fine, Aiden! If you want to go alone, then just go!" Zach shakes his head. "Better yet, I'll go!" He pushes past me, then runs over to one of the bikes, grabbing his backpack on the way. He jumps on and starts the engine.

"Zach, wait!" I run over toward him.

He revs up the dirt bike. "Goodbye, Aiden."

"How will I find you again?" I yell desperately as he speeds away.

I run to the other dirt bike. Maybe if catch up, I talk some sense into him. I only want to split up as long as I still carry the vials. It would be too dangerous to have him around.

The vials. Where's the box?

Wayne was holding it when Curtis saved us. I run over to Wayne's body to search for it. The little aluminum box I've been protecting lies on the ground beside him. There's a hole in the side of it. I swipe the box off the ground and open it. A bullet has entered and exited cleanly through. But the bullet smashed one vial to pieces.

Oh fuck.

The bullet's impact would have dispersed XT58 throughout the tunnel. Zach *must* have been exposed. There's a pain in my chest, and my heads swims, nearly falling over.

"Zach!" I cry out with all the air in my lungs. But it's useless. The sound of his dirt bike has faded into the distance.

I grab my backpack, stow the vials, then hop onto the other bike. But the engine won't start. That's when the smell of gasoline hits me. The gas tank is riddled with bullet holes with a puddle of fuel collecting on the tunnel floor.

"Fuck!" I smash my fists on the instrument panel of the bike.

How did I handle that so terribly? I didn't think he'd run off like that. I thought we could work it out. But with everything that happened, it's hard to blame him. And as usual, my efforts to protect Zach have put him in even greater danger.

I've got to try to find him. I hop off the bike, then push it by the handlebars until I'm out of the tunnel. A gravel trail runs to the west, heading downward and cutting through the forest. I'm right at the top of Snoqualmie Pass, so hopefully, this trail descends for a long time, and I can coast down.

I run along the trail, holding on to the bike to work up some speed, then hop on. The bike picks up momentum on the sloping trail, which continues as far as I can see. I tuck my head and use the brakes sparingly. At one point, the speedometer hits forty. With any luck, this bike can get me most of the way to Seattle. Or, at the very least, to a town where I can try to find a car.

The entire way down, I process my new reality. Zach is probably *not* immune, and he's most likely been exposed. If that's the case, his symptoms will start soon. I glance at the Casio watch Zach gave me. It's Saturday, 11:45 a.m. Tomorrow morning, he'll start coughing and feeling fatigued. By tomorrow night, he'll feel terrible, with fever and chills. On Monday, he'll barely be able to move. Most people don't make it much past day three. But those who do...*fuck*. The thought of Zach going through that makes my whole chest ache.

He's most likely headed to his parent's home on Vashon Island, but I have no idea where on the island it is. The only thing I know is that their house is on the water. But Vashon Island is huge, so that doesn't narrow things down enough for me to try to find him there.

As much as it tears me up, my best bet is to finish the job. I'll head to the bunker at UW Medical Center and deliver the vials so they can synthesize a cure. Without that, I'm of no help to Zach, anyway. Then maybe I can figure out a way to track him down. I shake my head. My plan seems hopeless.

As I continue downward, I'm wracked with this overwhelming guilt. Even if I deliver the vials, find the cure, and somehow find Zach, will he ever forgive me? I may have ruined the best thing that's happened in my life. Only time will tell.

Chapter Thirty-Four

Secrets Can Kill

ZACH

The world flies by in a blur as I race down Interstate 90 through the foothills of the Cascade Mountains, weaving the bike around stopped cars and the occasional multivehicle pileup. A glance at the speedometer shows 110 miles per hour. It's reckless, but I don't care.

There's an aching in my chest. None of the heartache I felt with Felix has been anything like this. I love Aiden so fiercely, and I feel betrayed. An actual pain aches right under my skin.

How could Aiden have done that after everything we just went through? He promised me we'd stay together. He didn't trust me enough to tell me about the vials, make my own decisions, or take my own risks.

This is probably for the best. Aiden will never change. Better to end things now than fall further in love with him and have to dig out of a deeper hole later. He's doing me a favor.

I only wish I could believe that.

Maybe I should have told him about my uncle and that I didn't think I was immune. It might have prevented this mess. But I kept quiet. I feared he'd think less of me and might even leave me. Given how he reacted, that's probably the truth.

But I should have heard him out. I ran off so upset. He was only trying to protect me, as always. Maybe if I turned around now, I could still catch him. Maybe we could work things out.

I slam on the brakes, making black streaks on the pavement, and turn the bike around. On the entire trip back, my mind is a mess. What will I say? What will *he* say? Can we repair the damage done? But all those thoughts are for naught. When I roll up to the tunnel exit, the scene of all that carnage, my hopes are crushed. The second dirt bike is gone.

And Aiden is gone.

I'm too late. And I have no way of finding him. I'm all alone.

Helplessness spreads over me. How could I have acted so rashly? I was blinded by anger and hurt. With my head hanging low, I speed away. There's only one thing left to do. I'm heading home. To Vashon Island to track down Mom, Dad, and Felix.

Before the Great Collapse, a ferry ran between Seattle and Vashon. But that's not an option now for obvious reasons. Instead, I'm headed to the family sailboat, which I can use to sail home. It's moored in a marina just south of Seattle.

As I race down the interstate on the bike, small towns nestled into the foothills fly by me. I take the occasional peek to either side as I enter the sprawl of the Seattle area. Vines have taken over many structures, and several buildings have burned to the ground, but for the most part, things don't seem too apocalyptic. Just deserted and run down.

But the farther I go, the more the destruction wrought by the Great Collapse rears its ugly head. A large section of South Seattle, once dominated by shipyards and warehouses, is now below several feet of water and an extension of Elliott Bay.

To the north, the skyline of downtown Seattle is like a scene from a disaster movie. Half the skyscrapers are gone. Collapsed, likely from saltwater entering their foundations. The remaining ones are in ruins, some charred black from fires long ago, all with broken windows and toppled facades.

I shudder at the thought of what I might find at my parent's house. Suddenly, Aiden's absence is harder to bear. He was going to help me through this. He'd be here to comfort me and would know what to do if I encountered problems. But what's done is done. I don't know where he is, and I'll likely never find him. I can't undo that choice now, as much as I'd like to.

I continue heading west, cutting through the southern part of Seattle, changing course several times, navigating water-covered streets, collapsed bridges, and fallen trees. After countless detours and backtracking, I get to the South Seattle Marina. The briny scent of Puget Sound assaults my nose.

But I'm met with a scene of devastation. Where row upon row of boats used to be moored in floating docks lining the shore, now, twisted hunks of metal and fiberglass lie, half submerged in water. Masts, ripped sails, boat hulls, and pieces of dock tangle together, stretching a hundred feet in both directions along the shoreline. The only intact boats sit lopsided in lawns and parking lots, deposited by a storm surge that receded months ago.

The few remaining marina buildings are submerged up to their roofs. The new shoreline is two hundred feet inland from where it once lay.

"Well, crap," I say to no one. There goes my plan to sail home.

Just to my west, the emerald-green island of Vashon rises from the waters of Puget Sound, dotted with trees. It's a mere two miles away, across a long channel of icy water. So close, but no way to get there.

I get off the bike and search around, getting a sense of the damage, trying to see if anything resembles a seaworthy vessel. And that's when I spot it—a large metal structure a few hundred feet down the coastline—a dry dock for boats needing repairs out of the water. My family used one when we damaged the keel of our sailboat.

Before the sea-level rise, the dry dock would have been at the shore, but now several feet of water surround it. And to my delight, a thirty-foot Catalina sailboat is suspended by several large straps attached to large chains.

I wade into waist-deep water to check it out. The water chills me to the core, but I press on. After a quick inspection, the boat seems to be in decent sailing shape. It was about two-thirds of the way through having its underside repainted. But other than that, there aren't any apparent problems. Protective blue canopies cover the sails and the cockpit, keeping out the harmful effects of salt water and inclement weather. I couldn't be luckier.

It doesn't take long to figure out the winching system to lower the sailboat. Fortunately, it's an all-manual affair. A large handle attaches to multiple gears, which raise and lower the boat.

In a short while, I've got the sailboat into the water, the harnesses removed, and the mainsail unfurled. A quick inspection of the rigging all checks out. It looks like a pretty simple boat to sail. Easily handled by one person who knows what they're doing. It's been well over a year since I did any sailing, but it should come back to me quickly.

A short while later, I'm in the cockpit, using the power of the wind to head to my home on Vashon Island.

*

AIDEN

The trail has gone steadily downward for miles, with a few exceptions where I had to kick along the ground for a while. But my luck doesn't last forever. After two hours of coasting, the trail levels out completely. It continues, totally flat, as far as the eye can see. So, I hop off the bike and walk, pushing it by the handlebars, hoping there's more downhill to come. As best I can tell, I've made it about halfway from Snoqualmie Pass to the outskirts of Seattle.

I can't get my mind off Zach. That look he gave me when I told him we should split up was of someone deeply betrayed. I'll never unsee that expression.

I'm such an idiot. Every time I get the least bit scared for his safety, I push him away. I should have trusted him. Let him make his own decisions and take his own risks. With *all* the facts. And my actions always make it worse for both of us—at Elk Springs, the Columbia River, and now the Snoqualmie Tunnel.

I can only imagine how he felt being left alone on the side of the Columbia River, waking up to find me gone. I didn't even have the courage to tell him myself. He had to read about it in the note I left for him. The thing is, I always intended for us to get back together. Our separations were never supposed to be permanent.

The note. I just remembered.

I gave him instructions for reuniting if we got separated. *There's a chance to find Zach.* We'd meet at noon at the Black Sun statue in Volunteer Park every Sunday.

Lightness fills my whole body—assuming he remembers what I wrote on the note. And assuming he forgives me and even *wants* to find me. Or, if he started showing symptoms and realizes he's sick. That thought makes *me* feel sick. It's a long shot, but at least it's something. A glance at my watch shows it's 1:45 p.m., Saturday. I have under twenty-three hours to get there.

I pass by a sign by the side of the trail.

Welcome to North Bend

Easy to Reach… Hard to Leave

I make a sad laugh. *That's some bitter irony.* But the good news is, going through a town increases my chances of finding a car. *And increases my danger.* Gradually, homes and abandoned cars show up along a street running parallel to the trail.

A new model Honda Civic slants haphazardly across the road, with a dead body in the driver's seat still decomposing. A grizzly metric for sure, but one that gives me hope this car's battery may be more recently used than many of the others I've found.

The keys are in the ignition.

I reach across the dead body and turn the key. The instrument panel lights up, but the lights are dim. Not totally dead, so that's far better than anything I've seen recently.

That's promising, but I may only get one chance at it. I tug at the passenger. Despite the decomposition, the person in the seat is quite large and hard to budge. I dig deep with all my strength until I drag the body outside the car and onto the ground.

In the driver's seat, I do my best to ignore the sickeningly sweet scent of decay as I put my hand on the keys.

Come on. Please.

As I turn the key, the engine turns over, sounding weak but close to catching. The next time, I give the slightest bit of gas to the engine. The noise gains in tempo but still won't quite start.

Deep sigh. Try again.

This time, the engine sounds weaker. "Fuck, fuck, FUCK!" I slam my hand on the steering wheel. My palm is throbbing and red from the impact. One more try confirms my worry. I've depleted the precious bit of juice remaining in the battery.

Back to fucking square one.

I head out on the trail again, leaving the bike behind. At this point, it's only slowing me down. I don't find any more working cars, and soon, I leave the town behind and enter a dense forest. A thick grove of evergreens lines the trail on both sides.

Then, a glint of something gets my attention in the distance, deep in the trees, almost impossible to see in the light of day. A house nestled in the forest. But there's something unique about it—a barely perceptible splash of light. As I cut through the trees, approaching the property, the forest opens up into a large, neglected lawn. Then what attracted my attention becomes clear.

"The lights." I say out loud to myself, smiling. Sure enough, outdoor sconces line the garage and front door, glowing a subtle shade of amber. Maybe something in there can help me charge the battery of the car I left behind.

Approaching any house has an element of danger. But one that has power is especially likely to be occupied and defended. I carry my rifle at the ready as I walk around, keeping my guard up.

The sprawling house is built in the modern craftsman style, with ga-bled roofs, wood and stone accents, and a massive attached four-car garage. As I circle it, the mystery of the electricity is answered. A bank of whole-home batteries lines the edge of the garage next to the power meter. The back side of the roof is nothing but solid solar panels.

This house has been creating and using electricity for over a year, as seen on the spinning dial of the meter. The house, deep and remote enough in the woods, hasn't attracted attention. Or so I hope. I'll need to keep alert and proceed with caution.

But, if anybody lives here, they haven't mowed the grass in a long while. It extends halfway up my thigh. Nothing else provides any hint that the place is occupied. The lawn furniture in the back has a thick layer of dirt on it, and the cushions are moldy. I walk up to the back door and try the knob. Locked.

Thinking about Zach picking this lock makes me smile but fills me with melancholy. It wouldn't take long for him to make short work of it.

The thought of him hunched over the lock, a look of concentration on his face, gives me a pang. But he's not here. So, like a wrecking ball, I kick the door with all my might. It flies open, taking half the frame with it in a flurry of wooden shrapnel.

"Well, that's another way to do it." I laugh to myself. Zach would have thought that was funny. I miss his laugh.

I walk through the door, gun in hand, eyes darting back and forth. "Hello? Anybody here?"

I carefully search the house. The air is stale, and dust covers every horizontal surface. All signs indicate the house is empty.

But as I head from the family room to the kitchen, a flash of movement stops me. I square up and cock my gun. "Who's there!"

Barreling around the corner, someone knocks me to the ground, and my gun clatters to the floor. A man is on top of me in a flash, frantically trying to scratch me with his jagged nails. Purple veins bulge from his neck. Infected. I grab his wrists before he's able to tear into my flesh.

I'm stronger, but what this guy lacks in strength, he makes up for in intense, manic energy. He's snarling at me like a wild animal, trying to wrench out of my grip.

He snaps his jaws at my face. I have seconds to act with his mouth inches away, so I butt my head against his as hard as possible. It startles him enough for me to shake him off.

On my hands and knees, I scurry to the rifle on the floor beside us. The moment I snatch it, his hand grabs my ankle. His open jaws reach to bite my Achilles. As his teeth start to clench, I swing the butt of the rifle around and whack him on top of the head, and his body crumples.

I lie on the ground momentarily. *Goddamn Infected.* Rare enough that they always manage to take me by surprise. Even with my guard up, I barely escaped unscathed.

After a moment to capture my breath and regain my composure, I get up off the floor. Judging by the man's beard length, I'd guess he only recently got sick. Maybe a month or two ago. He must have been holed up here for a long time, defending this house.

His chest moves, so he's still alive. I leave him behind and search the rest of the house. I plan to be long gone before this guy wakes up.

As I wander farther, I come upon a grizzly sight, but one I'm familiar with. Several other bodies lie in a heap in the hallway. His family, I can only assume. I avert my eyes, not wanting to see what state they are in. I turn the other way and focus on the task at hand.

I hope *something* in this house might help jump-start that car. Maybe a jumping kit like the one Jo gave us. The house is so large it takes some time to find the garage. I accidentally stumble into the wine cellar, the study, and finally, the home theater with multiple rows of black leather recliners.

Doesn't compare to the bank lobby theater. I smile, thinking of Zach and how excited he was to show me a movie. But then the thought of him getting sick enters my mind. Somehow, the images of seeing Marcus dying have morphed with my memories of Zach, and I nearly break down from the thought. After a moment of concerted effort, I collect myself and continue.

I finally find the garage door, open it, and have a reason to smile again. There before me is a navy-blue Audi e-tron electric SUV. The plug sticking out pulses green.

"Holy shit," I say with a wide grin.

To my left, a row of pegs poke out of the wall. One set of keys hangs from them, with a key fob emblazoned with the Audi logo.

I run to the car with keys in hand.

Chapter Thirty-Five

Best Laid Plans

ZACH

The sailboat cuts through the waves of Puget Sound with ease. My sailing technique comes back to me quickly. A northerly wind blows, and I need to head southwest, so I'm doing a lot of tacking and jibing.

Despite constantly adjusting the sails to catch the wind, I'm making good time. I've already crossed the channel from the mainland to Vashon. Now, I'm following the island's perimeter until I reach my parent's home. Nearly there.

I've waited so long for this moment, and now that it's upon me, a horrible dread fills me. I don't think I'm ready to find out the answers I'm about to discover. If only Aiden were here to help me through this. I expected him to be here with me. But the kindness and empathy he's shown me are replaced only by emptiness. How could we have both been so stupid, clinging to our secrets? Protecting them until they tore us apart.

I round the last bend in the coastline. A little cottage sits up on the ridge. The place I grew up. It's an unsettling mixture of familiar and foreign. The house looks in good shape, but the landscaping is unkempt. Ivy and morning glory grow up the side of the house and extend to the roof. Our little beach is gone, submerged beneath feet of seawater. The zigzagging staircase that used to lead down to the shoreline is halfway into the sea.

Normally, I'd have to anchor the sailboat offshore and ride a dinghy to our beach. Instead, I pilot the boat up to the stairs, rising from the water. The wood is slippery and unstable, covered with algae, and never intended to be submerged. I climb the steps with care.

When I reach the top, it's clear the house has been untouched for months. A nervous pit forms inside me. This could mean they abandoned the house and fled elsewhere. Or it could mean the worst.

The house is secure, all the doors and windows locked and intact. The overgrown garden is a maze of weeds and overgrowth. I find a flat rock etched with the phrase *Garden of Weed'n*, and under the rock, the spare key. Still there after all this time.

But something else gets my attention as I turn around to unlock the house—two large stones, deep in the garden. These are new. I've never seen them before. Written across the stones are the names Martha and Frank. My parents' names. The pain of seeing them overwhelms me, and I drop to my knees and start weeping.

Despite what I hoped, this is what I expected to find. But that doesn't help much. Expected or not, their deaths hit me like a sledgehammer as I sob over their graves.

I hoped that somehow, against all odds, fate would reunite me with them. I'd come home, see their smiling faces, and run up to hug them. I'd take in the scent of my mother's hair, with her back from the garden, smelling of flowers and earth. My dad would get a hug so strong I'd never let him get away. Instead, this place is like everywhere else in the world. Dead. Empty. Alone.

After a long while, when my sobs have subsided, I go through the house and find any belongings of theirs to remember them by. I only take a few items. Some family photographs, my dad's watch, and the golden necklace my mom's worn since I was a child.

When I'm done, I let out a long, drawn-out breath. There's one more task on the island—another piece of my past to reconcile. I have to find out Felix's fate. My parents' burial gives me a glimmer of hope that maybe he's alive. Maybe he did it. Felix loved my parents and treated them like his own.

The path from my house to his is forever etched into my memory. I've hiked this route a thousand times. Before we fell in love, we were best friends. We've known each other since the sixth grade.

His family's old farmhouse looks similar in condition to my parents' house. Unscathed but overgrown. As I approach the front door, two wooden crosses staked into the yard come into view. When I get closer, a chill goes over me; I'm afraid of what the markers will reveal.

Scrawled across one is *Allison*, Felix's mom. And on the other, *Felix*.

I'm numb. I have no more tears left to shed. They've all been spent.

For the last year, getting back here was the only thing I wanted. It was my singular focus. And now that I'm here, I've found nothing to return to. It was a fool's errand. All that's left here are the empty shells of my childhood memories in the form of graves. I shouldn't have expected anything else.

And the only thing left in this entire world that I care about is somewhere out there, but I don't know where. Aiden. I'm hollowed out and filled with regret and loneliness.

It's too late to return to the mainland before nightfall, and I'm unsure where I'd go next even if I could. So, I return to my parent's home in stunned silence, barely looking where I'm going.

With so much loss in the last twenty-four hours, my mind can scarcely contain it. I've lost Aiden, lost my parents, lost Felix, and had to witness Curtis's horrific death.

Wait—Curtis's letter.

I reach into my pocket for the envelope Curtis had tasked me to deliver. But as I take it out, another piece of paper drops to the ground. A lump forms in my throat. It's the letter Aiden wrote me the night he left me at the dam. I read through half of it and get swept up in conflicting emotions. It's the closest thing to a love letter that Aiden has ever written me. But it's also a stinging reminder of his repeated betrayal. I shove it back in my pocket, not wanting to relive those memories any longer.

Then I refocus and inspect Curtis's letter. The name *James* is written in careful cursive, with an address below it. It's in the Capitol Hill neighborhood in Seattle. I know that area well.

I'm relieved I have something else to do—a new goal. Maybe if I find James, we can have some common ground with our connection to Curtis.

Tomorrow, I'll work on heading back to Seattle.

*

AIDEN

There's no being discreet or careful now. I put the Audi in gear, then tear out of the driveway and head straight for the interstate. Carjackers and Connor be damned. Bring them on. See if they can mess with me when I'm trying to save the guy I love. *The guy I love.* I love him. The feeling has been simmering for a while, but now it's a full boil. I *have* to find him.

The Audi responds with precision. I've never driven an electric car before. The smooth, linear acceleration is a kick. Heading onto the freeway entrance, I'm thrust into my seat as I push the accelerator to the floor. The freeway is clear. Only the occasional wreck slows me down as I navigate past. But the road is wide, so I cruise as fast as possible, teetering on the edge of control.

The onboard navigation still works. The car has all the map data downloaded, so I'm not reliant on a nonexistent Internet, and the GPS satellites haven't malfunctioned yet. My destination is the UW Medical Center in the middle of Seattle. I enter it into the navigation system and blast down the road.

The outskirts of Seattle don't seem that bad. No worse than many smaller towns I encountered across the country. Run-down, but not destroyed. But the deeper I get to the middle of the city, the more the apocalypse is apparent. Entire neighborhoods are burned down. Graffiti is everywhere. And Mother Nature seems to be especially eager to swallow up the city, as many structures are covered by vegetation.

After such a long journey with so many obstacles, it's remarkable how fast this last leg goes. I cruise through Seattle's University District in less than an hour. My final destination is minutes away.

I pull the Audi up to a massive complex of buildings and get out. The UW Medical Center appears to have been built over many decades, with each new architect taking their inspiration from whatever drab, institutional buildings looked like at the time.

I wind through the maze of towers, outbuildings, and parking garages. But I know exactly where I'm going. I've studied the maps and the pictures extensively. Finally, I find a nondescript door on the side of an unremarkable building. A tiny camera protrudes from the building's facade.

I wave to the camera and speak clearly so the mic will pick up my voice. "Emergency Medical Bunker Gamma-six, this is Aiden Torres, courier from EMB Alpha-one, with a priority one package. Please acknowledge."

Nothing.

I wait for a moment, then repeat the message and wave to the camera again. Still no response.

This bunker was offline when I left Boston over a month ago. This was always a worry, but I'd kept it tucked into the back of my mind, never wanting it to stress me too much or let it cloud my judgment. Now, it's hitting me over the head.

The door should have been locked, but the doorknob turns freely.

Shit.

With pistol in hand, I ease the door open to reveal a large cement room and a freight elevator shaft, very similar to the one in Boston. But the inside is trashed. The biometric scanner next to the elevator, has been smashed beyond recognition. The metal gate that should guard the elevator shaft lies in a heap in the corner, ripped from its hinges.

I'm hit with a wave of panic. Any hope of finding the cure and saving Zach took a major blow, but I still need to press on. Maybe something down there will provide a hint to what happened.

I peer down the deep hole, which descends over a hundred feet. I shine the flashlight down it. Even the powerful beam cannot penetrate the darkness at the bottom. To my right, a metal access ladder descends the entire length of the shaft until the shadows obscure it. A narrow ledge, no wider than six inches, provides access to the ladder.

I press my body up against the side of the shaft and shimmy my feet along the ledge. My pulse rises as I shake off a minor spell of dizziness. Now is not the time to freak out. I grab the ladder rungs with all my strength and descend into the darkness.

My forearms, shoulders, and back muscles scream, but I continue downward. After over a hundred feet, I finally reach the bottom.

I'm standing on the top of the elevator car. Pointing my flashlight around, I find the access hatch into the cab. But it's already been opened. Someone has been here before me.

I poke my head down through the hatch to see what I'm getting myself into, shining the flashlight around in the darkness. Beyond the elevator car a large concrete room opens up, and a massive circular metal door provides access to the bunker. The door is ajar.

After gently descending into the elevator car, I creep toward the bunker, pistol in one hand, flashlight in the other. Large chunks of cement debris litter the floor and rest against the bunker entrance. The massive door won't open any further, with just enough room for me to squeeze through.

Inside, tables are overturned, smashed lab equipment is strewn about, and shattered TVs line the walls.

I search the large main room, shining my flashlight, looking for any signs of what might have happened here. I come across a series of letters and numbers spray-painted along the wall.

VXTZ UAR +11

Next to the text is the three-dimensional drawing of a rectangle in red paint. It almost looks like a shoe box.

I recognize the text immediately. This is cyphertext. An encoded message. Hopefully, it's a hint about the lab's new location.

Thank god. There's still hope.

Encoding is standard procedure for the Scientific Collective when leaving a message in the open. The plus-eleven is part of the key to unlocking the message, but we also use a private rotating key that changes weekly. Luckily, I have them all committed to memory—part of my training. I take a pen and paper from my backpack and jot down the writing.

A quick peek at my watch shows 7:38 p.m. Less than seventeen hours until the meeting time. That'll be cutting it close if Zach turns out to be sick. By then, he'll have a terrible fever. But at least it gives me more time to decipher this code and hopefully have a clue for what to do next.

I turn to search the rest of the bunker for more clues when a faint noise off to my left breaks the silence. It's quiet but unmistakable. Something down here moved.

I spin around on my heel, shining the light and pointing the pistol in the direction of the noise. "Who's there!"

A moment later, three figures holding guns walk into the beam of my flashlight. I don't recognize them, but their combat gear and how they carry themselves scream militia. One turns on a flashlight and points it at me, shining it in my eyes and obscuring any more details.

"You with the other one?" a woman calls out.

"I'm alone. What do you mean, *other one?*" I keep my voice calm.

"Blond bastard. Tall," she replies.

Fuck. Connor's been here. But I play ignorant. "No. Just me."

"Good answer," she says in a level tone. "If you said yes, we'd shoot you on the spot. He killed two of our men. But nobody has to die here. Just drop your gun and your backpack, and you can walk away."

That's not going to happen, so I say nothing.

"Drop the damn gun!" a man yells cocking his pistol.

"I'll be on my way," I reply, my voice firm. "But I need my supplies."

"I think you'll find we need them more," the woman says. "Is what you're carrying worth dying for?"

I sigh. "Yes," I say quietly.

My instincts kick in at the sudden movement from the three armed people. I dive for the cover of an overturned lab table to my left. Gunshots ring out, and a strobe of muzzle flashes brighten the room as I hit the floor hard. Dust rains down as the bullets impact the cement wall behind me, creating large divots.

Footsteps head toward me, closing the distance between us, so I act quickly. I pull the pin of the last grenade and throw it over the desk. It clatters along the floor. "Better run!" I shout.

"Shit! Grenade!" one of them yells, and there's the sound of frantic footsteps running away. I plug my ears.

A concussive blast fills the entire bunker. The table I'm behind, which has a soapstone top and must weigh several hundred pounds, slides back a few inches. The sound of metal shrapnel embedding into the overturned tabletop makes a staccato rhythm inches away from my head.

Wasting no time after the blast, I jump up and race for the door. I shine my flashlight around the bunker as I run but see no sign of them—just a big cloud of dust. But then gunfire erupts out of the darkness. I crouch down. With the door only feet away, I shoot several times for cover, then sprint toward the entrance. After sliding through the narrow opening of the circular bunker door, I shove it closed with all my might and drag a large chunk of broken concrete against it.

I race up the ladder as fast as possible, going two rungs at a time. Every ten or so feet, I peek back down but see nothing. When I reach the top, I shine my flashlight down into the abyss. No movement.

Without looking back, I run to the Audi and drive off as fast as the electric motor will go. My destination is Volunteer Park on the top of Capitol Hill, a neighborhood in the middle of Seattle. There, I'll wait at the Black Sun statue and hope against hope Zach remembers the rendezvous details I wrote in my letter.

When I get to the park, I leave the car a short distance away, not wanting to attract attention. I head directly to the statue, hoping to see Zach's warm smile. The rendezvous isn't until tomorrow, but maybe he got here early.

But he's not here. I miss Zach so much. I miss his smile, I miss his humor, I miss his smarts. I even miss his tendency to panic sometimes. I miss *him*. I desperately want to find him. And I'm worried beyond belief that when I find him, he'll be sick.

Or that I'll never find him.

I shove that thought away and continue on.

The statue is a black, round disk about ten feet in diameter with a hole through the middle, standing on top of a pedestal. It resembles a large misshapen doughnut. Through the hole, the Space Needle is framed directly in the middle. Clearly, this was the intent of this statue.

With no Zach in sight, I search for a place to set up camp. Nearby, an old stone water tower from over a hundred years ago rises up. The tower is no longer in use, but its doors are open. Plaques on the wall make it clear this is a historical marker.

Spiral staircases wind their way up to the top of the tower over seventy feet above the ground. At the top is a large flat surface. It's a good spot to set up a tent. Windows line the perimeter of the wall, providing an excellent vantage point for the entire area.

With my camp set up, I settle down with the pad of paper, the encrypted code, and local maps, and I try to find some clue or pattern to reveal the bunker's new location.

Zach's life depends on it.

Chapter Thirty-Six

Black Sun

ZACH

Cough…cough…cough…

I wake up with a start, hacking. For a moment, I forget where I am. But a quick look around reorients me. I'm lying on my old bed in my childhood bedroom. Posters of Tom Holland as Spider-Man and classic movies like *Star Wars* and *Jaws* fill my walls. Then, the fate of my parents and Felix returns, and the pain comes rushing back.

But another fit of coughing interrupts my thoughts. There's a tickle in the back of my throat. I've learned through the years that I'm a hopeless hypochondriac. Every sore throat and cough doesn't mean I'm sick. I shake off the worry and get out of bed.

I'm glad I have a purpose today. Find James and deliver Curtis's letter. Retracing my steps, I head to the sailboat moored to our half-submerged beach staircase and start on the trip back across Puget Sound.

Overall, I'm finding the effort of sailing much more taxing today than yesterday. I probably needed a better breakfast. I'm winded and sweating a bit when I finally get to shore. The breeze blows through and gives me the chills. I rub my torso to warm up but find it doesn't help much, so I put on a light jacket from my pack.

My destination is Capitol Hill, just east of downtown Seattle. I weave the bike through back roads and side streets, trying to find a way free of water and obstructions. It takes some time, but soon I'm heading north on I-5.

As I approach, the devastation of downtown becomes more apparent. Seeing how fragile these giant skyscrapers are is startling. Toppled buildings have flattened entire city blocks, and towers have collapsed into each other. Some stand precariously as if a strong enough wind could knock them over.

I scan the freeway ahead. One building has fallen onto the lanes, forever blocking the progress north. I take the next exit and head the rest of the way via surface streets.

I'm thankful for the motorcycle. In remote rural areas, the Infected are rare. But driving through the city, it's not uncommon to see movement on either side of me. The occasional figure chases after me down the road. Quick acceleration is all it takes to lose them, but it still makes my pulse skyrocket every time it happens, and I keep a vigilant eye.

When I finally arrive on a tree-lined street in front of a classic craftsman house, I double-check the address in Curtis's letter. It matches up.

I'm hit with a pang of sadness as I head to the porch. Aiden and I had planned to deliver this note together. It feels wrong doing it without him. I miss him deeply.

I knock on the door. No answer. Reaching for the knob, I find the door unlocked. The air is stale, but there's no hint of death. I spot some old mail on the dining room table. The letters are addressed to *James Nguyen*. This confirms I'm at the right place.

Searching for any signs of life, I spot framed photographs on the fireplace mantle. Many are of two elderly men. Some with their arms around each other, some surrounded by other people. In all the photos, they are smiling and happy.

And then, one photo catches my eye. I recognize a familiar face standing with one of the two men from the other photos. Both are considerably younger in the photo, but one is unmistakably Curtis. He looks so happy. They both do. A tear streaks down my cheek, and I wipe it away.

After searching the entire house and finding nothing, I head out to the backyard. There, I find what I was worried I might discover. In the middle of the lawn, there's a mound of dirt. Grass grows over it, but it's clearly a grave and, at the top, a makeshift cross. Somebody has written *James* across it. I let out a deep sigh as more tears flow down my cheeks. I so hoped I might find James alive.

All I wanted was to deliver this letter for Curtis. To do this one thing he asked me to do. James and I could have shared memories of Curtis together. And there might have been one person I'd have some connection to. Instead, like everywhere else, I only find death.

Tears drip on Curtis's letter, making the ink run in black streaks. I contemplate burning it and spreading the ashes over James's grave. That would be the respectable thing to do, but I miss Curtis too much. With some trepidation, I open the envelope and read it, hoping to have this one last connection.

It's a beautiful letter filled with loving memories of a better time between James and Curtis. As I read the words, I'm overcome with melancholy joy at their wonderful life together, but a life that was interrupted. When I get near the end, a particular passage stands out.

> *As I recall all these beautiful memories with you, James, I have only this one regret. I couldn't find it in my heart to forgive you in time, even though I knew you did what you did from a place of love. Forgiveness is a cornerstone of love. By not understanding that soon enough, I lost you. But I never stopped loving you. And I hope you can say the same about me.*

As I read the words, it's as if I'm reading about Aiden and myself. There's a lump in the back of my throat.

Oh god.

I can't make the same mistake.

I love Aiden so fiercely it hurts, and having him gone only amplifies that hurt. I reread the letter he wrote at the dam.

Why do I keep torturing myself like this?

As I read the letter, I'm hit by longing and anger. But when I get to the end, my jaw drops open.

> *PS: If we both make it through this, I'll wait for you every Sunday in*

Volunteer Park in Seattle. At the Black Sun statue at noon.

Oh, my god. Aiden left explicit instructions for us to meet if we got split up. It was under my nose the whole time, and I forgot about it.

My watch says 1:29 p.m., Sunday. *Crap.* I'm an hour and a half late. But Volunteer Park isn't far. Maybe I can still catch him. I run out of the house, jump on my bike, and race to the park as fast as possible.

*

AIDEN

I've been waiting for Zach all day.

I woke up this morning at first light and stared at the statue from on top of the water tower. By 9:00 a.m., I'd packed up camp and waited nearby, alternating between standing next to the statue, sitting at a park bench, and pacing around the area. I spent the whole time poring over my maps and trying to make sense of the encrypted writing. I have some leads but no breakthroughs yet.

Noon came and went. Then one.

Now, it's one thirty, and I'm fighting despair. Zach hasn't come. He either doesn't remember the note or hasn't forgiven me. And if his symptoms haven't progressed enough for him to realize he's sick, he'll die before next week. Or worse, he'll go on living as one of those *things*. I'm a total wreck.

I want to stay longer, but this place weighs on me heavily. This statue now symbolizes Zach's rejection of me—a monument to my failure. With a heavy heart, I walk down the tree-lined path back to where I parked.

As I approach the car, I become aware of a rumbling sound in the distance. It's getting closer. It's the sound of a motorcycle engine. I jump in the air, pumping my fists.

I spin around and sprint back to the statue. My lungs burn, but I keep going the whole way. As I reach the statue, a motorcycle approaches with a lone rider.

It's Zach. He made it. He's alive.

Zach parks the motorcycle near me and hops off it. He doesn't even set the kickstand, and the bike hits the ground with a nasty crunch. But neither of us cares as we both run toward each other. Zach leaps up and jumps into my arms.

I lift him and spin him around. We're both laughing and crying at the same time. I squeeze him tightly and whisper into his ear. "Zach, I'm so sorry I didn't tell you about the vials, and for wanting to leave you. I should have trusted you. Let you take your own risks. I never want to be gone from your side again."

Zach chokes out a response between sobs. "I'm sorry I didn't trust you enough to tell you about my uncle and ran off like I did. You were trying to protect me, like always. I should have waited to hear you out."

We both hold on tight. And then Zach starts coughing. Not a short cough or two, but a full coughing fit. I set him down, my heart wrenching. I put my hand on his forehead. He clearly has a fever.

"I think I might be coming down with something." Zach's sad eyes gaze into mine.

I'm wracked with unimaginable worry and guilt. I have to tell Zach about the broken vial, but I fear he'll be so upset that he'll hate me and run off again. But I have to do it.

"Aiden, what's wrong?"

"In the tunnel—" My voice is shaking, and I barely form words. "A bullet hit my aluminum box. One vial was smashed."

Zach takes a step back from me. His mouth falls open, and his eyes are wide. He backs into the base of the statue and sits down with a blank expression. He says in a totally flat voice, "Did you find the lab?"

I take a deep breath. "The lab is abandoned. But I think it's just moved. I have a lead."

"How long do I have?"

"Zach, let's concentrate on trying to find the—"

"How long?" he says forcefully.

"It's been twenty-six hours since you were exposed. In the next twelve hours, you'll be going downhill fast. By tomorrow, you won't be able to move much."

"And after that?"

I'm unable to meet his gaze. "Nobody makes it much past day three."

Zach stares past my shoulder off into the distance. "Everyone's dead. Mom, Dad, Felix, James, Curtis."

"I'm so sorry, Zach."

"And now I'm dead."

"You aren't dead yet!" I take him by the shoulders. "There's still hope."

Zach's face crumples. "I don't want to die."

I pull him into a hug. "You're not going to. Not if I can help it." I rock him back and forth in my arms, rubbing his back. "It's okay, Zach. We can beat this."

He looks at me and nods, his face an iron resolve. "I'm not going down without a fight. What do we do now?"

I let out a long breath. He's trying to be so strong. "Now, we get to work. At the lab, a code was spray-painted on the wall." I point to the piece of paper where I copied it down.

VXTZ UAR +11

"Next to that was a red 3D rectangle," I say. "It's standard practice for the Collective to encrypt messages. The plus-eleven is half of the key. It's a simple Caesar Cipher. The other half of the key, I have committed to memory."

Zach nods. "That makes sense. I learned about ciphers in my comp-sci class in high school." The gears in his head turn. Now that he has something to focus on, he looks more hopeful.

"Yeah, but the results don't mean anything to me." I point to more scribbles below the original code. "When I decode it, I come up with this."

AGXN VZB

"It looks like the decryption didn't work," I say. "Does that make any sense to you?"

Zach scrunches his face up. "No, not really. Here, let me see that code again."

I hand Zach the note, and he stares long and hard at the original letters. Then his face brightens. "Wait. You said the first part of the encryption was a Caesar Cipher, right?"

I nod.

"Are you sure that's a plus-eleven?"

"I think so. What else could it be?"

"Are those capital *I*'s, maybe? Instead of ones?" Zach asks. "As in Roman numerals. Get it? Roman and Caesar?"

I drop my jaw. "You mean like Roman numeral two. So, the first part of the key is a two!"

I use the number two in the key, work out the new solution, then write it on the paper.

PSNS DD4

Zach points at it. "PSNS. Puget Sound Naval Shipyard. That's in Bremerton, Washington, right on the other side of Puget Sound."

"Oh, my god, Zach! You're a genius!" I hug him so tightly that he grunts a little. "What does the DD4 mean, do you think? And the red rectangle?"

Zach shrugs. "Not sure. Guess we'll have to go there and see." His whole demeanor has changed. He's filled with hope. And so am I. He gets up and heads toward the bike. "But not sure how we'll get there. The bike is running on empty, and it kinda got smashed when I jumped off it."

I walk in the other direction and gesture for him to follow. "C'mon Zach. Our chariot awaits."

When I approach the Audi and make it chirp with a click of the key fob, Zach's face lights up. "Wow. I'm impressed."

I tell him all about how I found the car as I enter our destination into the navigation system.

"It's sixty-six miles to the Puget Sound Naval Shipyard," I say. "We still have one hundred and three miles of electric range left. That should get us there with miles to spare."

Zach slaps the dashboard. "Let's see what this baby can do." His resilience is astonishing. Even sick and staring down death, he's still his same wonderful, quirky self. I'll never take him for granted if we somehow make it through this.

With all the ferries gone, the only way to get across Puget Sound is to go south, around it. From Capitol Hill, we get on Interstate 5 heading south, which will take us to Tacoma and then across the Tacoma Narrows Bridge. Bremerton is just north of that. We're making good time. The freeway heading south out of the city is seven lanes wide. I weave the car back and forth like a skier on a slalom course, navigating around the wrecks while going nearly eighty.

After about a half hour of uneventful driving, we race past downtown Tacoma and take Highway 16 toward Tacoma Narrows Bridge. Soon, we'll cross Puget Sound and onto the Kitsap Peninsula. Just a few more miles, and we'll be home free.

We're cruising around the last bend before the approach to the bridge. The Audi is cruising fast along the wide-open freeway. And then I slam on the brakes. We come to a shrieking stop, leaving a dark streak of burned rubber on the road. I step out of the car and gape, trying to process the sight before me. A massive twisted hunk of metal, concrete, and wire sits where two massive suspension bridges used to stand tall, built side by side, spanning the Tacoma Narrows waterway.

Zach walks up to my side. He looks onward at the carnage before us. "I can't believe what I'm—"

But he can't complete his sentence as he doubles over and lands on his hands and knees, overwhelmed by a fit of coughing.

Chapter Thirty-Seven

Nothing Unsaid

ZACH

The coughing comes swift and brutal. The ferociousness consumes me. A sense of malaise descended on my earlier, but now it feels as if I'm choking up a lung. A wave of panic hits me as I fight for air. Blood rushes to my face and neck. It feels like I might suffocate.

Aiden consoles me, rubbing my back. "I'm here, Zach. I'm here." Gradually, the coughing subsides, and I catch my breath. That was a scary moment. Having Aiden by my side is comforting, even though there's nothing he can do.

I get up, and we walk over toward where the road collapsed to better see the wreckage that once was the twin Tacoma Narrows bridges.

Two bridges once stood side by side, one built long ago, the other more recently. Both were over a mile long and had giant towers on each side supporting the suspension cables. The pier that held up the east tower of the older bridge appears to have crumbled. Most likely destroyed by the sea level rise and the enormous storm surge that spread through every waterway in the world. The massive tower toppled into the main span of the newer bridge.

The way forward is utterly impassable.

"I guess we'll need to go the long way around," I say. "Down to Olympia and around the south side of Puget Sound."

Aiden looks at me, his face wracked with worry. "We'll never make it. That'll take us a hundred miles out of our way. We don't have enough range."

"And there aren't exactly any charging stations around."

Aiden shakes his head. "We can take our chances to find a vehicle with fuel, but all that is going to take time. And that's time we don't have."

My head is swimming. I'm already feeling ill, but now panic is rising. I don't want to die. I close my eyes and clear out unwanted thoughts, continuing until my terror ebbs.

I open my eyes. With a fresh mind, sometimes, a solution presents itself. That's when it hits me.

"Aiden, how far are we from south Seattle?"

"About thirty miles. But we just came from that way."

A smile grows across my face. "How do you feel about learning to sail?"

*

We're back in the Audi, heading north the way we came. I plug the South Seattle Marina into the navigation system. According to the car, it's thirty-five miles away, but I know it'll be longer than that.

"The roads are a mess on the way, so we'll have to use the GPS as a guideline," I warn Aiden. "But I learned some tricks to getting there. I hope we'll have enough range."

"Just tell me where to go," Aiden responds. "We'll make it."

A sense of dread grows as each mile of range ticks away. We're nearing the marina, only a few miles to go, and our range is down to five miles. The Audi keeps warning us that the battery is low, but we ignore it. We'll keep going until we hit zero, then continue on foot the rest of the way if necessary.

But we get lucky. With two miles of range left, we drive up to the marina.

"See, nothing to worry about," Aiden says with a sheepish grin.

"Yeah, two whole miles to spare. Why was I worried?"

The sailboat is where I left it, tied up to the dry dock.

On the boat, Aiden looks a little anxious. "I don't know anything about sailing."

"It's easy. You only need a few principles. I'll give you a crash course."

"Hopefully, no crashing involved."

I let out a little laugh. "You'll do fine."

After we navigate the boat to open water, I show Aiden the lines that raise and lower the different sails and how to tweak them. He picks it up immediately. With the mainsail raised, it cracks and whips in the wind until

Aiden adjusts the trim. The sail catches the wind just right, making a satisfying *snap*.

"Awesome." Aiden has a broad smile.

"See? You're a natural."

I give Aiden a quick tour of the rest of the lines, showing him the genoa sail and how to tack and jibe. He picks it all up quickly. It's important that he knows all the basics. I'm not sure how much longer I'll be of much help. The work to get the boat going has tired me out, and my face is flushed, with heat radiating from me. I bury the fear and focus on our task at hand.

The chill bites into me as we cruise through the water, so I put on a sweatshirt and settle down on a bench in the cockpit. Aiden is at the helm. The wind pushes his hair back. His eyes dart back and forth between the mainsail and the genoa. He makes minor course corrections and an occasional tug on a line. He's a joy to watch, even in my rapidly deteriorating state of mind. He's instantly talented at whatever he does. I love him so much.

We're making good time. The wind has held up, and we've been averaging just over seven knots. At that rate, it should take about four hours to get to our destination. We're headed north along a long narrow waterway between Vashon Island and Seattle. Small houses tucked into the trees dot the landscape. Occasionally, a house built too close to the shoreline is half-submerged below the new waterline. It's a surreal sight.

"Hey, Aiden. Remember one thing I wished we could do from before the Great Collapse?"

"What was that?"

"Going sailing." I wave my hands around.

Aiden looks at me with a little laugh. "I have to admit, it's pretty nice. But it doesn't beat ice cream, does it?"

"I can't argue there. I could really use some ice cream now."

We both laugh, but a lone tear runs down Aiden's cheek. He wipes it away quickly.

We've been sailing for a few hours, and I'm feeling worse by the minute. My coughing comes back in fits and starts, chills run throughout my body, and I'm shivering and sweating at the same time.

I'm hopeful we'll find the bunker, and they can make a cure, but it feels like a long shot. I don't know how much time I have left, and there are things I need to say to Aiden. I pause for a moment before I speak, choosing my words carefully.

"Aiden?"

He looks away from the water, and when his eyes meet mine, he can tell something's up. "Yeah?" he asks tentatively.

"I have some things I need to tell you. Before it's too late."

He opens his mouth, about to say something, but then shuts it with sad nod. He looks as if he's dreading what I'm about to say.

"If, for whatever reason, we don't find a cure…"

Aiden's face starts to crumple. "Zach—"

"Aiden. Please. I need you to hear me. If I make it through the fever—if I live through it, you have to—" What I'm saying feels surreal, like someone else is speaking. "I don't want to live as one of them. Do you understand?"

Aiden wraps his arms around me, crying, and chokes out a reply. "I don't know if I can do that."

"I need you to, Aiden. Please."

He nods into my shoulder and whispers a simple reply, "Okay."

"One more thing I have to tell you." I look deep into his silver eyes and calm descends over me. I cup my hand on his cheek. "I love you."

He gives a joyous laugh through his tears. "I love you, too, Zach. So much."

We hold on tight like we'll never let go. I want to live in this moment forever. Hit a pause on life and simply be here with him, in his warm embrace. Together, forever with the guy I love, who loves me back.

We stay that way for a long while, but my energy is fading. I finally pull away. "I need to rest. And you need to pilot the boat."

I sit on a bench in the cockpit as Aiden takes the wheel. A few minutes later, I'm weak and lightheaded.

"I'm going to lie down for a bit." I get up and take the first step down into the cabin and have to steady myself as I nearly fall over.

Aiden's brow furrows. He puts a hand on my forehead. "Oh man, you're really burning up now."

He takes a bottle of ibuprofen from his jacket and taps out a few pills. "Take these. It'll help with your fever. And try to get some rest."

"You don't have to tell me twice." I pop the pills and wash them down with water from my pack.

Lying down on the bed in the cabin is not very restful, and the boat's motion isn't helping the unease creeping over me. A wave of nausea hits me, and I run for the sink just in time. The violence of the act sends waves of pain through my entire body.

So much for all that ibuprofen.

Soon I'm huddled up on the bed in the boat's bow. I gather all the blankets I can find to cover myself up while shivering uncontrollably.

Closing my eyes, I remember my mindfulness. I clear my thoughts and focus on my breathing. Meditation is difficult with the ever-present undercurrent of pain and discomfort. But it's not impossible.

Somehow, I manage. My body and mind quiet. I push away all external senses and internal pain to make a place of darkness and solitude. Here, I'll wait—a castaway on an island in my mind. I'll wait to be rescued. I'll wait for a miracle.

Chapter Thirty-Eight

Homestretch

AIDEN

This sailing stuff isn't so bad. I've got this.

No sooner does that cross my mind than the mainsail snaps wildly, losing the wind. I tug on various ropes, hoping to correct it. But now the genoa is snapping too. Damn it. The wrong rope. I undo my original error and finally get both of the sails trimmed. The boat is now cruising, cutting a course through the choppy water.

We're getting close. We've made it all the way north, and the Puget Sound Naval Shipyard is to my left. Turning the boat will mean running perpendicular to the wind. It can be done. *In theory.* Zach described it to me, but I have yet to try it.

Down in the cabin, Zach is under a mountain of covers.

"Zach, are you awake?" I call down. "I might need some advice on tacking."

No answer. My heart skips a beat.

I run down to him. Zach is burning up, and his breathing is labored. He's not doing well. He looks so helpless and fragile, and it tears me up.

I head back up and try my best on my own.

I release the tension on the rope holding the boom. The sails immediately start flapping, making loud snapping noises as the wind rips through them. I turn the wheel to the left, and the boom flies to the right. The sail catches the wind with a loud snap.

I did it.

The sails are a little turbulent, so I let out more rope until they quiet down.

The boat slows as it cuts across the wind, but we're still moving. It's actually working.

The shipyard looms larger as we approach. Even with the sea level rise, the docks are awe-inspiring, with massive aircraft carriers, each the size of a small city, anchored alongside them.

With the boat headed in roughly the correct direction, I get ready for our approach. I put on my backpack, then head down to wake Zach.

I give him a little shake. "Zach. It's almost time to go."

He moves a little but only makes a grunting noise.

I shake him harder. "Zach. I need you to get up. We need to be ready!"

Nothing.

He won't be able to move on his own. My only option is to dock this boat as best I can, then carry him out. This is going to be tricky.

As the shipyard approaches, I scan for the best spot to land. Next to one of the massive aircraft carriers is a floating dock. Moored to it are a few patrol boats. The dock bobs and weaves with the waves that splash against it. I get the sailboat close enough, drop the sails, and let the boat coast.

When we're twenty feet away, I drop the anchor to stop the boat's momentum. But the anchor doesn't catch, and the boat keeps moving, heading straight for the dock. I try to course correct, but it's far too late. The bow of our boat rams into the dock, and there's a massive crunching noise as aluminum and fiberglass collide in an explosion of shrapnel.

The boat is taking on water through a hole in the bow. I throw our dinghy over the back and tie it down with a quick knot. Then I run to the cabin, splashing through the water that has already leaked in, and cradle Zach in my arms.

"Aiden?" Zach's eyes flutter open as I carry him.

"Hang on, Zach. We're getting close." I keep my voice calm and soothing.

Back on deck, I set Zach into the dinghy, and I get in behind him.

As we paddle away, the sailboat sinks until, finally, only the mast is above water.

"Well, I guess it was a crash course after all." I say under my breath.

Bit by bit, I paddle us to land. Massive aircraft carriers loom on either side of us, blocking the sun. I'm met with a new problem when we get to the dock. How will I get Zach and myself off the dinghy without tipping it over? Zach is like a one-hundred-fifty-pound sack of potatoes. Still, I hoist him over my shoulders in a fireman's carry. The boat shimmies under my feet, but I grab the dock with my free hand to steady myself and crawl ashore. We're on land.

Now to just find this damn place. DD4 and a red 3D rectangle. What in the hell could that mean?

I carry Zach up a long flight of stairs and along the main dock towering above the water. Eventually, I come across a sign reading *Dry Dock 2* with an arrow pointing left.

Dry Dock 2. DD2.

"DD means dry dock!" I'm filled with hope. "Now I just need to find Dry Dock Four. We're almost there!"

Zach responds with a barely audible grunt.

I keep on until I pass a sign that reads *Dry Dock* 3. Getting closer. Finally, the *Dry Dock 4* sign is before us.

I turn and walk along the edge of the dock. It's currently empty and falls a hundred feet. Peeking over at the precarious drop makes the hairs on my neck stand on end. I'm not afraid of heights, but this drop is bone-chillingly long, with no protective railing.

This is where they built these massive aircraft carriers. I saw it on History Channel. Once the ships were complete, they filled the entire dock with water until they floated on their own. But now, the dry dock is empty— just a massive hole.

Various buildings, cranes, and construction materials skirt the edge. I scan everything, looking for something that resembles a red rectangle. Then I see it. A hundred feet away, a bright red shipping container. *A 3D rectangle.* Against all odds, we've made it.

But as I approach, my worst-case scenario unfolds before me as

Connor steps out from behind the container, holding a gun and wearing a smug expression.

Fuck.

I should have known. I should have been ready. But here I am, with my rifle attached to my backpack and Zach hoisted over my shoulder.

"Hello, Aiden. Finally here. Did you take the scenic route?" Connor aims the handgun directly at me.

I say nothing.

"Didn't expect to see me?" Connor asks. "That code was easy to crack. Remember, I still have some connections at the Collective."

I stare at him, frozen, not knowing what to do.

"But it was clever of the Collective to disable my biometrics." He points over at a panel on the side of the shipping container. "I didn't expect that. They still worked for me back in Boston after I 'died.'" He makes air quotes to emphasize the word.

My anger builds, and the words spit out. "What are you talking about, you sick fuck?"

"Language, Aiden. After you left me for dead on that bridge six months ago, you took the vials. If you'd simply left them, none of this would have happened. Marcus would be alive. You'd be with him right now."

My pulse rises and anger takes over. "You had something to do with Marcus's death?"

"The vials you stole from me. They contained the same thing you're carrying now—the weaponized version of XT58. Of course, you were kind enough to spill some onto the road, a bit of which I was able to salvage. It wasn't enough to accomplish my plans. But it was still enough to kill."

Connor's words hit me like a freight train. "You didn't. Tell me you didn't!"

"Like a good worker bee, you finished our mission and delivered the vials to DC while I went back to Boston. I got there at 3:00 a.m., when the whole bunker was asleep. I tried to synthesize more XT58 from what you left on the road, but the sample was too contaminated. That's when Marcus ran into me. I guess he always had problems sleeping when you were away. I didn't have anything against Marcus, honestly. He just walked up behind me. He was as good as dead the moment he entered the lab."

My blood is boiling, and my pulse thuds in my head. "You fucker!"

"I guess it was poetic justice. You left me for dead on the side of that bridge and took the vials from me. So I took Marcus from you. Being presumed dead was too valuable to me, so I knocked him out with a sedative. By the time he'd wake up, his fever would be so bad that nobody would believe he saw me. Ravings of a fevered mind."

"Why?" I cry out.

"We want the same thing, Aiden. To find the cure. But the Collective will never do it. They have to be stopped. You'll never understand that. You're too naïve. So I'll do what I must. I'll kill who I must."

"You bastard!" That's all I manage. The world is crumbling around me. Connor is the architect of all my misery. He wanted the weaponized Infection all along, from our first mission together. And he infected Marcus. He *killed* Marcus. I want to strangle him with my bare hands. Now Marcus's dying words finally make sense. He wasn't accusing me of cheating on him with Connor. He was *warning me* about Connor.

"Now listen carefully. I need your handprint on that scanner." Connor gestures to the control panel on the side of the container. "If I could,

I'd just shoot you and drag your lifeless body to it. But it only works if they detect a pulse. If you try anything stupid, I'll shoot Zach. First, set him down."

I have no choice, so I do as he says. I lay Zach down, resting against the side of the container.

"Good. Now give me the vials."

I take off my backpack, then fish for the aluminum box.

"Slide them over." Connor gestures with the barrel of the gun.

I push the vials along the ground, but they only get halfway between us.

Connor rolls his eyes. "Just leave them. Come with me and open this door. Try anything stupid, and Zach dies."

"Nobody in this bunker will help you while they are still breathing." I spit the words out.

"Of course not. I don't need them. Remember, I've recruited my own scientists. I just need to get into the lab so I can take their research. I'll shoot anyone who gets in my way."

Connor backs away, leaving lots of space between us. He gestures to the control panel on the container with its handprint scanner.

I walk up to the scanner and raise my hand. And I wait.

"Go on! What are you waiting for?" Connor yells.

This is my last chance. I'll have to stop him or die trying. I draw in a deep breath as my training kicks in. My body winds up like a coil, ready to spring.

"Fine, I'll shoot Zach instead." Connor turns the gun away from me and aims at Zach.

His hand flexes, about to squeeze the trigger. I dive for the gun. A gunshot rings out, and a searing pain bursts into my side. I crumple in front of Connor. The pain is unimaginable, as if somebody ran me through with a molten hot knife, then twisted it. The sharp, searing pain fills all my consciousness.

Connor looks down at me, disgusted. "You had to be the fucking hero, didn't you?" He grabs my palm and starts dragging me, streaking a trail of blood behind. I didn't think the pain could get worse, but somehow it does.

"Well, I'm okay with doing this the hard way too," Connor says as we reach the panel. He raises my hand to press it to the console. "Please, stay alive long enough to—"

The sound of a rifle shot rings out, and a bullet strikes Connor in the left shoulder. He howls in pain. The impact sends him staggering back, teetering toward the edge of the hundred-foot dry dock wall.

I turn my head. Zach is barely conscious but holds the rifle from my backpack next to him. Smoke rises out of the barrel. With one last burst of energy, I grab a metal cog from a scrap pile next to the container and throw it at Connor. It hits him squarely in the head.

Connor staggers back, his feet half over the wall edge. His hands pinwheel as he tries to regain balance, but his weight is shifted too far back. He disappears off the edge. His scream echoes through the dry dock, punctuated by a dull thud and then silence.

"I thought he'd never shut up," Zach says just before I black out.

*

ZACH

I lie there, weak, fever raging, every muscle in my body screaming and aching. Aiden lies unconscious, with a pool of blood forming under him. I try to move, but my arms and legs don't respond. So, I close my eyes and remember Curtis and his kindness. I remember my mother and father and how much I miss them. And I remember Aiden and my love for him. I dig deeper than I've ever dug before. Energy wells up inside me. It won't last for long. I need to act quickly.

I crawl over to the aluminum box resting on the ground. The one that's caused all this pain but also has the power to cure it. Getting to my feet, I lumber over to Aiden, lying next to the container. He's still breathing, but his breaths are shallow. I put his hand up to the panel. A light flashes green, and the door opens up to an elevator.

I hook my hands under Aiden's arms and pull with all my might. Somehow, I find the strength to drag him onto the lift and press the button. As we descend, Aiden's eyes open slightly.

"Hold on!" I cry. "We're almost to the bunker!"

He looks into my eyes. "I love you, Zach."

I kiss his forehead. "I love you too, Aiden."

He smiles, and then his eyes close. His face goes slack.

"Aiden! Stay with me!" I slap his face to wake him.

But he doesn't respond, and I'm spent. I crumple beside him, with my arm draped over his chest.

The elevator takes forever. When it gets to the bottom, my reserves are depleted. All I can do is sit and stare at the large circular bunker door in front of us. Our goal is so close. But I've done everything I can. I have nothing left.

Even now, Aiden's face is beautiful. I love him. If I have to die, this is how I want it to be. Next to Aiden. Together in a broken world. For eternity.

I'm barely aware of the bunker door opening. Shapes approach, and voices shout. Someone lifts my eyelid, and a bright light shines into my eye. The box I'm clutching is pulled away.

Then darkness.

Chapter Thirty-Nine

A New World

ZACH

When I wake, my vision is fuzzy. The world is impossibly bright. A loud ringing buzzes in my ears, but the sound subsides, replaced by the deep murmur of voices.

My vision slowly focuses. First, I'm aware of a room. A hospital room, I'd guess. Then, objects around me take shape. The IV bag to my left snakes down and goes into my arm. A large instrument panel to my right makes beeping noises.

Then faces. An older man in a lab coat. A woman with gray hair tied back into a ponytail beside him. And then I see him. Aiden. He's alive, and

I'm alive. Either that, or this is some kind of afterlife.

I reach out to touch him to be sure. "Aiden?"

He squeezes my outstretched hand. "Zach, you're awake!"

"You got shot."

"Yep. I'm on the mend. Thanks to you." He lifts up his shirt. A bandage wraps around his waist.

"Everyone here owes you their life. You stopped Connor."

His name brings a cascade of memories. It was me. I shot Connor. Aiden helped, and the fall killed him, but that's a technicality. I had to do it. He was going to kill Aiden and everyone else in the lab. But that doesn't make it feel better. I didn't want to take a life. Even one so despicable as Connor. Now, I'll carry this burden.

But Aiden is alive. And I'm alive.

Wait. I'm alive.

"What about the Infection?" I plead.

Aiden grabs my hand. "The treatment worked. It's in remission. You're the first person ever to survive."

*

AIDEN

We spend the next few weeks in the bunker, fully recovering.

When Connor shot me, the bullet went directly through. It missed my lung by a centimeter. I was very lucky. They stitched me up once they stopped the bleeding, and I recovered quickly. Yet, weeks of rest are still called for.

They combined the vials we delivered with the protein they isolated.

From that, they synthesized a strong drug that immediately neutralized the Infection in Zach.

Zach gets blood tests daily to measure the XT58 in his blood. After a week of treatment, it's undetectable. And when they stop the treatment, there is no rebound. Still, it's something they'll observe long term.

My physical wounds are all healing, and maybe the mental ones can also. Finding out Connor was the source of all my misery was like having my heart ripped out of my chest. But knowing the truth somehow makes everything easier to bear. For the first time since Marcus's death, I shift the guilt from myself. The scar will always be there, but now a path forward exists.

Zach and I spend as much time together as possible. We have a room together in the bunker. Before this, the only life we knew was on the run. It's nice to get some normal time with him. To truly get to know him. There's still so much we have to learn about each other. And I look forward to every minute.

Zach is lying on the bed, reading a book, when I walk in with my hands behind my back.

"Okay, I know something's up." Zach looks at me with narrow eyes, but a smile is on his face.

"Close your eyes and put out your hands."

"What is it?"

"A surprise. You'll find out in a second. Do what I said."

Zach sits up and puts his hands out. He lets out a yelp when I hand him something freezing cold. "Aggh! What's this?"

"Okay, open your eyes."

He holds in his hands a bowl filled with two gigantic scoops of chocolate ice cream.

"Oh, my god! Where did you get this?"

"I made it." I beam. "You just need the right ingredients. The rest is simple chemistry."

Zach digs into the ice cream ravenously.

"Hey, slow down. Give me some." I scooch beside him and try to edge my way into the bowl, but Zach swats me away with his spoon. Then he gives me a big smile, scoops out a sizable portion, and feeds it to me. A dribble of ice cream goes down my chin.

"Oh. You've got a little something there." Zach licks it off. And since his lips are in the vicinity, I kiss him. The kiss is cold, chocolaty, and wonderful.

*

Deciding to leave the Collective wasn't hard for me. They saved Zach's and my life, and for that, I'm grateful. But I've paid my dues, and I'm optimistic about the future for the first time since this all began. The Collective will need a lot of help to make the world aware of the treatment they've developed. But that's a job for others. I've done my part.

After discussing it, Zach and I decide to take over Curtis's farm. It isn't a hard choice. We were both so happy there. Before returning to the farm, we travel to collect Curtis's body. We bury him alongside James. That seems like the right choice. Reunited, finally.

After that, we pack up enough supplies to get us on our feet and return to the farm. Without the FLA on our tail, the drive is fast and uneventful.

Curtis's desire for simplicity was admirable, and we hold to that spirit.

But Zach still loves to tinker and improve. So he rigs up a big solar farm from some equipment we scavenge and installs a bank of whole-home batteries. All the conveniences of modern living include central heating, an electric oven, a refrigerator, and, of course, a big-screen television with many old DVD movies. I improve our defenses by rigging up cameras around the property's perimeter.

We also establish some trading routes with Curtis's old contacts. It's clear that Curtis planned on handing off the farm for a while, and we were happy to find he had people watch the animals while we were away. He took detailed notes of all the different people, what they traded, and strategies for working with them. In no time, we have a good supply of cheese, cured meats, and we even have some people specializing in scavenging supplies for us. It's fascinating to see the seeds of civilization taking root. And I love experiencing all of that with Zach.

*

ZACH

On a warm autumn evening in late September, Aiden and I are around a fire pit we set up outside the farmhouse. He strums the guitar, and I'm spread out on a blanket, singing to the melody he's playing.

When the song ends, I smile at Aiden. "This reminds me of that night in Elk Springs when we sat by the fire. I knew right then I wanted to spend the rest of my life with you."

Aiden lies beside me on the blanket and gives me a gentle kiss and a warm smile.

I run my hands through his hair. "It took you a little longer, didn't it?"

He stares into the fire and contemplates his answer. "I was in a terrible place back then, and you rescued me from it." Then he looks me in the eye. "But if I'm being honest with myself, and I really think about how I felt, I already cared for you deeply. I came back to rescue you, after all. Even if you ended up rescuing me."

I laugh, then kiss him. "I love you, Aiden. And I'll love you forever."

Aiden smiles. "I'll love you forever too."

We hold each other for the rest of the evening. The sun dips below the horizon turning the clouds a deep orange and red, casting Homestead Farm in a golden glow. When the sky darkens, and the fire's last embers fade to black, we walk hand in hand back to the farmhouse and onward to the rest of our lives.

Acknowledgements

Writing itself may be a solitary pursuit, but getting the written word into a completed book, ready to publish, takes quite a crowd of people. If somebody told the lonely gay boy I was at age thirteen, writing my first short stories, that so many people would encourage me in my writing journey, I would have been quite surprised and delighted.

First, I need to thank my best friends, Tyler Ross and Nick Laken, who endured many early drafts and spent hours reading and critiquing, helping make the story what it is today.

Thanks to my wonderful husband Peter, who was always willing to listen to "just one more chapter," even if gay romance books aren't really his thing.

Thank you to my early developmental editor, Chris Barcelona, who helped shape the story, particularly the third act. Your advice and encouragement were invaluable.

Thanks to my two superstar beta readers, Sonja Shepard and Gina Handley, who spent an enormous amount of time being very thoughtful about their feedback and answering my long list of questions at the end of each chapter. I owe you two a lot. Thanks to the other beta readers from my novel writing course, including Catalina & John.

Thanks to my entire Gay Romance Book Club for letting me hijack our reading schedule and turn it into a beta-reader think tank. Andy & Brian Magee, Eric Loewenthal, Kiyon Ross, Peter Oehlert, Beau Preston, along with Tyler and Nick, you all have been a huge help, and your encouragement propelled me through many ups and downs.

Thanks to the members of the Seattle Writing Group who critiqued early drafts of many of the opening chapters, with a special call out to RE Andeen and Michele Cacano.

Thanks to the entire NineStar Press team, who believed in my story, including Raevyn McCann, and a special thanks to my editor, Elizabetta McKay, without whose help and encouragement, this story would not be in front of you right now.

Thanks to Micah Epstein for bringing Aiden and Zach to life in the stunning cover illustration.

Thanks to Talia Carver for giving a voice to Aiden and Zach, bringing emotional depth in a way I could hardly believe.

Thanks to my family for providing encouragement through my writing process. I love you, Mom, Dad, and Sis!

Thanks to Oreo and Minou, who kept me company with lots of purring, meowing, and the occasional forced power snuggle.

Finally, thank you, the reader, for taking the time to go on the journey with Aiden and Zach. Without your enthusiasm and support, my writing dreams would not be possible.

About the Author

Paul is a lifelong creative writer whose life is filled with queer joy. His passion is to spread that joy through storytelling, writing books where you might not typically see queer characters. He lives in the Pacific Northwest with his husband and two tuxedo kitties and might have a slight addiction to reading gay romance. But it's not a problem. He could stop any time he wants. Honestly.

Email

paul@pmwinters.com

Facebook

www.facebook.com/paulmichaelwinters

Twitter

@pmwintersauthor

Website

www.pmwinters.com

Instagram

@pmwintersauthor